Items should be returned on or before the last date
shown below. Items not a... borrowers may be renewe...
telephone. To renew, plea...
barcode label. To renew c...
This can be requested at your local library.
Renew online @ **www.dublincitypubliclibraries.ie**
Fines charged for overdue items will include postage
incurred in recovery. Damage to or loss of items will

ath

MIGUEL GARNETT

Also by Miguel Garnett

Rondo, winner of the Amalia Puga de Losada Prize for the most read novel in Cajamarca

Cañadas Oscuras and *Tiempos Van... Tiempos Vienen,* historical novels about the War of the Pacific, 1879-1883

A Ojo de Pájaro,

Polvareda, Don Jasho, short novels

Los Preguntones de Nolandia, for children.

ISBN: 978-0-9934220-0-3

First published in 2015
© Miguel Garnett
Santa Apolonia 146
Apartado 319
Cajamarca
Peru
miguelgarnett@yahoo.es

The quinde 🐦 and condor 🦅 used as dividers in this book are birds that are often found in northern Peru where this story is set.

Cover painting by the author

Designed and printed by: Genprint Ireland

Publishing consultant: Fergus Mulligan Communications, www.publishing.ie

For Anne and Walter, Michael, Jacky, Jo, and Carrie
Always present, in spite of distance and the world's tempests.

Only men of peace die,
warriors are immortal.

(Chinese proverb)

Too long have I been dwelling
amongst those who hate peace.
I am for peace;
but when I speak,
they are for war.

(Psalm 120)

Author's Note

The action of this novel takes place in the northern Andes of Peru during the *Shining Path* emergency. The *Shining Path* – *Sendero Luminoso* – led by Abimael Guzmán Reynoso – *Presidente Gonzalo–*, with a philosophy based on Marxist-Lenism, as interpreted by Mao-Tse-Tung, began its armed insurgency in the central Andean Department of Ayacucho during the general election of 1980. The insurgency soon spread throughout Peru, was to last 12 years, cost the country 70,000 deaths, and left the economy in ruins. Initially the democratically elected government treated the insurgency as a matter to be dealt with by the police. However, it soon became apparent that it was far more serious and the armed forces became involved. A lack of understanding as to the nature of the insurrection and how to confront it resulted in terrorism being employed to crush terrorism. As the subsequent *Commission of Truth and Reconciliation*, set up in 2001, revealed, there was violence and disregard for Human Rights on an appalling scale, committed both by the members of *Sendero Luminoso* and the armed forces. 70% of the deaths occurred amongst the Quechua-speaking peoples in the central and southern Andes. Some Catholic priests and sisters, plus a few Protestant pastors were also killed.

Guzmán was captured in September 1992 and condemned to life imprisonment. *Sendero Luminoso* still exists, operating in remote jungle areas of the country in conjunction with cocaine producers and dealers; and there continue to be deaths amongst the police and military. Its attempt to be recognized as a political party – *MOVADEF* – has so far failed.

The town of San Agustín de Yanacancha is imaginary, though based on a number of provincial northern Andean towns where the author has lived and between which there is a striking similarity. There is always a central square, called the *Plaza de Armas*, dominated usually by the parish church. Grouped round the square are to be found the municipality and other administrative offices. The Holy Week customs described in the novel are based on those of a number of these towns, whilst some of the background scenery is based on that to be found in the Cordillera Blanca of the Andes, a bit further to the south.

All the characters in the novel are fictitious and any similarity with persons either living or dead is purely fortuitous, for which sincere apologies.

Miguel Garnett,
Cajamarca,Peru

One

$\mathcal{M}$ANUEL DASHED DOWN the street, sticking as close as possible to the tumble of two storey adobe houses that lined one side, so as to take advantage of their wide tiled eaves to protect him from the worst of the rain. His sneakers slipped and slithered on the wet rough stone pavement, but he didn't fall. He was 22 and lithe. Tall for a youth reared in the Andes, he was noted in the town for his good looks; raven eyed with long black curly hair that flip-flopped over the collar of his loose anorak as he ran. He kept his eyes on the slippery stones, untroubled by the dirty water splashing onto his jeans. He seemed to be the only person in the town of San Agustín de Yanacancha* prepared to brave the tempest.

Lightning flashed violently, followed by an immediate roar of thunder. The storm was overhead now and the rain deluged down. Manuel felt the afternoon suddenly become colder as the rain turned to driving hail that clattered in fusillades against the twisted tile and galvanized iron roofs of the buildings, whilst the wind bent the tall palm trees in the Plaza de Armas in the centre of the town.

The rainwater cascaded through the narrow cobbled streets in raging torrents, sweeping away accumulated dirt in a mad swirl of flotsam: old boxes, paper and rotten fruit, plastic bags, kitchen waste and even the occasional guinea pig; whilst at the same time depositing a clutter of mud and stones from the mountains above the town. The flood waters then hurtled into a gully where the usually

---

* Yanacancha is the Quechua for *Black Field*. Many place names in the Andes are a mixture of Spanish and Quechua, especially when the name includes that of a town's patron saint, as in this case, St. Augustine.

happy babbling stream had become a roaring predator, propelling to their deaths unwary animals which had been grazing placidly along its banks, and wrenching up by the roots many of the gentle willows that grew there.

Since its foundation in the mid-sixteenth century by the Augustinian friars and Spanish conquistadores, San Agustín de Yanacancha had stood for four and a half centuries on a small plateau some 8,000 feet up in the Peruvian Andes, nestling below the fifteen thousand foot snow-capped peak of Condorrumi —*The Stone Eagle* —. The lower slopes of the mountain were covered with irregularly shaped fields of maize, alfalfa, potatoes and wheat, whilst eucalyptus woods dotted the landscape in darker patches of green. A rough dirt road wound down from the town into a wide valley below, filled with rich pastures, small sugar and coffee plantations, and fruit trees.

When the province basked under a deep cobalt sky with the peak of Condorrumi glistening and a heavy scent floating up from the valley, the local inhabitants had every right to call it 'The Pearl of the Andes'. However, on this late March afternoon there was nothing pearl-like in the sludge and grey lashing rain engulfing the landscape. Indeed, it seemed as though Catequil, the ancient storm god of the pre-Inca inhabitants of the area, had finally risen in rebellion against both the Inca Sun and the Christian Cross which had successively supplanted him; and as the storm progressed, he looked like regaining his position. There was no sign of the sun, and the large stone cross that stood on top of a small hill behind the cemetery on the outskirts of the town crashed to the ground when it was struck by lightning. Whole fields of maize were being flattened by the wind and shredded by the hail, whilst in the town itself every house reverberated to the roaring of the tempest.

As Manuel ran through the rain-sodden streets women and children huddled over back-kitchen fires, choking on the damp smoke which eddied in every direction except outside. In the cantinas and drinking dens, men countered the deluging rain by swilling down calabash loads of *chicha*, a beer made from fermented maize. Raucous singing, obscene jokes and smoky camaraderie, punctuated by increasingly incoherent cries of '¡Salud!' filled the gloomy peeling rooms, each, in the custom of the place, presided over by a picture of San Agustín, the town's patron saint, sharing wall space with naked girlie calendars flashing themselves provocatively at the drinkers.

In one of the cantinas, old Ma Vásquez's joint, down by the market, Lucio Benites, a 23 year old unemployed school teacher, had spent the earlier part of the afternoon getting drunk. He had gone about the task deliberately, enjoying the increasing sense of freedom that each swig of *chicha* gave him. As the alcohol had penetrated his blood stream Lucio had first revelled in a diatribe against the supervisor of education who yesterday had denied him a teaching post for this year; then against the government, then against everyone who had crossed his path recently, and finally he had shaken his fist at San Agustín shouting: '¡Qué se vaya a la mierda*!' —which is one way of telling someone to piss off—. After a while this expletive euphoria passed and now, crying his anger and frustration, Lucio staggered out of the cantina into the storm. For a few minutes he enjoyed letting the rain pour over him as he lurched from side to side towards the upper part of the town until he stumbled and sprawled semi-comatose, uncaring as the tempest intensified.

In another corner of the same cantina an animated conversation was taking place. 'I'll bet you were really scared, Sif,' wheezed a thin-faced individual sat on a rickety stool and looking across the bare wooden table at his cronies with whom he was sharing a plastic bucket-load of sweet *chicha*. Alcides Sifuentes shifted uneasily on his own stool and, by way of reply, looked furtively at his mates before aiming a gob of spit onto the floor.

'Of course he was,' chortled Santiago, another member of the group.

Sifuentes rubbed his chin pensively and then said slowly, using the accepted slang for the guerrillas now operating throughout the country: '*Terrucos* are right dangerous bastards and I didn't want nothing to do with 'em. That's why I hid.'

'Where did you hide, Sif?' asked Eladio, pulling off his battered straw hat to wipe his brow, and then clapping it back on his head brusquely.

---

* Mierda: shit.

'I jumped in amongst the *penkas**.'

'You should have seen him when I came by,' sniggered Santiago. 'Arse up in the *penkas*.'

Laughter erupted from the other members of the group in great burps and the calabash was dipped into the bucket of thick yellow *chicha* for another round.

'That explain the scratches you've got on your mug, Sif?'

'Course it does.'

'Don't you believe him. He's made up all that about the *terrucos* and the *penkas*. What really happened was that his old woman gave him a right scratching when she found out what he was doing with Rosa María,' spluttered Eladio gleefully.

'Bloody lies!' shouted Sifuentes indignantly. 'Santiago, you saw the place and helped to pull me out of the *penkas*.'

'Sure I did,' replied Santiago. And then with a wink, following Eladio's teasing lead, he added: 'But I didn't see no *terrucos*. I'll bet Eladio's right and your old woman pushed you there. We all know that she's got a temper worse than a scalded cat.'

'Go to hell,' snarled Sifuentes, angry as he jumped to his feet and knocking over the stool. 'Come on, square your fists and we'll settle this like men!'

'Calm down, Sif! There's no need to take on so,' interrupted Antenor, the most rodent-like member of the group who had kept quiet until now.

'Have a drink and let's forget about it.' He swung a dripping calabash load of *chicha* towards Sifuentes, whose anger melted before the heady liquid which he downed almost at one gulp and then spluttered: 'Alright, but you watch what you say about my old woman, Santiago, because next time I'll belt you like you've never been belted in your whole bloody life.'

'I didn't mean no harm, Sif,' muttered Santiago as Sifuentes picked up his stool and resumed his seat at the table.

---

* *Penkas* are sharp pointed cactuses, almost bush-like in size, and in the area which the novel depicts they are to be found like hedgerows along the sides of the country lanes and between the fields.

With that, good humour was restored to the group and they settled back to the more serious business of finishing the bucket of *chicha*. Whilst they did so the conversation turned to the subject of the *terrucos*.

'What are they doing here is what I want to know,' mused Eladio. 'We never had the likes of them here before.'

'Right bloody scary they are,' offered Antenor with a shudder. 'From what I've heard about them they act like brutes, but they say that they're here to help the poor.'

'Like hell!' burped Sifuentes by way of reply. 'You're poor and I'm poor. We were born poor and we'll bloody well die poor, and no-one will give a damn. I've heard say that we're poor because we're lazy and booze too much. But what about the big noises in this town? I tell you that they're a right lazy shower of bastards and they booze more than we do. But they're not poor! And the *terrucos* aren't poor either. Look at the sodding great machine-guns they use! They'll kill as soon as look at you. As for the police, they spend the time just lounging about doing nothing or getting pissed, until some poor bugger falls into their hands and then they amuse themselves by beating the shit out of him. Doesn't matter how you look at things, life's a bloody misery these days.'

On concluding this lengthy speech, Sifuentes stared satisfiedly at the other members of the group. None of them was normally given either to much deep thinking or to much talking, so on this occasion Alcides Sifuentes had surpassed himself and his friends looked at him with a mixture of admiration and skepticism.

Then Antenor said slowly: 'You're right, Sif; but life for the likes of us has always been a misery.'

'At least we didn't have *terrucos*,' said Eladio.

'No, but there were the hacienda owners and the bands of thugs that they employed.'

'I agree, Antenor,' intervened Santiago. 'There's always been someone to kick us up the arse, but at least we knew who was who. *Terrucos* are different. Most of the time, we haven't a clue who they are. They attack a place, kill people, and then they're gone; just like the plague that steals up on a wet night and destroys all your potatoes before you've had a chance to realize what's happening.'

The guerrilla, or terrorist, problem was new in the province, but it had already made such an impact that everyone talked about it and the children had begun to play *terrucos* versus the police, with the former always winning. Opinion, gossip, rumours, all did the rounds of the cantinas, the offices, the small workshops, and every back-kitchen of the town, but no-one seemed to have a clear idea of what was happening; least of all the civic authorities and the police force. There was the vague assumption that everything had been fine and then, out of the blue, the terrorists had arrived and started making life unpleasant: blowing up installations, cutting communications, and killing a number of people. In fact, had there been any serious study of local history, everyone would have realized that there was nothing new about terrorist activity in the Andes.

At the end of the nineteenth century and the beginning of the twentieth, bandits were rife, and again, in the thirties, there was a lot of trouble in the north when the military hunted down the left-wing sympathizers of the day. Furthermore, the police had always come down heavily on the *campesinos** who lived in semi-slave conditions under the hard yoke of the hacienda owners. In the early 1970s the haciendas were taken over by the State and turned into cooperatives; but in many cases the majority of the *campesinos* continued to live in grinding poverty, with the result that there were sporadic outbreaks of violence, always heavily crushed by either the police or the military.

Then, in 1980, a new wave of insurgency broke out. It started in the centre of the country, but soon spread. It was well armed and employed an extreme Marxist ideology, whilst at the same time creating an air of mystery. It was this guerrilla movement, known as the *Shining Path*, which had now reached the province of San Agustín.

Amongst the mass of the population there was little idea as to where the *Shining Path* was supposed to lead. Leaflets urging people

---

* Campesino is often translated into English as *peasant*, but this does not really convey the full meaning of the word which refers to all those live in the country-side, either as small-holders owning their own land and probably some cattle, or as agricultural labourers owning virtually nothing.

to join the armed struggle were occasionally to be found blowing about in the streets of Yanacancha, and plenty of slogans had been painted on the walls, with the hammer and sickle very prominent. However, the only people whom the police had managed to capture were a couple of drunken students from the teacher-training college, and they'd been painting slogans for a bet.

Then two incidents occurred which brought it home to people that the terrorist presence was no laughing matter.

A few days ago an assault had been carried out on the large cooperative farm of Santa María del Valle. Not only was extensive damage done to the buildings and farm machinery, but the administrator and the chief accountant had been shot dead in front of their families and the assembled farm workers. After that their bodies had been strung up on the goalposts of the football field. Worse still, a couple of young agricultural engineers, who had been sent by the government to help improve the cooperative's production, had also been shot, in spite of the workers' pleadings on their behalf. When the police arrived the day after the attack, one died of terrible wounds as a result of a booby-trap left at the foot of the flagpole from which he had been ordered to haul down the terrorists' Red Flag.

News had also reached Yanacancha that last night the terrorists had killed Gilberto Llacta, the district officer of the village of Llangodén. These incidents had sent a shaft of fear through the province.

'I don't know what's worse,' muttered Eladio. '*Terrucos* killing folk or the government screwing us to death by putting up prices every bleeding day.'

'If you ask my opinion,' spat Santiago, 'it's the government. The *terrucos* just kill rapidly with a bullet or a knife, but the government's killing us all slowly by starvation. When the mayor wanted our votes he told us that the bleeding APRA* Party was going to give work to us all; there'd be plenty of money, and medicines and food would be

---

* APRA: Alianza Popular Revolucionaria Americana. Political party founded in 1924 by Víctor Raúl Haya de la Torre. It won the 1985 general election in Peru under the leadership of Alan García Pérez. In the following years the terrorist insurgency increased dramatically, and hyper-inflation overtook the economy.

cheap. And now, thanks to APRA, there's hardly any work, we've got no money, there isn't even bread half the time, and it'd be cheaper to buy bloody diamonds than it is to buy medicine. We can't afford to live and we can't afford to die because even a funeral costs too much. Fact is we're fucked!' And with that another ample gob of spit hit the floor to emphasize it.

Sifuentes shambled to his feet and muttered morosely: 'Got to go.'

'Where? You'll get soaked.'

'Up to the municipal depot. If I'm late the mayor'll sack me. I reckon that he's looking for any excuse so as he can give the job to some APRA jerk.' He held out a grimy hand to his drinking companions by way of saying good-bye.

'Have a last drink, Sif,' said Eladio, handing him the calabash.

Sifuentes took it and dipped into the nearly empty bucket of *chicha*.

'¡Gracias y salud!' He downed the *chicha* as though his throat were a drain, and then spat on the floor with satisfaction. 'The *chicha*'s great! You've got to give it to Ma Vásquez that she really knows how to brew *chicha*. See you all.'

''Bye Sif,' they chorused as he lumbered towards the door.

Once out in the street Sifuentes splashed his way in the direction of the Plaza de Armas. As he did so, Manuel came along one of the side streets dragging Lucio Benites with him. Sifuentes took no notice of them and stopped to empty his swollen bladder into the storm water swirling across the square. Lucio was sufficiently conscious to have started again to abuse all and sundry who had conspired to make sure that he didn't get a job this year, especially 'that bastard supervisor of education'. He hung with one arm round Manuel's neck and when he caught sight of Alcides Sifuents urinating placidly into the flooded square he laughed drunkenly and shouted: 'Piss on 'em all, Sifuentes! Piss on 'em!'

Manuel dragged Lucio up the steps that led to the church and the parish house beside it. The door of the latter was open, as always during the day, and Manuel hauled the drunken Lucio inside, sat him down on a bench in the patio and called out: '¡Padre Alfonso!'

The clock in the tower on the other side of the church forecourt struck four-fifteen.

DRINK WAS ALSO circulating freely in the office of the supervisor of education, Don Juan Ortiz. A small group of men were gathered there sorting through the applications for teaching posts, which should have been done a couple of months previously so as to ensure that all schools could start functioning on March 1st with a full complement of teachers. However, that had never been known to happen, and it is doubtful whether it had occurred to anyone that it should. Every year saw the same chaotic scramble as teachers with qualifications and years of service sought better postings, particularly in the town, instead of being stuck for another year in some remote valley; whilst unqualified, or third-class, applicants tried to get any job that was going.

The supervisor and his staff were going through the apparently arduous business of deciding where their favours and patronage should fall, sitting under the benign stare of a vast photo of Víctor Haya De La Torre, the founder of APRA. As might be expected, this eminent politician had to share wall-space with San Agustín and a floosie calendar or two. There was also a collection of lithographs of the nation's heroes which are obligatory in all dependencies of the Ministry of Education, though none of this particular collection of ideological icons in the supervisor's office —figures of integrity and courage— impinged much on the lives of the men gathered round the table, imbibing generously and working sporadically.

At first it would seem that the processing of over a hundred super-deck bureaucratic sandwiches should be a mammoth task since each folder presented by an applicant would inevitably contain layer upon layer of documents —a birth certificate, since one does not exist in Peru if a birth-certificate cannot be produced, even though one knows perfectly well where and when one was born; a residence certificate, a good-conduct certificate, education certificates for every year in secondary school, plus, of course, further education certificates—. Apart from these, any extra certificate that could be added to the pile played its part, such as a course in cookery, a series of lectures attended in the departmental capital —even though one hadn't actually attended the lectures but had signed onto the course and been present when the certificates were handed out at the end—. A few letters of recommendation are always a vital part of any folder's contents, and, of course, a flowery petition seeking a post. All this is the basic sine qua non when applying for a teaching job.

However, there were other documents which, in the last analysis, were more important. Applicants who could prove membership of the governing party took preference over mere university and teacher-training graduates, whilst a straight-forward financial offer would always be a great obstacle remover. Party cards and cash were usually presented in discreet envelopes apart from the rest of the documents.

In order to sort the wheat from the chaff the supervisor and his staff had only to attend to the small envelopes. In at least 60 of the folders there were no such envelopes and so these had quickly been cast to one aside. Of the remainder, it was a question of getting the envelopes into the order of advantage, and so everyone was relieved of the more difficult task of bothering about the order of merit. Since the liquor circulating was courtesy of a couple of applicants, they were already fairly high on the list.

'Ana María Robles Castillo,' droned the group's secretary as he opened another folder.

'That's old man Robles' daughter isn't it? asked the supervisor, tossing off another glass of beer and then leaning back in his chair, scratching his crotch reflectively.

'Sí, señor supervisor.'

'I owe Robles a favour or two, so I've already told him that his girl can have the Llangodén posting. I presume that's alright with the rest of you.'

There was a general nodding of assent. Robles was too important a man in the town to offend. He owned a couple of large trucks and had a well-stocked general store, which was known to be a front for his drug-dealing. Besides, Robles was liberal with funds for the Party and for any good cause in the town.

As he watched the staff of the Education Office nodding their assent and appreciation for Robles and his dim-witted daughter, the supervisor recalled the wretched incident which had occurred yesterday with the applicant who had held the Llangodén post last year, Lucio Benites.

SOMEHOW BENITES HAD got past all the minor functionaries whose task it was to prevent people from reaching the supervisor, and he had barged in to confront Ortiz: 'You gave me the job last year, so why not this?'

The supervisor had sucked his breath and then said in measured tones: 'You must understand that we make appointments on merit, and this year a number of people of outstanding accomplishments have presented themselves.'

Such as Jorge Robles' daughter I suppose!'

'Yes, a girl of great academic promise.'

Academic promise! The girl's as thick as a plank and you bloody well know it!'

Unnerved at the young man's vehemence and lack of respect, the supervisor had added: 'Besides there are other factors that must be taken into consideration, señor...er....'

Lucio Benites.'

Si, Señor Benites.'

'Sure there are other factors, like who your father is, how much cash you can offer, a crate of beer, sleep around, or whether you belong to the bleeding APRA Party,' retorted Benites bitterly.

'Señor Benites, you are being insulting and rude, and there is absolutely no reason why I should tolerate such behaviour in my own office. I must ask you to apologize or you can take it from me that no future application of yours will be considered here.' He had then leaned back in his ample chair and folded his arms over his stomach whilst he looked uncomfortably at the young man in front of him. Lucio Benites was dark-skinned with lanky unkempt hair.

He needed a shave. His shirt was stained and his jeans and sneakers were shabby. As far as the supervisor was concerned, Benites' appointment to the post in Llangodén last year had proved to be of no advantage to anyone, except perhaps to that of the children he had been teaching; but they didn't count. Benites was in fact an excellent teacher, but his political views were known to be left-wing and he had upset some of the parents.

'Because I wouldn't pass their bloody brats who had hardly attended school the whole year and had learned nothing?'

'May be, may be,' murmured the supervisor soothingly. 'But you know, it doesn't do to go around upsetting people. The campesinos are not the submissive folk they used to be, and I can promise you that I'm not prepared to have droves of angry parents coming down here to cause trouble. Should you obtain another post you'll have to be more careful.'

'So whether the kids know anything or not just doesn't matter!' snarled Benites in reply.

'I think we've discussed your case sufficiently. Now if you'll excuse me ....'

Lucio Benites knew that he had been foolish and that for the time being he was beaten, but he vowed vengeance, turned on his heel and walked out of the office.

As HE RECALLED the incident, the supervisor writhed uncomfortably and looked round at the faces of his staff, all men of small established respectability. He had cut Benites down to size and had got rid of him, but there had been no enjoyment in it. The angry and frustrated young man had touched a deep personal chord in himself, largely covered by years of accommodating to the system. There had been a time when he had been a radical left-wing student in the University of Trujillo, and the flash in Benites' eyes, his lean figure and shabby clothing had reminded him for a moment or two of his own student days. He too had nurtured ideals, but these had then withered under the necessity of earning his keep and making his way in life. Besides, there is perhaps nothing so effective as the monotony of provincial town life in the Andes for suffocating ideals and creativity.

Juan Ortiz came out of his reverie and realized that another candidate was being discussed: 'She's from a poor family and can't offer much,' said the deputy supervisor. 'But she deserves a posting.'

'You interested in her or something?' asked Ortiz sneeringly.

The deputy shot him a look of anger, but then swallowed his bile and snapped: 'Of course not!' 'Hernández, this is a branch of the Ministry of Education, not a bleeding charity. If the girl wants the job she pays properly.'

'I'll have a chat with her, señor,' replied the deputy quietly

'Good!' The supervisor poured himself another beer, downed it with a satisfied gulp and then handed the glass to his secretary as he levered himself out of his chair. 'I'll take a look outside before the next one.' He lumbered across the room and went out. He walked through a small waiting room and then opened the door that led into the street. The rain was still pouring down and just a few yards away Sifuentes was urinating placidly. Ortiz looked at him and muttered indignantly: 'Bloody Indian, peeing in the street just like he was one of us!'

Then he glanced at his watch and saw that it was four-fifteen.

THE TEMPEST WAS making enough noise with its lashing rain and howling wind to drown the cries of two young *campesinos* who had been arrested a day or so back, Pablo Huamán and Eriberto Huaripata. Naked and blindfolded they were both plunged repeatedly into a cylinder of icy water laced with excrement.

'Mierdas, I want names!' hurled the captain of police who was supervising the interrogation. Water and filth ran off them as they choked and spluttered, crying that they knew nothing. Captain Vargas looked at them with a deep loathing. These were the kind of bastards who were sowing havoc throughout the country, blowing up electricity pylons and bridges, assaulting isolated police stations, and killing anyone they considered to be an *enemy of the people*—especially government officials, technicians, individual members of the armed forces, and those who had shown initiative and managed to make some money—. And here were these two bloody *terrucos* who refused to say anything! In his anger the captain gave one of them a well-aimed kick in the testicles which sent the young campesino sprawling and howling with pain. 'Names, carajo*!'

As he writhed on the ground the crying youth babbled that he didn't know anyone amongst the terrorists and that he had never had anything to do with them.

'Always the same! The whole bloody country is crawling with *terrucos* and every suspect we haul in swears on his mother's grave that he knows nothing. There's only one way to deal with you bastards and that is to beat the shit out of you until you do talk.' The he turned to the sergeant at his side and snarled: 'Give them another working over!'

'Sí, mi capitán,' came the reply with military precision. Then he added with a grin: 'It'll be a pleasure, señor.'

The captain lit a cigarette and inhaled deeply as he watched the sergeant and a couple of young policemen punch the *campesinos*. Finally one pleaded for mercy and said that he'd talk.

'About bloody time! Who?'

'Humfri Becerra.'

'What do you know about him?'

'He came and talked to us.' The phrase was spluttered between broken teeth and a swollen mouth.

'What did he talk about?'

The campesino was heaving and found it difficult to speak, or even to get a clear idea formulated in his head. He paused and looked round the room with glazed eyes.

'Mierda, what did he talk about?' shouted Vargas. 'Or do you want a bit more help to remember?' He grabbed the young man's testicles and squeezed.

'No, jefe, please!'

'Then talk, damn you!'

'He told us that we've a right to organize our community as we

---

¡Carajo! A common expletive in Peru, pronounced with a gutturual j. The English equivalent is 'damn it!' or 'fuck it!'

like without any interference by the town authorities.'

'Oh he did, did he?' observed Vargas cynically. 'And you agree with him?'

' Sí, jefe.'

The captain gave him a kick which sent the campesino sprawling.

'Get on your bloody feet, mierda!' shouted the sergeant, dragging the young man back to face the captain.

'And what else did this rabble-rouser have to say?'

'This what?'

'¡Carajo! What did Becerra have to say? Did he tell you to fight or take up arms against the government?'

'He told us to fight for our rights.'

'You agree with that too?' hurled Vargas.

This time the campesino didn't reply.

'Do you agree!'

'Sí,' spluttered the campesino. The he cried 'Oowww!' as more blows rained down on him. 'No!' he gasped.

'Did Becerra tell you take up arms?'

'I don't remember.'

'Then I'll help you to remember,' said the captain drily. He lit another cigarette and applied it to the campesino's torso.

'Oowww!'

'Now do you remember?'

'I don't think he said anything about arms, jefe.'

The cigarette was applied again.

'Oowww! No, please! I'll say whatever you like.'

The interrogation went on for another half an hour or so with little useful information being gathered. Finally Captain Vargas turned to the sergeant and asked: 'Have we got anything on this Becerra?'

'I could tell you a few things about him, señor. I'm from the same village, Llangodén. I knew Becerra when he was a kid. Always had a chip on his shoulder, ever since the day he was born. He reckoned that people began messing about with him right then.'

'Tell me all you know about him,' said Vargas, sitting down and stretching out his legs.

'Bien, señor, it was like this ....'

*T*HE BABY HAD *come into the world quickly and lustily, but then something began to go wrong with his mother and she sank rapidly owing to an internal haemorrhage. The women folk who attended her did all they could to stop the bleeding, but to no avail; and when they realized that Domitila Becerra was slipping out of this life they asked her what name she wanted to give her child since there was no known father to do the honours.*

'Humfri,' she whispered.

'What?' exclaimed her mother.

'Humfri.'

'What kind of a name is that supposed to be?'

'I like it. It's got a good macho sound and I want my boy to grow up macho, like his father.' A smile crossed her face and had the hovering women known it, Domitila was recalling the coupling which had produced her son. Just once, during the annual celebrations in honour of San Cayetano, with a brawny youth who was one of the itinerant vendors that are always to be found at the religious fiestas in the Andes. He took her at the back of his stall on a pile of unsold cloth and cheap clothing. She never learned his name, but Domitila remembered that he was macho.

Domitila's mother made one more effort to persuade her daughter to give the child a decent Christian name; without success.

'I want him called Humfri.' And with that she closed her eyes for good and there could be no further discussion on the subject. So Humfri had to bear the strange name, though perhaps not quite so strange in a land where children are baptized with names ranging from Bismark to Stalin, or with weird concoctions like Reeder and Nanciregan. Nevertheless, it remained a sore point with Humfri that people had started messing about with him on the day of his birth, and he soon learned that life harboured a lot more messing about both with him and his class.

When Humfri was born, his grandfather was still a peón on the great hacienda of San Cayetano de Llangodén, which sprawled over the mountains until dropping finally down in the east to the vast gorge of the River Marañón. It was here, along the banks of the swift-flowing river and in the sheltered valleys that large quantities of fruit and coca were grown, some of the former going up to the big house to be turned into preserves and jams, whilst the latter guaranteed a good proportion of the income of the hacienda's owner; an income that also came from the cattle, the maize, the potatoes and the wheat that thrived in the extensive uplands.

The owner of the hacienda was called 'la niña', an enigmatic aristocratic lady whom no-one who lived at San Cayetano had ever seen. She lived in a fine mansion in Lima and had inherited the hacienda from a distant cousin. Every year there were rumours that 'la niña' was coming to visit her lands, but somehow the trip never materialized; though she showed none of the same reluctance to receive the income from San Cayetano that enabled her to live in style, entertain lavishly, and give generously to charity.

In order to ensure that the hacienda was not mismanaged, 'la niña' let it out to the Góngora family in Trujillo, who in their turn sub-let it to the Zúñigas of San Roque. These last used to turn up at San Cayetano for the sowing and harvesting of the crops, and also for the annual fiesta in honour of the patron saint. Then the dilapidated rooms of the big house would ring with drunken laughter, mixed with the explosions of the rockets that are an essential part of any religious celebration. Over the open hearths of the kitchens massive cauldrons and pots would simmer and bubble all day long, ensuring a constant supply of food. The chicha would flow in quantities and the older workers of the hacienda would nod happily to see life coursing with such abandon, as it had done in the old days, when the owners had actually lived there. However, by the 1960s the younger men had begun to chafe at a system whereby they had to slave away in order to maintain their own families, the Zúñigas, the Góngoras, and the never-seen 'niña' in Lima. So when the Agrarian Reform decreed by the military government reached them in 1971* *they welcomed it with open arms, and the hacienda became a cooperative.*

---

* In October 1968 there was a military coup which overthrew the democratically elected government of Fernando Belaúnde Terry. There followed a dictatorship under General Juan Velasco Alvarado which attempted to reform the social structure of Peru on the lines of what Nasser had done in Egypt. One decree put an end to the haciendas.

The change was celebrated by slaughtering and eating some prize cattle. Everyone got gloriously drunk and the government officials made off with a number of works of art that had remained in the chapel. Before doing so they told the campesinos: 'You are the owners now! No longer will you be exploited by absentee, bloodsucking landlords! Everything is yours to run as you will!' This, in practice, meant that it didn't run at all, since no-one was accustomed to planning or decision making. Whereas in the days of the hacienda the workers had never been allowed to think or speak their mind, at least there had always been seed and fertilizers. After the Reform there were continuous meetings in which everyone had plenty to say, but somehow neither seed nor fertilizers ever materialized. So the cooperative just fell apart and the land was divided into small-holdings. Families like the Becerras came out of this very badly, whilst others, like the Llactas, did very well for themselves, and between young Humfri Becerra and Gilberto Llacta there was bitter hatred.

At the school which now functioned in part of what had been the big house Humfri and Gilberto quarreled continuously and one day, after a particularly acrimonious discussion Humfri had shouted: 'I'll screw you Gilberto Llacta.'

'You miserable little jerk, you couldn't screw a cat!' jeered Gilberto. 'Your family are losers. Always have been and always will be.'

Then they had fought like two wild dogs, punching, screaming, kicking, and rolling in the dust. The other boys had stood and watched, saying nothing, but ready to cheer the winner. It was Gilberto who won finally with a well-aimed kick in the crotch of his opponent. That had been the turning-point in Humfri's life. He was determined that this was the last time he'd ever be down on his knees. He vowed revenge against Gilberto and his family, and made no secret of the fact.

Humfri had one advantage over Gilberto. The schoolmistress in Llangodén was his godmother, and once she realized that the little boy was intelligent she did everything she could to encourage and help him. Eventually he made it to the university in San Roque, and there he managed to combine being a university student with remaining at heart a campesino. Unlike others from the countryside, he was not ashamed of his origins and returned to Llangodén whenever he could, sliding back into the local dialect, slipping a poncho over his head, and wearing car-tyre sandals just like any other campesino youth. However, his family and close friends knew that he had undergone a profound change, and when he squatted round the fire with them in the evening and *shared a bottle of cañazo*, he'd manifest his admiration for the Shining Path and would talk about a society based on Marxist-Leninism.*

Humfri's loathing for Gilberto Llacta increased. He spat out his scorn and called him 'a bloody government turd.' However, Gilberto didn't care. He was the rooster in Llangodén now that he had been appointed the district officer, and he knew that so long as he didn't steal too blatantly he was on to a good thing with a steady source of income from government financed projects. Once or twice he overstepped the mark, but a timely present to the judicial authorities in Yanacancha had smoothed things over. Gilberto wasn't a political fanatic, so it didn't really matter much to him which party won the elections, and he found no difficulty in changing cards in 1985, when the present APRA government came to power. He was confirmed in his post as district officer and was able to filter sufficient money into his own pocket to allow him to build a fine house in Trujillo.

'LLACTA?' SAID CAPTAIN Vargas, interrupting the sergeant's flow of information.

'Sí, mi capitán.'

'The guy the *terrucos* shot a couple of days ago in Llangodén?'

'Sí.'

'So Becerra was probably involved.'

'Could be, señor. The universities are all on strike, so Becerra may well be around in the Llangodén area.'

'Good, now we've got something to go on I'd like you to send a man out to Llangodén to investigate a bit further. Use Sánchez. He can pass easily for a campesino and knows the lie of the land; and tell him to report directly to me when he gets back.' Vargas stood up and stretched himself. He gave a contemptuous kick at the campesino still moaning on the floor and said: 'Before Sánchez leaves, have another go at these two creeps we've got here, and see if you can

---

**Cañazo:* A fiery spirit made from sugar cane, sometimes called in English 'firewater'.

some more out of them.' Then he left for a hot shower, a change of clothes, and a stiff drink.

Outside the rain continued to sheet down. It was around four-fifteen.

HUMFRI BECERRA SAT under the low eaves of the house where the wake for Gilberto Llacta was taking place, huddled against the impact of the wind. Like everyone else present he was cold and morosely he watched the hailstones piling up in the muddy patio in front of him. Under every available piece of shelter other *campesinos* sought to avoid the ravages of the tempest, the men combating the icy wind with harsh cigarettes, masticating *coca*, and downing fiery *cañazo*, whilst the women squatted by the smoky fires over which they were preparing food for the large gathering. Nobody said very much, not only because of the storm, but also because of the stunning effect of Gilberto Llacta's death had had on them.

IT HAD OCCURRED a couple of nights ago, a night without rain in this part of the province, but cloudy and cold. A silent column had advanced on the village of Llangodén, and the barking of occasional dogs had not been enough to bring folk out of their houses to see what might be happening, because dogs always bark during the Andean night. The column had reached the cottage of Gilberto Llacta which was set somewhat apart from the rest and had been easy to identify because it had a new corrugated sheet-iron roof which glinted silver when the moon peered through the clouds. The leader of the column had knocked sharply on the door: 'Open up!' There was no reply. The next knocks were more insistent and then a woman's voice, muffled by sleep and terror, answered: 'Who is it?'

'Don't ask questions! Just open the bloody door!'

The door was opened a crack and it was barely possible to make out the unkempt figure of the woman who had answered. She looked at the masked group and croaked: 'What do you want?'

'Gilberto Llacta,' came the curt reply.

'He isn't here.'

They pushed her aside roughly and entered the cluttered room, typical of the country cottages of the area, with everything jumbled about all over the place. The only furniture consisted of two beds, a table, a couple of chairs and a sewing machine. Clothes and blankets hung on cords suspended from the roof beams, and there were sacks of maize and lentils, plus several piles of potatoes heaped against a bare adobe wall.

'Light!' snapped the leader of the column.

The woman made no move and seemed paralyzed. The masked figure gave her a shove and repeated: 'Light, carajo!' and then added, 'or I'll blast you and your bloody cottage to bits!'

She still hesitated, half from frozen panic and half from sheer blind obstinacy. One of the group produced a torch and shone it round the room. Then he advanced purposefully towards the sacks of maize and pulled them apart. The beam of his torch fell on the cowering figure of Gilberto Llacta.

'Mierda, come out!' he ordered the terrified man.

Llacta crawled out of his hiding place and was told briefly that popular justice demanded his death for being a lackey of the corrupt bourgeois government and for stealing from the people. 'You've been on to a good thing ever since you became district officer. Recently you've got yourself a nice new roof, thanks to stealing half of what was intended for the medical post.'

'It's not true, I swear it!'

'And this land, which you and your family grabbed when the cooperative collapsed, I suppose that that's not true either? Nor the prize cattle you were able to buy out of funds for the irrigation scheme?' sneered his interrogator.

Two small children who had been woken by the noise were now clinging to their mother's skirts and watched the scene wide-eyed with fear. Suddenly the women herself intervened: 'You're not going to hurt my Gilby are you?' she pleaded. 'We'll pay for the roof or whatever.'

'Shut your trap, Martha!' spat Llacta.

'I don't want you to get hurt,' replied the woman stubbornly.

'Come on, jefe, we can't waste all night gabbing,' intervened another of the hooded figures. 'Shoot the mierda and let's go.'

'*No!*' *screamed the woman sinking to her knees imploringly.*

The leader of the group fired at Llacta's temple at point blank range and the campesino crumpled onto the floor. His wife collapsed and burst into uncontrollable sobbing, accompanied by that of her children. The leader grabbed her and hauled her to her feet saying brusquely: 'You can cut out that noise! You know what your husband was like and you helped him steal. He never did a bloody thing in this village that wasn't to his own advantage. And you can think yourself lucky that we're not the police or the military because the next thing we'd do is gang rape you and kill your sniveling brats.'

With that they left her and she flung herself onto the floor beside the corpse and sobbed and sobbed. The door of the cottage swung open and shut in the cold wind, adding its dismal creaking to the macabre scene.

'*I'll bet it was Humfri Becerra who put the terrucos onto you, Gilby,*' *cried the woman.* '*And I swear you'll get your revenge!*'

THE HATRED WHICH had existed between Humfri Becerra and Gilberto Llacta was no secret in Llangodén and Nasho Quiroz, sat on the bench next to Humfri during Gilberto's wake, wondered whether the rumours about his being responsible for the district officer's death were true. As Nasho chewed his *coca* reflectively, sweetening it with an occasional dab of lime on a pin which he prodded rhythmically into a small calabash container, he looked at Humfri and took stock of his lean face, his knit brow, and the deep hard look in his eyes. The young *campesino* had always been a loner; always been different. It was difficult not to respect him, but there could be no question of liking him. Nor could Nasho ever quite understand what Humfri talked about: the *Shining Path*, President Gonzalo, and some Chinese guy called Miaowse-Tung, whoever he was.

Humfri himself glance round the scene and could see that a number of the poncho-clad mourners were obviously talking about him and were throwing hostile glances in his direction. Suddenly there was a movement amongst the women and one came running across the muddy patio in the pouring rain. Hatless, her long plats streaming behind her, she made straight for where Humfri was sitting. It was Martha, Gilberto Llacta's widow, and she threw herself on the young man screaming: 'It was you who denounced my Gilberto to the *terrucos*! You're the one to blame for his death!'

Humfri tried to fend her off without hitting her, but she was like a tigress and continued to hurl accusations as she scratched and clawed at him. Someone grabbed her and managed to pull her off Humfri, though they couldn't stop her screaming like one of the furies, soaked in the pouring rain: 'You killed him, you bastard!'

He replied deliberately: 'Martha, I didn't kill him. I never liked him, I'll admit; but if I'd wanted to kill him I'd have done it myself and not sent others.'

'¡Mierda! Coward!'

'Martha you're upset, and you've a right to be, but I've got nothing to do with Gilberto's death and you don't call me a coward,' replied Humfri stiffly.

'Coward!' She yelled again at the top of her voice.

In spite of the deluging rain there was an electric tension in the air. Humfri looked at the hostile faces surrounding him and knew that he couldn't avoid some kind of a fight. He took a deep breath and then threw down a challenge: 'Martha I can't fight you, but I'll fight one of your bloody brothers.'

'You'll fight no-one!' came a peremptory order, and everyone turned to see that three hooded men had approached silently whilst their attention was riveted on Martha and Humfri. If the atmosphere had been electric a few minutes previously it was now doubly so as the mourners found themselves covered by the light machine guns in the hands of the menacing figures. 'No-one needed to denounce Gilberto Llacta. He was well known to us as scum and we decided to eliminate him when he didn't heed our warning and resign as district officer.'

'Gilberto didn't do us any harm,' spoke up Nasho to everyone's surprise, including his own.

'He stole from you as much as he could,' one of the masked figures spat out harshly.

'It wasn't much,' persisted Nasho.

'So you're defending him?'

'Sort of,' replied Nasho slowly. There was a crack! Then with a remarkably graceful movement Nasho slid into the mud. He had been felled by a single shot.

'Anyone else want to defend Llacta?' asked Nasho's killer.

No-one dared to say a thing, and the intense silence was broken only by the hiss of the continual downpour.

'Are you coming with us?' the killer called across to Humfri.

Humfri stood up, all eyes on him again. He didn't say anything and just crossed the patio to join the three terrorists. As he did so Martha broke free and came up behind him screaming: 'May the blood of Gilberto Llacta take revenge on this mierda of a Becerra!'

That was the last that the people of Llangodén saw of Humfri Becerra.

It was about four-thirty.

IT WAS *Friday of Sorrows*, the Friday before Holy Week, which is still dedicated in many old parishes of the Andes to the sorrowing Mother of God —*La Dolorosa*—, and custom dictated that her statue be carried round the town in procession, dressed in solemn black, with the silver swords of her seven sorrows piercing her heart. The devotion to *La Dolorosa* was deep in San Agustín de Yanacancha, probably because the women knew only too well from the experience of their own lives about suffering, especially in a society still dominated by machismo.

Most religious processions in the Andes have their sponsors, or *mayordomos*, who have to ensure that the *andas* —the great platforms on which the statues are carried— are suitably adorned for the occasion with flowers and candles, and sometimes with elaborate confections in crepe, velvet and muslin. The *mayordomo* also pays for the band and arranges for food and drink to be served after the procession is over. He, or she, will pay for the rockets to be let off during the Mass and the procession, and often for a firework display to be held at the end of the proceedings.

Here in Yanacancha, these duties for the procession of *La Dolorosa* were carried out each year by Señorita Flor Delgado, one of those spinsters without whom no Andean parish is complete; selfless in her devotion to the needs of the local Church. For over 50 years Señorita Flor's mother had sponsored the procession of *La Dolorosa* and then, after the old lady's death, her daughter had carried on the tradition alone these last 20. Señorita Flor was now well into her 70s, but no year went by without her providing generously for the procession of the Mother of God. 'I've promised to do this until the Good Lord takes me, and so I shall,' she had announced categorically to the parish priest, Father Alfonso, recently when he suggested that she ought not to continue incurring the heavy expenses involved. 'I can't take the money with me, Father, and what little I've got I've earned honestly, so I'll spend it as I please, if you don't mind.' With that the priest knew better than try to interfere further since Flor Delgado was a formidable lady, in spite of the delicate flower-like implications of her name.

Señorita Flor was hard at work with a small group of friends putting the finishing touches to the statue of *La Dolorosa* and the *andas,* all of them oblivious to the storm outside, and interested only in making sure that everything would be ready for the procession that evening. The old lady presided benignly, thinking of the great pots of food cooking down at her house. Times might be hard, but she wasn't going to stint her hospitality and, like Elizabeth of old, she was only too happy to attend Mary.

For over 30 years Flor Delgado had been the school mistress in Llangodén. 'I really enjoyed teaching those children,' she confided to Doña Leonor Gil de Verástegui, wife of the local bank manager and mother of Manuel, who was outside somewhere in the storm.

'There's not many who can stick the country schools for so long,' observed Doña Leonor. 'In fact I reckon that most teachers regard them as a penance to be completed as quickly as possible.'

'Half the trouble is that they despise the *campesinos,* and the other half is that they want all the comforts of the town,' replied Flor in a no-nonsense tone.

'Living rough never bothered you then?'

'Not really. Besides, it was not all that rough. Once you've gained the confidence of the *campesinos* they're very generous, and I remember that almost every day someone would bring me a gift of food.'

'That's strange, because a lot of the teachers complain that the *campesinos* are thoroughly uncooperative.'

'I reckon that it all depends on the teacher. Let's face it, there are plenty who arrive late on Monday and are off back to town before lunch on Friday, at the latest so the children don't receive a full week's schooling. And besides that there are other problems such as drunkenness and even violations. The *campesinos* are no fools and they can tell at once whether a teacher is really committed to working with them or not. In my own experience I never had any problems and loved working amongst the folk of Llangodén.'

'But it must have been frustrating to know that no matter how hard you worked the majority of the children you taught would either stay on the land and grub a living as their fathers and grandfathers had done, or drift into the shanty-towns that cluster round the coastal cities.'

'I never saw things that way, and besides, there was the occasional bright child who wanted to carry on with his education. My greatest joy came when one of them finally made it to the university. He was an orphan and I took him under my wing and became his godmother —though I had to put up with his being baptized Humfri—. I suspect that his mother saw one film in her life and Humphrey Bogart starred in it. Well, my Humfri was a clever little monkey at school, and always fighting. The other youngsters used to pick on him, especially a nasty brat called Gilberto Llacta. However, Humfri struggled through and made it to the university in San Roque. He's there now and doing well. He dropped in to see me just the other day on his way up to visit Llangodén. Another strike, or something, has paralyzed his studies he told me.'

'Yes, it's affecting all the universities and that's why I've got Manuel at home. As far as I can see the boy'll be a grandfather before he finishes his studies because of the number of strikes and delays.'

'Humfri's worried too. He keeps on telling me that he doesn't want to be a burden; but I'm only too happy to help him, and my other *campesino* godchildren too.' The old lady's face crinkled into a happy smile. 'I've got several. Since I never married and had children of my own I thought that the least I could do would be to give some poor kids a helping hand. I don't know whether I've achieved much though. When you reach my age and begin to look back over your life you can't help wondering whether you made good use of the time that God has given you.'

Doña Leonor gave señorita Flor a friendly pat on the arm and said: 'I hope that when I reach your age I can say that I've done half of what I know you've done.'

Flor Delgado smiled happily as she replied: 'You've got some fine children and frankly I envy you. Humfri's a great lad, but he's not really mine, and when I see your brood at Mass I think how the Lord has blessed you, especially with Manuel. He'll make a wonderful doctor when he finishes his studies.'

Tears welled up in Doña Leonor's eyes as she heard this praise of her eldest son and she replied quietly: 'Gracias, Señorita Flor.' Then she added: 'You know I worry about him a lot. He's spent much of his life in this small town and now he has to live in the hurly-burly of Lima. Sometimes I wonder whether he'll get involved with drugs or tangle with a girl before he finishes his studies. Then there is this nightmare inflation that we are suffering, and on top of that all the violence that has broken out. I'm beginning to wonder what kind of a country we're handing on to our children.'

'I can understand your feelings, because if things carry on the way they are going there won't be any country left. We're as near to a civil war as we can be without actually calling it that; and there doesn't seem to be any end in sight. For a few days we hear nothing and then suddenly we are told about a military operation or an attack by the *terrucos* with goodness knows how many people killed and how many families plunged into mourning.'

Doña Leonor sighed bitterly and said: 'At the beginning of the emergency I don't think that the killing and the fighting meant much to me. It all seemed so far away from here and concerned the terrorists, the police, and the military. The civilians killed were almost always Quechua-speaking *campesinos* down south. I didn't know anyone involved. But now the killing and the violence are right here in our own province, and the news of the deaths in Santa María del Valle really hit me because when we lived in Chiclayo I got to know the family of one of the agricultural engineers who was killed. Carlos was such a nice lad, and he stayed here with us before going out to the cooperative. I can't understand why the *terrucos* had to kill him. When one of them has been killed I've just shrugged my shoulders and said that they knew what they were letting themselves in for when they joined the *Shining Path*. When a young policeman or soldier has been killed I suppose I've simply hardened my heart and said to myself that's the risk they run when they join up. When a *campesino* has died, awful as it may seem, I don't think I ever gave that much thought. Now the son of a friend of mine has died. And why? God only knows! Why on earth should anyone want to kill an agricultural engineer who is doing his utmost to improve the lot of some *campesinos*. I just don't understand.'

Doña Leonor began to cry and Señorita Flor put a gentle arm round her as she too felt a deep grief and tears welled up in her eyes as she said: 'You know, as I look at *La Dolorosa* I think how many women like her, mothers here in Peru on both sides in this war, have had to receive the broken bodies of their sons and daughters as a result of the fighting and the violence.'

A silence fell between them, tears trickling down both their faces, echoing the crystal drops on the Virgin's cheeks, glistening in the half-light.

By this time the work of decorating the *andas* was almost complete and the other ladies who had come to help Flor Delgado were standing back to admire their handiwork. Realizing that she herself hadn't been doing anything to help during the last ten minutes, Flor left Doña Leonor's side with a word of apology and walked round the *andas* several times, checking that everything was in order and just as she wanted. She straightened a candle here and the folds of a drape there, until finally she pronounced herself satisfied. Then she said that she'd go and check that the band would turn up on time, 'Not like last year when we had to wait ages for them.'

'Because it was the band-master's birthday and he was as drunk as an owl,' said one of the severer looking members of the group.

'I hope that it'll stop raining before the procession tonight,' murmured another of the ladies, a timid person who had treated every candle as though it were made of the finest porcelain.

'Of course it will,' insisted Flor Delgado emphatically. 'Never in all my life has it rained on the procession of *La Dolorosa.*'

'But this tempest is quite different, señorita,' observed one of the others. 'I can't remember anything like it. Just listen to the rain!'

'Fiddlesticks!' retorted Flor. 'It's always rained hard here in Yanacancha. Perhaps that's why our pagan ancestors worshipped Catequil, the storm-god.'

'I'm sure that I've not got any nasty pagan Indian blood in my veins, thank you,' sniffed the most impressive of the helpers, Doña Dagoberta Castillo de Robles.

Flor Delgado snorted without offering any reply, and then shepherded the ladies into a small semicircle in front of *La Dolorosa* and began to pray the Sorrowful Mysteries of the Rosary.

The clock in the church tower struck four-thirty.

MUDDY RAIN-WATER ran in rivers down the side of the Plaza de Armas and threatened to flood the dingy office of Emilio Santillán, Doctor of Law, who sat behind a desk piled high with the dusty folders of pending cases —most of them pending for a long time—. Like all provincial lawyers, Dr. Santillán was dressed in a suit, though in his case it had obviously seen better days and belonged to the style of at least a decade ago. Although unshaven, the lawyer exuded eau-de-cologne, injecting an incongruous scent into the deep musty atmosphere. There was something feline about his twitching face, accentuated by a wispy moustache that jerked impatiently as he listened to the sobbing pleas of a woman sat saggedly in front of him on the edge of a chair. She was a *campesina*, as could be seen at once from her indigenous Indian features and colouring, and by the way she was dressed.

'You must help me, señor,' she cried, tears rolling down her furrowed nut-brown face. 'The police say they haven't got my boy, but I'm sure they have. The other day they came to our village looking for all the young men. Turned everything upside down, stole our chickens and any money there was. Then they went off firing into the air and threatening us with bloody hell.'

'They took your son, Eriberto?'

'No, he was hiding in the woods with other boys from the village.'

'So what happened?'

'When Eriberto came back that evening he told me that he was going to take the pig to market, sell it, and then leave for the coast because he was fed up with things here.'

'And?'

'He took the pig the following day and I haven't seen him since.'

'So he's gone down to the coast.'

'He left all his things at our cottage. I'm sure that the police have got him.'

'You may well be right,' mused Dr. Santillán. In fact in his own mind he was pretty certain the she was. As he turned this over, Dr. Santillán remembered the times when he'd got happily drunk on free whisky, thanks to his friendship with successive police officers; and young Captain Vargas had already proved himself to be exceptionally good company. He may not have been long in Yanacancha but he had already obtained excellent contacts to provide a discriminating man with excellent liquor, women —decent ones not being all that easily available in a small Andean town— and drugs. And now this wretched Indian woman wanted him to go and plead with the Captain for her son, who was probably a *terruco*, whatever the mother might say to the contrary.

With a sigh, Dr. Santillán muttered that he would do his best.

'Please, please! Eriberto's all I've got.'

The lawyer remained unmoved, watching the crumpled woman, her heavily lined brown face running with tears and her hands trembling as she tried to untie a grubby handkerchief in which her money was wrapped.

'I'll pay you something now, señor. I haven't got much, but I want to save my boy.'

'The money'll do for a start,' said the lawyer drily as he received the screwed up notes. 'Come back in a few days.' He looked at her feeling ill at ease. He had always found the *campesinos* difficult to deal with. Either they were excessively obsequious or, especially when they had got a few drinks inside them, truculent and offensive. So this woman aroused little compassion in him since she was as alien to him as though they lived on different planets instead of a few hours walking distance apart. However, he had just enough humanity to feel that he'd have to do something for her and asked if she had a photo of her son. She produced a tattered picture taken the previous year during the annual fiesta of San Agustín.

The lawyer took the photo and squinted at it in the gloom of the afternoon. It portrayed a youth who could have been any one of the thousands of young *campesinos* who lived in the province: a young man with a new straw hat pulled down rakishly to one side of his face, a short red poncho hanging slightly askew, and widely cut trousers over car-tyre sandals. He held a radio in one hand and looked slightly tipsy, which would be normal during the fiesta.

'That's my Eriberto.'

'Fine. Let me keep it and I'll see what I can do.'

'Please, please!' sobbed the woman as she rocked back and forth. It was about four-fifty.

WITH NO GUTTERS on most of the roofs that straddled and sagged crazily over the houses of the town, the rain fell from them like a curtain, making the vision of anyone looking out distorted and opaque. The mayor of San Agustín de Yanacancha, Don Nicolás Leal, a thin, hunched individual, had stood for almost an hour gazing with just such a vision from his office window that gave onto the Plaza de Armas.

The municipality had once been one of the larger town houses of Yanacancha, belonging to a hacienda owning family. However, when the Agrarian Reform had brought the haciendas to an end, the family had sold up and gone to live in Trujillo, whilst their onetime residence became a warren of pokey offices filled with rodent-like clerks: some mice and others rats.

Gloomily the mayor had watched the flood waters swirling in the street below, with the palm trees in the centre of the square looking as though they might snap at any moment in the howling wind, whilst the flowers and bushes in the gardens around the trees had become a bedraggled battered mess. The mayor had also glanced towards the church at the upper end of the square and could just see the blurred figure of Alcides Sifuentes adding his quota to the flood water. Then Manuel and Lucio had staggered into view and up the steps. As he had watched Sifuentes, Don Nicolás thought of what a useless night-watchman he made for the municipal depot; but the old man had been given the job thanks to the insistence of one of the left-wing councillors, and any attempt to remove him would cause an uproar from the small, but vocal, radical left-wing party, so it was easier to leave things as they were.

Don Nicolás must have stood at the window mesmerized by the storm for quite a time before he muttered bitterly to himself: 'The *terrucos*'ll enjoy this bloody tempest. Perfect weather for them and it'll clog up any police movements, if they bother to stir themselves at all.'

'I beg your pardon, Don Nicolás, did you say something?' asked his middle-aged secretary who dominated the municipality and had just entered the office without knocking and with a large pile of papers requiring a signature.

'Nothing, Señorita Janine,' replied the mayor with a disgruntled shrug of the shoulders. Then, indicating the papers, he asked: 'What are those?'

'There's a bit of everything, señor, and all requiring your signature.'

'Put them on my desk and I'll sign them later.'

'Some of them are urgent,' ventured the secretary with what passed for her idea of a seductive smile.

'I told you to leave them on the desk,' snapped Don Nicolás impatiently.

Señorita Janine was surprised at this outburst of irritability because normally the mayor was an undemonstrative individual who showed her suitable deference. Furthermore, she had no intention of letting herself be intimidated by him because she could feel the crisp notes in her bodice which she had received in order to ensure prompt signatures. 'One of the documents is Señor Robles' plan for the extension of his house,' she said, holding it out towards the mayor. 'Señor Robles,' she repeated emphatically.

'Oh alright,' sighed don Nicolás resignedly.

He signed with a flourish and before he could object the secretary slipped another document under his nose. 'Nothing like doing it at once, is there señor?' She smiled again, spider-like this time, and then, with an apparently obsequious 'gracias,' flounced out of the room, or rather, as nearly as possible that a woman of her age and proportions perched on high-heeled shoes could flounce.

Don Nicolás returned to the window and continued to gaze at the tempest outside. He had been mayor of Yanacancha prior to the military seizure of power in 1968, and then was elected again when there were free elections in 1980, also in 1983 and the last time, in 1986. Within the limits of his narrow background and provincial life in a small Andean town he was as good a mayor as could be expected. He had neither the funds, nor the vision, nor the energy, to get involved in extensive public works; though at least some progress had been made during his administrations. Also he was sufficiently intelligent to realize that in a place like Yanacancha it made life pleasanter to be on friendly terms with everyone, so he had kept party favouritism within bounds. He gave the two left-wing councilors just enough leeway to keep them satisfied, and he had managed to rub along with the succession of judges and police officers appointed by Lima.

Everything had been going alone quite well until the terrorists arrived on the scene, and since then Don Nicolás knew that the place was falling apart. He had no clear idea of what was happening, though he could see that events were overtaking him and the pleasant feudal society in which he had lived all his life was finally disintegrating; and he felt impotent in the face of the rising storm. Alone with himself, as he was this afternoon, he could honestly say that he had no solutions to offer to counter the violence that was lashing the province. Nor, he realized, had the government any constructive plan. As in everything over the past few years, the government spent its time dithering and prevaricating, and had nothing concrete to offer.

The rain continued to cascade down and the mayor wondered how many landslides would block the only road out of the province. He then looked at his watch and saw that it would be five o'clock in a few minutes.

THE TERRORIST COLUMN had enjoyed the hot chicken that the woman had served them. Now it was time to move on again. It was still raining hard, but this was proving a boon because it enabled them to move almost to the edge of the town without fear of being detected.

'What do we owe you?' one of them asked the woman who cowered in a corner of the room.

'Whatever you'll give me,' she stammered, frightened to death by these rough looking youths and the girl.

'We're not the police and we're not thieves,' said another in a softer tone. 'You've prepared food for us and it made good eating, so what do we owe you?'

The woman smiled nervously and stated her price.

'Fine!' They paid her and then the leader of the group said: 'But don't you go telling anyone we've been here, because we wouldn't like that. Just remember, what we're doing we're doing for you. We're doing it for the Revolution.'

'I see,' she replied in a tone which indicated that she didn't see at all.

Then they left and went out into the rain, oblivious to it and intent only on their objective, a three-pronged attack on the town. In spite of the fact that several members of the group were little more than sixteen or seventeen years old they had the look of seasoned fighters, and they had had the *Shining Path's* ideology so drummed into them that they were impervious to set-backs or difficulties.

The rain continued to deluge down and low cloud scudded across the landscape getting caught up in the eucalyptus woods like rent muslin. The terrorists padded their way through the mud and wet undergrowth, protecting only their weapons, until finally they were within striking distance. They stopped and listened to the last orders.

'Remember, no prisoners, and if any of you fall, you fend for yourselves.'

'What about Vargas?'

'If you get him, castrate him before you slit his throat. Shove his penis in his mouth, and then string him up somewhere where the whole town can see him.

'A pleasure, compañero!'

They moved off and within seconds the cloud and the rain had swallowed them all.

It was almost five o'clock.

JUST AT THIS moment Father Alfonso Calderón stood looking out of his study window across the forecourt of the church. He was a slight man, clean shaven, with a sharp jaw and a trace of indigenous Indian features in his olive-skinned face. His deep black eyes were fiery. The priest was 36 years old, a native of the province, and his old mother still lived in the district of La Quinua.

After he finished his studies for the priesthood the Bishop had sent him to Yanacancha. 'I know a man's not reckoned to be a prophet on his home ground', the prelate had sighed when appointing him, 'but there's nothing else for it at the moment. There's no other priest available and I can't leave Yanacancha unattended any longer. It's a couple of years since old Rengifo died and the tares amongst our pretty ragged wheat are multiplying daily. The evangelical sects have sown discord and division, the communist teachers in the schools spread their own materialistic form of unbelief, and the whole parish is falling to pieces. What a thing to have to admit over 400 years after the cross was first planted in Yanacancha!' The Bishop had laughed bitterly and added: 'You're a bright lad, so perhaps you can pull the place together.'

Thus, at the age of 26, Alfonso Calderón had taken over the pastoral care of roughly 10,000 people in the town of San Agustín de Yanacancha and some 50,000 more who lived scattered in the villages and isolated farms throughout the mountainous province. He became used to walking for days and weeks from valley to valley, across the mountain ranges, and bit by bit he established close links with his flock, even in the most isolated corners of the moors, or in the remotest valleys which gave onto the great gorge of the River Marañón.

At first the *campesinos* were wary of Alfonso. He wasn't like old Father Rengifo who used to visit them to celebrate their fiestas, riding on an ancient mule, his cassock tucked up about him. No, this young man walked everywhere, used the same car-tyre sandals as everyone else, and replaced the cassock with jeans. Out in the villages, or on the farms, Father Alfonso shared the life of the people. He enjoyed taking a hand at plowing with a yoke of oxen: 'Nothing like keeping in practice', he'd grin. 'I used to help my old man when I was a youngster, and I reckon that I could plow as straight a furrow as any man in La Quinua.' In the evenings, after Mass, he'd share a meal with any family that invited him, hunched on a low stool near the fire, swapping anecdotes and jokes, and swigging at the bottle of *cañazo* as it did its rounds.

Whenever he was in the town of San Agustín, Father Alfonso fulfilled his priestly duties to the letter, and his house was always open to those who had need of him, and he managed to be discreet and kind. He tried to comfort and shrive compassionately, to instruct his people in sound doctrine, to celebrate the sacraments reverently, and to give himself unstintingly to whatever service was asked of him. However, after ten years of this Alfonso had come to feel like a squeezed-out orange; and, according to the teaching he had received in the seminary, the only one defence guaranteed to maintain his priesthood intact was prayer. Prayer!? That's all very fine when one feels as though there is a communion or dialogue with God, but recently it had become little more than talking to the wall and listening to silence. Also, what they had forgotten in the seminary, or perhaps his professors had never had first-hand experience of it, was the sheer loneliness of an Andean priest which can undermine his humanity; and Alfonso was sharply aware that should his humanity collapse, his priesthood would quickly follow. Sometimes as he passed the town's cantinas and saw men drowning their sorrows he longed to join them, and even if he still hung on to his celibacy, he often craved a woman's arms.

Alfonso was under no illusions: as a man and a priest he was extremely vulnerable. Now, on top of everything else there was the added strain of the terrorist presence in the province, and it had been in response to a plea from the villagers of Chugurmayo that he had left Yanacancha early yesterday morning to visit them. There had been a police raid on the village and the people were very frightened.

WHEN HE ARRIVED, Alfonso had gone from house to house and listened to what the people had to tell him:

'They came at dawn, Father, firing and shouting: "Out of your houses you fucking terrucos!"'

'They kicked down our doors.'

'They scattered everything all over the floor.'

'They stole things.'

'Never have I heard or seen the like, Father, not even in the worst days of the haciendas. They treated us like animals then, but this was worse,' said old Fortunato who had seen a few things in his time.

Segunda Chilón, whose 15 year old daughter Luisa, had been raped, said bitterly: 'Father, when I've heard that the compañeros had killed a policeman, I'd weep for his mother. But not now, Father. I wish they'd kill all the bastard police after what they've done to my Luisa.'

'There were two of them. One threatened us with his weapon and forced

43

us to watch, whilst the other raped my child. Then they changed round,' spat Adelberto Quispe furiously, the girl's father, as they stood amongst the blackened ruins of the cottage. *'There was nothing we could do because they'd have killed us.'*

'Did the police burn the house?'

'Sí. When they'd finished with our Luisa they set fire to the thatch and laughed about lighting the stove to cook the bun they'd left in the oven.'

As a priest, Father Alfonso knew that he had to preach forgiveness and reconciliation, but he found his anger and bitterness rising as they had never done before. He had given Luisa Quispe her First Communion the previous May, when the whole village had been a joyful scene of celebration. The beautiful dark-eyed girl had approached so trustingly with flowers in her rich black hair, as he had held the Host in front of her. Now she writhed inconsolable amidst the ruins of her parents' cottage and relived the nightmare of the rape.

After listening to the sorrows of the Quispes, Father Alfonso had walked up the hill to the cottage of Pablo Huamán. He took out a cigarette and smoked pensively. What had these simple folk in Chugurmayo done to deserve being so abused and beaten up?

Although the priest didn't know it, they were paying for the aftermath of the terrorist attack on the cooperative of Santa María del Valle, where a booby-trap had been left at the foot of the flag-pole on which they had run up their own emblem with its hammer and sickle. The young policeman ordered to haul down the flag had been so severely injured that he had died screaming. There and then, Captain Vargas had vowed *'to scorch this bloody province until every 'terruco de mierda' has been killed!'*

The first victim of this policy had been Chugurmayo which lay on the moors above Santa María del Valle. There was no love lost between the two communities, their enmity dating way back to when the hacienda owners had decided to devote themselves to cattle-raising and had driven the indigenous owners off the rich pasture land of the valley up into the bleak moorlands of Chugurmayo. The Agrarian Reform did nothing to right this historical injustice and the people of Chugurmayo found the cooperative just as hostile as the previous hacienda had been. There had been several confrontations and then when the police asked the members of the cooperative whom they suspected of being behind the attack, the reply was simple: *'Los Chugurmayinos.'*

'Who's their leader?'

'*Adalberto Quispe.*'
And so his family bore the brunt of the police reprisal.

As Father Alfonso thought about the rising storm of violence that was engulfing the province and ruining the lives not only of girls like Luisa Quispe, but also of the fresh-faced policemen who were being ordered to loot and burn, and encouraged to rape, he saw a young campesina emerge from behind the cottage. She was obviously pregnant and carried a bundle of kindling in her arms. She called him over and invited him into the low lean-to kitchen. He squatted beside the reluctant fire over which the girl was trying to heat some maize gruel in a broken earthenware pot.

'*You don't know anything about my Pablo do you?*

'*Did the police take him?*'

'*First they wrecked everything we had and then they dragged him away like an animal.*'

The priest looked across at the girl, Dolores Vergara, 17 and Pablo's partner. Perhaps her condition had saved her from Luisa's fate, but all the same her dignity had been violated as she watched the police wreck her cottage. The priest moved over beside her and put his arm round her, letting her sob out her anguish whilst every expletive in the book rose in his gorge. 'For Christ's sake! What does one say to people in this situation? What comfort can I give that isn't pious blurb?'

Father Alfonso then spent the night in the village and realized that there was little that he could do except be there. He celebrated a quiet, almost stilted Mass in the church, grateful for the dignified formality of the Latin Rite which gave him protection from the violent emotions he felt within himself and from those of the villagers which came at him in waves. Luisa Quispe was there with her parents and brothers who had escaped arrest. They were bitter young men now. Dolores Vergara arrived alone and went to sit on the floor beside her mother. Eriberto Huaripata's mother swayed back and forth, weeping rhythmically; someone had just found his bag and she knew now for certain that the police had taken him. The small chapel, the scene of so many joyful Masses in the past, was hushed and dark with the few statues of the saints cowering in the shadows as if ashamed at what they had heard here yesterday. Captain Vargas and his men hadn't even respected the chapel, but had used it to interrogate the terrified villagers. Vargas himself had sat in the priest's chair, laid his gun on the altar, and supervised the systematic humiliation and expletive laden questioning of the older folk and children.

During the Mass the people hardly responded, but just let the words and actions that have come down through the centuries and extended to the remotest regions of the world flow over them: 'This is my Body…. This is my Blood.' As Father Alfonso elevated first the Host and then the Chalice the campesinos bowed their heads in reverence. God was with them on this cross of a village.

This morning, Father Alfonso had left Chugurmayo before dawn because he wanted to get back to Yanacancha by the afternoon so as to attend to a few matters before the evening Mass and the procession of La Dolorosa. He had walked rapidly along the stony paths, climbing steadily to the high moorland that stretches out below the mountain peaks. The climb took several hours, and the fast movement and perspiration began to assuage his aching spirit, whilst he was glad to suck the cold mountain air into his lungs. There was dampness everywhere and all the signs were for more rain. However, it rarely rains in the morning in the northern Peruvian Andes, and all being well he'd make it before the next downpour.

Once up on the open moors Alfonso felt better. At one point he paused and looked back towards the valley from which he had climbed, and he could see beyond it to range after range of distant mountains, like some frozen sea. The clouds were boiling up between the peaks and a few shafts of early morning sunlight fell like giant spot-lights on one or other of the mountains. After enjoying the view for a few moments the priest continued on his way, crossing the moors at a good pace.

The path from Chugurmayo brought Alfonso above the Yanacancha valley from behind Yawarrumi, —The Stone of Blood—, the twin peak of Condorrumi —The Stone Eagle—, and so called because on a summer's evening the peak would turn a deep red in the setting sun. As he swung round the base of the peak and the Yanacancha valley below came into full view the priest experienced a surge of joyous feeling. It was at a moment like this that Alfonso knew that there was something superbly primal in the bond between man and the world. Maybe it needs a poet to express this emotion as it deserves to be expounded, and Alfonso could make no such claim, though in his gut he knew that he was one with the vast landscape and for a moment or two could exult with the psalmist: 'The world is the Lord's and all that is contained therein!'

The scene was peaceful enough this morning, but Alfonso had only to look behind him at the massive black clouds piling up to remind himself that the Andes are untamed and shortly another violent tempest would unleash itself over the mountains.

It was here, beside Yawarrumi, that a couple of people came into view, a man and a woman walking towards him. Alfonso knew that they were not campesinos, for all their country dress, and the poncho of the man barely concealed the weapon he was carrying. The faces of both were muffled in thick scarves and Alfonso eyed them narrowly.

'Buenos días, padre,' said the man in a matter-of-fact tone.

'Buenos días,' replied Alfonso briefly.

The pair didn't stop and just kept walking ahead. For his part, Alfonso felt unnerved that a couple of terrorists could be walking around quite openly and unconcerned. He shuddered and continued swiftly in the opposite direction.

By the time Father Alfonso reached the town the rain was tumbling steadily out of the sky. He glanced into the church and saw Señorita Flor Delgado and her friends decorating the andas for La Dolorosa; then he went into the house for a change of clothes and a meal. Before he had finished, the storm was unleashing its full fury over the town.

THE PRIEST HAD just finished eating when he heard Manuel call: '¡Padre Alfonso!' He left the room and went into the patio where he saw Manuel and Lucio Benites.

'Good heavens, Manuel! What on earth are you doing out in this weather?'

'I knew that mother was down here at the church and I thought I'd better come to escort her home. On the way I found Lucio lying in the gutter, drunk; but the wetting he's had seems to have sobered him up.'

'You're both soaked, so get those wet clothes off and wrap yourselves in blankets whilst I put on some coffee.'

A few minutes later they were sat in the kitchen wrapped in blankets and enjoying the hot coffee.

'By the looks of it you went on a right bender, Lucio.'

'Sure thing! Are you going to tell me what a sinner I am?'

'No, I don't think so; but still, what's the problem?

'That bastard of an education supervisor, Juan Ortiz, won't give me a job. He chucked me out of his office yesterday. Since I'm only a third-class teacher I can be thrown on the dung heap like so much shit whenever the supervisor likes, and I've got no redress. I desperately need a job because my mother's sick and I've got brothers and sisters. As you know, my old man buggered off to heaven-knows-where ages ago.'

The priest let Lucio carry on spewing out his anger and frustration whilst outside the storm increased in intensity. The rain was sheeting down as though old Catequil were really mad at the place and was hurling the Second Flood at Yanacancha. Another crash of thunder brought the three men to a window overlooking the Plaza de Armas. There came a brilliant flash which struck the tower of the church and caused the bells to jangle diabolically. This was followed by an eerie silence, broken only by the continued hiss of the rain. Then the watchers saw a group of figures dash into the square. They were hooded and carried weapons.

'Bloody hell, *terrucos!*' murmured Lucio.

'Listen!' ordered Alfonso.

Above the sound of the storm they could hear explosions and gun fire.

'¡Puta madre*!' Exclaimed Manuel.

The clock in the church tower struck five.

¡Puta madre! A common expletive. An English equivalent would be something like *holy shit* or *bloody hell!* The same expression can be used to express admiration or contentment, for example: '¡*Una fiesta de la puta madre!*' 'A great party!'

THE STORM WHICH had provided such excellent cover for the terrorists also did much to lessen the impact of their attack. There was no collective panic because most people remained huddled in their houses and so were totally unaware of what was happening. The attempted assault on the police post failed because Captain Vargas had served in Ayacucho and had experience not only of how to defend the place but also how to mount a counter-attack.

Whilst the assault on the power plant only succeeded in destroying one pylon, and the explosives set to destroy the generating machinery failed.

The most successful part of the operation was the attack on the municipal depot. The grenades which blew open the doors also killed Alcides Sifuentes who had arrived a short time before. The terrorists ran into the building and set the store rooms alight, consigning hundreds of sacks of food to the flames. Some well-placed charges of dynamite wrecked the vehicles parked in the courtyard, including the only bulldozer that the town possessed.

'Get a bloody move on!' shouted the leader of the group. With that, another loud explosion rent the air and a truck burst asunder, sending a jet of fire skywards. But the flames were brief and soon fizzled out under the impact of the rain. Only the food stores continued to blaze under the protection of their roofs.

This same group had the task of destroying the telephone exchange, but as they ran into the square they saw that the police had driven off their attackers and were advancing. '¡Vámonos!' yelled the leader. The terrorists barely had time to do more than loose off a few shots that shattered some of the windows in the municipality, and give bedraggled vivas for the Revolution as they fled.

Apart from the parish priest and the two young men with him at the window of the parish house, virtually the only other person who witnessed the terrorist attack was the mayor. He had remained hypnotized by what he saw and was a perfect target for the *terrucos*, but by some miracle none of the bullets hit him and he only moved when the window next to his desk was shattered.

'Thanks to San Agustín,' said his wife later.

'Thanks to *La Dolorosa*' said others.

The mayor looked at his watch and saw that it was five-fifteen.

A SHORT TIME later the driving rain and hail started to slacken off, and then, as though ordered by the storm-god Catequil, stopped abruptly. The wind blew the leaden sky clean and the day began to draw to a close, to the accompaniment of a glorious sun-set. The few remaining clouds turned gold and red as the sun dipped towards the western mountains and slid gently towards the distant Pacific. A million rain-drops, caught in the trees and the wreckage of the crops, glinted like so many diamonds, whilst throughout the battered province life stirred again.

It was only now that the townsfolk began to realize that there had been a terrorist attack, and what most called attention to the fact was the fire still burning in the municipal depot. Flames were leaping through its roof and a pall of smoke spread over the upper part of the town. Drinkers staggered from the cantinas and their commentaries flowed like the water had done down the streets, or the *chicha* down their throats. Suddenly Yanacancha found itself full of heroes of both the tempest and the attack as the drunks imagined what they would have done to fight the terrorists.

Just to emphasize the fact that full normality was returning quickly to Yanacancha a crackling sound over a couple of loudspeakers rigged up in the square announced that *Radio San Agustín* was about to go on the air. One or two spitting and burping noises followed the crackling, and then came the announcement that thanks to the foresight of the mayor and the APRA Party, the municipality possessed its own diesel motor which would enable the radio to function tonight, plus the cinema and the lights in the Plaza de Armas. This piece of news was accompanied by the inevitable slogan: *'APRA at the service of the people!'*

The cinema had its usual diet of *Kung-Fu* for youngsters, whilst for older youths and adults there was something called *Erotic Fury*. It would have been impertinent to enquire why there should be electricity for the showing of a porno film rather than for the maintenance of vital facilities in the hospital. Next came an appeal for calm, which was superfluous under the circumstance, and the mayor himself took the microphone to inform the populace that he would be asking the authorities in San Roque to send military aid. After that rock music began to thump out, shaking the old adobe walls of the houses with their twisted roofs and drooping balconies. Hot metal and a remote Andean town might seem strange companions, but a few youths began to gyrate expertly to the rhythm in front of the porno film poster, making it abundantly clear that they were fully signed up members of the late twentieth century, as did their hairstyles, their clothes, and their surreptitious drug taking.

A small group of *campesinos* who had been trapped in the town by the storm hastened by, hoping to reach their village before it became too dark. One of them was dragging a reluctant pig which squealed and protested, and they formed a tableau that might have been snatched from the eighteenth century, or even earlier.

Down at the police post a tight rein was kept on discipline. 'We don't stand down until light to-morrow,' ordered Captain Vargas when a sergeant came to ask permission for his men to relax. 'I'll bet that during the night the *terrucos*'ll have another slam at us, hoping to catch us celebrating this little victory with an almighty booze-up; so full alert will be maintained.'

Suddenly someone realized that there was something missing in the local landscape, the large cross that had crowned the hill behind the cemetery. As the notice spread people came out of their houses to look, comments began to flow freely, and even the youths stopped their dancing. The great cross, which was the first sign of the town when one travelled up from the valley, was no longer standing. It had always featured in photos and paintings, and now it was lying shattered on the ground.

'*¡Terrucos de mierda!*'
'Bloody atheists!'

'They deserve to be shot!'

'The cross must be replaced at once!'

No-one realized that it was the tempest that had destroyed the cross.

The sun sank splendidly, throwing the mountains into deep purple relief, and shortly afterwards darkness fell with the abruptness that is characteristic of this part of the world. People went to eat what they felt was a well-earned meal, and then slowly drifted towards the church for the Mass of *La Dolorosa*. Throughout the Mass the church continued to fill, and by the time the band arrived for the procession the place was packed. Señorita Flor Delgado was delighted, since normally this first of the Holy Week ceremonies only attracted a couple of hundred of the most stalwart faithful; but the events of the day had provoked a little heart-searching and a lot of curiosity. The old lady swelled with pride as she watched the beautifully decorated *andas* being lifted onto the shoulders of 16 young men, the candles flickering in what was now a gentle breeze. And so the serene figure of the Mother of God was borne along the streets of the town, infusing a renewed faith in the hearts of the Yanacanchinos.

When finally the procession returned to the church and the people had dispersed either to Flor Delgado's house or to their own homes, Father Alfonso felt too tired and too numb to do anything more than sink to his knees in silence in the church. Prior to the Mass he had been called to the municipal depot to attend to Alcides Sifuentes, though it was too late to do anything more than offer a prayer for the repose of his soul. But the sight of the mangled remains of the old man, still sprawled in the entrance of the wrecked depot, had brought the priest into a direct confrontation with violent death. Alfonso had then visited a number of houses where he knew lived old and lonely people in order to comfort and reassure them. He had returned to the parish to celebrate the Mass and walk in the procession, and now he just wanted silence. He was exhausted and felt that there was no making sense of what had happened during the past few days. He looked at the statue of San Agustín in the retable behind the altar; that extraordinary man, a brilliant libertine and then a profound Christian thinker who had died whilst the city of Hippo was under barbarian attack. Mentally Alfonso ran over the litany of violence: the deaths of the agricultural engineers and the young policeman in Santa María del Valle; those of Gilberto Llacta and Nasho Quiroz in Llangodén; the rape of Luisa Quispe and the disappearance of Pablo Huamán and Eriberto Huaripata from Chugurmayo, and now the attack on the town itself and the death of poor old Alcides Sifuentes. The destruction of the cross was the final icon.

Alfonso knew that he needed to pray, needed to feel the presence of God in order to guide his frightened flock; pray not just for those who had suffered, but also for all those who were causing the suffering. And with that he lapsed into a half-doze.

The clear starry sky clouded over and a light drizzle began to fall, creating a collective reaction of damp fear which settled over the town, exacerbated by the rattle of machine-gun fire as the terrorists tried another, and unsuccessful, assault on the police post. Alfonso shook himself awake and leaving the church walked slowly to the parish house.

It was nearly two in the morning.

Two

*T*HE NIGHT'S RAIN slowly petered out and Saturday dawned bright and cold. Most of the town awoke as if suffering from a collective hang-over, whilst down at the police barracks the men were jubilant.

During the years of the emergency the police had taken a severe roughing-up at the hands of the terrorists and morale in the force was low all over the country. Badly trained and poorly armed, the police had previously only received that respect from the civilian population which is given to bullies, though when times had been normal there had been no shortage of recruits because uniforms and guns are always attractive. However, since 1980 terrorist mobility and audacity had forced the police into check, and there had been a steady stream of deaths and failures. Barracks had been assaulted and burned, lone policemen had been cold-bloodedly murdered, and the civilian population had taken its quiet revenge in a lack of sympathy.

But this morning in Yanacancha things were different.

'We licked the bastards!' grinned the men as finally full daylight enabled them to relax.

The damage caused to the barracks by the terrorist attack during the night took on the aspect of honourable war rounds and provoked a hearty interchange of memories of the battle.

'Yeah, this time we showed the shits what to expect!'

'I thought I'd had it when a grenade exploded near the gate'

'Did you hear one of the bastards scream when we hit him?'

'I wonder whether we've killed any of them. Do you think so Quique?'

'Don't know, but I bloody well hope so.'

At dawn a patrol had left the barracks to search for traces of the attackers.

'I'll bet those two *campesinos* we picked up the other day knew all about the plans for the attack.'

'Of course, man! Though Vargas didn't get much out of them, even though he did string them up.'

'Too bloody soft, that's our problem. If I were given a free hand I'd have them singing like birds in no time.'

'What'd you do?'

'Stick an electric current up their backsides for a start and squeeze their balls. One's got to use modern technology. Just beating them is no use. The *terrucos* are trained to resist that.'

'Not like Vargas beat-up those two. He really gave it to them. He's a good type and knows what he's doing.'

'Agreed —intervened one of the others—. He showed us how to treat suspects up there in Chugurmayo.'

'The best part of that was the fun Quique Rojas and I had with the girl. What do you say, Quique?' Quique smiled maliciously and spat on the ground.

The conversation was interrupted by the return of the patrol and the men burst into cheers when they saw that their mates were dragging a corpse and a girl who was still alive. She was filthy dirty after spending the night in a muddy ditch. She had been hit in the leg and could hardly walk. She must have been in great pain, but she didn't utter a sound and even managed to flash a defiant look at her captors.

'Bitch!' snarled one of the policemen.

'Quique, you've a chance to repeat what you did in Chugurmayo,' laughed one of the others.

'Needs cleaning up first, then I'll show her a thing or two with pleasure,' he chortled.

'Cut the blather you men!' ordered Captain Vargas as he came out of his office. He pointed at a couple of the men and ordered: 'You two, lock up the woman and then report back here.'

'Yessir!' came the sharp reply in unison, accompanied by smart salutes.

The captain pulled out a packet of cigarettes and offered them round. He lit one for himself and then sat on a bench. It was good to see the men in better heart this morning. Like them, he was tired of having to take a frequent bloody nose and not be able to return one to the terrorists. But this time they had not only beaten off the attack, but had taken the initiative, killing one of the attackers and capturing the girl without suffering so much as a minor wound. Vargas knew that his men were good basic material, as they had shown when they had been in Chugurmayo and, given a free hand, he reckoned he could turn them into a real fighting force, just as he himself had been toughened up on the course that had turned him into a *sinchi* —a *brave*, a member of the crack police hit-squad—. What his men lacked were the motivation and determination to kill in cold-blood, because they were not going to win this war with men who were squeamish.

However, the captain was too intelligent to believe in dumb brutality. There was a philosophy behind the *sinchi* style training and it was known as *the Cisneros doctrine*. This was a kind of Maoist philosophy turned against the terrorists who were themselves inspired by Mao-Tse-Tung, and it preached quite simply that the *campesinos* are the water in which the terrorist fish swim. You dry-up the water by eliminating *campesinos*, even if it means killing new-born babies.

Chatting with his men now, Vargas hammered home this message and added: 'Remember, you'll be doing a great job for which no-one will thank you, just as no-one ever thanked a street-sweeper. Of course, folk raise merry hell when the streets are dirty, but they never give a moment's thought for the poor bastards who have to clean them during the night. We police are society's street-sweepers. We have to do the dirty work that others are too fucking finicky to do. Every great civilization depends on guys like us: men who sweat their guts out, get dirty, and keep the whole bloody works running. That's us. We won't appear in the history books, just like the soldiers of Julius Caesar, Alexander the Great and Napoleon don't. We'll get no medals, we won't be treated like heroes, and they won't even pay us what we're worth; but they'll scream blue bloody murder if we don't clean-up this country of terrorists.'

What Captain Vargas hadn't been taught during his training to become a *sinchi*, but had learned through experience, was that being a street-sweeper cleaning-up the country was fun. There was a deep satisfaction to be got out of battering down the doors of a house, smashing furniture, overturning everything, trampling someone's prized possessions into the dirt and hurling obscenities at cowering civilians. A man could let-off his pent-up frustration and anger.

Vargas continued to talk to his men: 'With a bit more preparation and a few more successes like last night's we could win the war here. We've got to get it into our heads that we're going to win and that we must be left to fight without having our hands tied by politicians and priests insisting that we respect people and don't violate Human Rights. Fuck Human Rights! The *terrucos* don't respect anyone and if they think that someone needs to be eliminated they just go right ahead and do it. That's the way we've got to fight, carajo!'

This last produced a cheer from the men. Then the captain stood up and said with a grin: 'And now I'll see what information the young lady we've captured will be so kind as to give us.'

'Need any help, sir?' asked Quique Rojas.

And everyone laughed.

UP AT THE church there was hardly anyone for the early Mass, however, Señorita Flor Delgado had never missed attending, and she didn't fail today either.

'Good morning, Father.'

'Good morning, señorita,' the priest replied quietly.

'You look tired, Father.'

'I feel it.'

'Is there anything I can do to help out?'

'Thanks. I don't think that there's anything special. Just pump hot coffee into me throughout the coming Holy Week so that I can keep going.' Then he added with a grin: 'And some of your excellent liqueur, of course.'

They both laughed. After that Señorita Flor became serious again and asked: 'Is it true that the watchman at the municipal depot was killed in the attack yesterday?'

'I'm afraid so. It seems that a grenade exploded at his feet.'

'Poor old thing! What did he ever do to deserve that?'

'Nothing as far as I know.

'Father, what are the *terrucos* fighting for? Old man Sifuentes was just a poor guy who had a miserable job because he wasn't fit for anything else; except boozing perhaps. What good has it done to burn down the municipal depot with hundreds of tons of food for ordinary folk in this province? Do they think that we're all going to applaud them for that? They're just savages, Father!'

'I reckon that the people who attacked the town yesterday thought that the food in the depot would probably be distributed only to members of the government party —and they could well be right about that—, and also they hope that the mayor will call in the military, who can be guaranteed to make a pig's ear of everything, and so turn the civilian population against the government.'

'The war will come to this province then?'

'It's already come.'

'It's madness and I don't understand anything. So, God help us! By the way, there are leaflets blowing about in the streets urging us to join the armed struggle.'

'Be careful that you don't pick one up. There's a prison sentence for being in possession of terrorist propaganda.'

'Even for a harmless old lady like me who couldn't possibly hurt a fly?'

'Sí, señorita.'

'But that's ridiculous!'

'We live in a ridiculous world.'

A chill breeze ran through the church causing the votive candles in front of the statue of Our Lady of Sorrows —*La Dolorosa*— to flicker and the priest to shiver.

'I'm sorry, Father. I can see that you're tired and all I've done is to keep you gossiping here.'

Father Alfonso smiled depreciatively and said: 'It's part of my mission to listen to people, and I reckon that in the next few days I'm going to have to do a lot of listening.'

Then he bade the old lady good-bye and went into the parish house.

This was a typical house of an Andean town, with its rooms grouped round a patio. The patio was full of flowers and in the centre there was an ornamental bird-bath in which several small birds were enjoying themselves. The priest crossed the patio and entered the kitchen where he found Lucio Benites and Manuel drinking coffee.

'Good heavens, Lucio, you've got up early!'

'There was so much banging in my head that I didn't know whether it was another *terruco* attack or the effects of old Ma Vásquez's *chicha.*'

'The latter I suspect,' commented the priest drily. Then he turned to Manuel and asked: 'What brings you here? Are your people alright?'

'Yes thanks, Father. We had a scary time because we wanted my father to hide. He must be on the *terrucos'* hit-list since he manages the only bank in this town. He wouldn't hide of course, so he and my mother had a furious row. He insisted that he had to protect his family and he wasn't going to run away, whilst mother spent her time screaming that the *terrucos* would be after him and not the rest of us. I can tell you that I was bloody glad when dawn came and the danger of a further attack passed. None of us slept a wink all night.'

'But everyone's alright?'

'Sí, gracias,' replied Manuel with a wan smile. 'By the way, mother reckoned that you'd probably be very tired yourself and in need of a good breakfast, so she sent this.' He opened a basket which was on the table and took out several plates of food.

'Manuel, your mother's great! Do you mean to tell me that after spending the whole night awake and trembling with fear she's got enough energy to cook this?'

'When it began to get light and we reckoned that the danger had passed she told me to kill a chicken and said that we might as well enjoy a good breakfast in thanksgiving for having passed the night safely. And since she considers you to be one of the family she sent me down with your portion.'

'We could do with a few more people like your mother around, Manuel. She's got both courage and common-sense. Not like some people.' He looked fixedly at Lucio; however the implication was lost on the young man who was smoking morosely and broke in suddenly.

'It's a pity that the *terrucos* didn't string-up some of the authorities of this town on the palm trees in the Plaza de Armas, starting with that shit of an education supervisor, Juan bloody Ortiz.'

Since the remark was greeted by silence on the part of both Father Alfonso and Manuel, Lucio then added aggressively: 'You don't agree?'

'Frankly no, Lucio,' replied Father Alfonso. 'Killing the authorities of this town isn't going to resolve anything —just violence in reply to violence—. Tell me, what good has the *terruco* attack yesterday done? Unless you think that killing someone like old Sifuentes is a great advance towards the creation of Utopia.'

'Look at what the police did in Chugurmayo!' shouted Lucio. 'You told me yourself last night that they had beaten hell out of the *campesinos* and raped a girl. At least the *terrucos* don't pillage and rape.'

'No, they just kill and destroy,' retorted Alfonso bitterly. 'And we might have less pillage and rape from the police if only the *terrucos* would take themselves off and leave us all in peace. It's thanks to them that the police have gone berserk.'

'The police have always kicked the shit out of the *campesinos*, and along with the military are what sustains the corrupt administration and so-called justice system that are the plague of this country,' spat the young teacher angrily.

'Okay Lucio; but you don't have to give me lessons in social history. I'm as aware as anyone that we've been a mess ever since the Spanish conquest, but I'm not all convinced that the *terrucos* are helping one bit. They're just another twist in the screw of violence,' said Alfonso earnestly.

'These are the birth-pangs of a new society,' urged Lucio. 'Blood has to be spilt.'

'For heaven's sake, Lucio! What you're saying might be acceptable in a student debate or in the cantina of old Ma Vásquez, but not here.

People like Alcides Sifuentes and those who died in Santa María are worth far more than some Marxist propaganda about a society which shows no signs of coming into existence, if what the *terrucos* are doing is anything to go by.'

'So everything just stays the same, with the police and local bigwigs buggering us about? I'm sick and tired of being kicked up the arse by bastards like Juan Ortiz!' snarled Lucio.

'You know perfectly well that I don't believe that things should stay the same as they are,' replied the priest calmly.

'What do you believe then?'

Father Alfonso paused before replying. He took a cigarette out of a packet lying on the table, lit it, and the said deliberately: 'A real change in any society can only come about if people change. We find that in the Bible when the prophet Ezekiel talks about replacing the stony heart with one of flesh.'

'Bloody hell, the Bible!'

'Why not? If we took seriously what it teaches we could have the just society that both you and I want; and for that I'm convinced that a change of heart is required.'

'If we're going to wait for that we'll all be dead and gone long before it happens. The only way to change things here is to impose a new order by force.'

'And if some of us don't want the new order that the *terrucos* seek to impose, what then?' enquired Manuel who had sat passively during the argument. Lucio made a throat-slitting sign with his hand and laughed.

'Then God help us,' sighed Alfonso. 'All you want to do is to replace one oppressive society with another.'

'If you really believe what you're saying, Lucio, why aren't you out there with the *terrucos*?' asked Manuel.

The teacher shot him an angry look and said: 'I suppose you're trying to be funny, Manuel.'

'Not at all. I would have thought that that would be the logical conclusion of everything you've said. However,' he added with a touch of amused malice, 'that's us isn't it, bla, bla, bla, and doing nothing.'

Lucio sprang to his feet in anger shouting: 'Go screw yourself Manuel! Since your old man's a bank manager he can afford to keep you at the university, but I'm just a poor bastard on the dung heap!'

'Calm down, Lucio!' ordered Father Alfonso.

A heavy silence fell between them and Lucio sat down slowly. He poured himself another cup of coffee, took a cigarette and lit it. Manuel looked at the table, embarrassed that his intervention had triggered off the teacher's reaction. Several minutes passed and then they heard the rumble of vehicles.

'What's that?' asked Manuel.

The three of them went to the window overlooking the plaza and observed a couple of trucks full of soldiers.

'Bloody army ¡carajo!' Spat Lucio.

The trucks stopped and the soldiers began to descend from them. They were obviously young men from the coast, and 'probably from the shanty-towns surrounding Lima,' sighed Father Alfonso wearily. He already knew from what he had read about the situation in the central Andes that sending in coastal troops was just like sending in a foreign army. The *costeños*, however poor their own backgrounds, utterly despised the *serranos*, and took a special delight in throwing their weight around in the Andean towns and villages.

A portly colonel appeared and shouted an order.

'So Pontius Pilate arrives with his legionaries,' muttered the priest whilst Manuel smiled at the comparison.

THE ARRIVAL OF the first army units in Yanacancha lifted the spirits of the town's authorities and was a source of delight to the youngsters who scampered about in the Plaza de Armas as the troops heaved their kit off the trucks and lined up in front of the municipality. The mayor and several other authorities were on hand to receive the colonel, and they proposed that a meeting between themselves and the military be held immediately.

'First I want to know where my troops will be quartered,' replied the colonel.

'We thought that perhaps one of the schools would be the best place,' replied Don Nicolás obsequiously.

'Major Cantuarias!' called the colonel to a tall thin officer. 'Go and check-out the place they're offering us. If it's suitable get the men installed. If not, look around for somewhere. Remember, we can requisition any place we need.

'¡Sí, mi coronel!' replied the major.

'Now, señor alcalde,' said the colonel to the mayor, 'I need some breakfast since I've travelled all night. After that I'll be only too happy to meet with you and the other local authorities.

'As you say, colonel.'

Whilst Don Nicolás took the colonel down to his own house for something to eat, messages were sent hastily to all the authorities and prominent citizens, asking them to attend the meeting in the town hall. *Radio San Agustín* also burst into life, urging loyal Yanacanchinos to come forward and show their support for the army unit. The result of all this activity was that within an hour of the army's arrival in the town there was a large crowd in the main saloon of the municipality waiting for the meeting to be called to order. Crystal chandeliers and a portrait of the President of the Republic, plus photos of former mayors of Yanacancha, gave the room a certain solemnity and splendour.

The mayor arrived, unshaven and sunken-eyed. He immediately took over the presidency of the meeting, sitting at a table covered with a blue cloth and on which there was a small Peruvian flag. At his right was the colonel and at his left, Dr. Emilio Santillán, in his capacity of stand-in for the judge, who was away. Don Nicolás coughed and cleared his throat. He invited everyone to stand and sing the National Anthem. That done, he launched into a florid speech of welcome for the colonel and his troops, and then asked Captain Vargas to inform about the terrorist presence in the province and the actions taken so far to counter this.

Vargas spoke of the attacks on the Santa María Del Valle cooperative and the town of Yanacancha itself. 'There have been a number of deaths amongst innocent members of the civilian population and one policeman has been savagely killed. We have visited a village that was attacked by terrorists and have beaten off the attacks launched against this town.'

'Gracias, capitán,' said the mayor at the conclusion of Vargas' information and also thanked the police for their courage and success. He then invited questions.

Father Alfonso rose to his feet and said: 'I would like to ask Captain Vargas if he has terrorist captives or any suspects under interrogation.'

'None, Father,' replied the police captain coldly. Then he added: 'I'm surprised that you should be interested in whom we may, or may not, have under interrogation, since clamping down on terrorism is the job of the police, not of the parish.

This remark caused a light ripple of laughter, and there was a gleam in the captain's eyes which suggested mockery. His whole bearing was in marked contrast to that of the priest. The latter was unshaven and disheveled, whilst the captain's high combat boots, tight green trousers with a holster slung across his hips, and an immaculately pressed shirt, accentuated his lithe manhood and alertness. Father Alfonso was fully aware that he cut a poor figure by way of a contrast with the police captain, but he persisted, saying: 'At least two young men have disappeared from the village of Chugurmayo, and, from the information that I have, one of them, Pablo Huamán, was arrested by the police on a charge of being implicated in terrorism.'

'Your information is incorrect, Father,' replied Vargas smoothly. 'We are holding no Pablo Huamán on terrorist or any other charges.'

'I'm sorry to insist, captain, but the man's wife herself told me that he was arrested by the police.'

'Then she is lying. And I presume, Father, you are not going to accuse me of that before this assembly of town worthies.'

A murmur ran through the room and the priest knew that the handsome young officer was gaining over him. However, he felt that he must press on and said: 'Captain, I have seen with my own eyes the ravages caused by the police in the recent operation carried out in Chugurmayo. You speak of a visit. Rather it was an assault!' Then his voice rose in anger as he turned to address the assembly: 'Doors smashed in, furniture broken, food scattered all over the place, and one house burnt down! This kind of thing is totally unacceptable from the so-called forces of law and order!'

'Meaning?' flashed the captain and leaving the word hanging in the air, whilst people in the room shifted uncomfortably and began to whisper to each other.

'None of this is hearsay I can promise you. I personally have seen the damage and spoken to Luisa Quispe who was raped by your men, captain!' These last words were hurled in accusation, but the priest might just as well have been using a pop-gun for all the effect they had on the policeman.

Vargas strode into the middle of the room, placed his hands on hips, and addressed the assembly: 'Señoras y señores, I admit quite openly that a police incursion took place in Chugurmayo, because the terrorists had attacked the village and caused the damage mentioned by the reverend father. Our incursion was conducted cleanly, speedily, and efficiently. The task of the police in this province has been a thankless one, and I can only express pain and surprise when the parish priest, far from supporting the maintenance of law and order, can do nothing better than launch unfounded and unjust charges against me and my men. With very limited resources the police have done their utmost to protect all of you present here today, and the battles we fought yesterday and during the night should show that we have been entirely worthy of the trust you have placed in us. Today let me be among the first to welcome the colonel and his troops who have come to help us in the difficult, but glorious, task of maintaining peace here in Yanacancha.'

The captain's words were greeted by a hearty round of applause and he sat down with a satisfied smile, whilst Father Alfonso could only regret his own foolishness in having allowed himself to be almost openly declared a terrorist sympathizer.

The mayor turned to the colonel: 'Perhaps, colonel, you would be good enough to inform us about your plans for the security of this town and its inhabitants.'

'Yes, let's get on with it,' intervened Jorge Robles in a loud undertone that could be heard throughout the room. 'Frankly I don't give a damn what's happened to the Indians in Chugurmayo, or whether anyone's being held for questioning. What interests me is to hear about the protection we can be offered so as not to be murdered in our beds.'

'It is to prevent such an unhappy occurrence that I and my men have come to this town of San Agustín de Yanacancha, señor,' responded the colonel almost jocularly. His quiet conversational manner immediately inspired more confidence amongst the assembled citizens and there was a perceptible leaning forward to listen intently.

The colonel explained that he had arrived with an advance guard of troops from the barracks in San Roque so that the Yanacanchinos could see that the army was responding immediately to their very justified cry for help. The bulk of the troops would not be arriving until late tomorrow evening because they would have to cover some 750 kilometres from Piura, and almost 200 of that would be over dirt roads, making a rapid advance difficult. These remarks were met with much nodding of heads, as though the colonel had just said something very profound. Then he went on to outline his plans and concluded saying: 'In brief, Yanacancha will be a province in a state of emergency and I, as the commander of the military forces, will be the chief authority here.'

Hardly had the colonel finished speaking when a left-wing member of the town council, Señor Lenin Izquierdo, was on his feet and saying: 'You must respect the Constitution and the elected representatives of the people.'

'My dear sir,' replied the colonel with a lynx-like smile, 'you can choose between sticking to the letter of the Constitution, or having the *terrucos* in here to shoot you in front of your family. I didn't ask to come here. That request was made by the elected mayor of this town; and now that I'm here I'll assume the necessary powers to carry out my task.'

'Hear, hear!' said Jorge Robles loudly. 'In the name of the long-suffering and hard-working shop keepers of Yanacancha I wish to thank you colonel for your prompt arrival. The only thing that matters here at the moment is to get rid of the terrorist menace. Whether it's done *constitutionally* or not doesn't matter a damn.'

In this, Don Jorge was backed up by one of the town's more pompous schoolteachers, Andrés Núñez, who launched into a florid discourse about Yanacancha as 'The Pearl of the Andes' and 'A Cradle of Virtue', concluding with asking everyone to give the colonel a round of applause.

The schoolteacher then continued, invoking the patriotic spirit of the parish priest to suspend the Holy Week ceremonies which would begin earnest tomorrow and would attract large numbers of *campesinos* to the town. By the way in which he used the word *campesinos* everyone understood that he implied *terrorists*. As the teacher lowered his portly backside onto a chair all eyes were turned once again towards Father Alfonso. The priest understood that he'd have to make an immediate reply, however reluctant he might be to do so. He also realized that if he were to make an honest analysis of the social reality of Yanacancha he would incur more wrath and hostility. At the same time he knew that most of the people present at the meeting would be unwilling to forgo the Holy Week ceremonies. He stood up slowly and, thanking the school-teacher for referring to his patriotic spirit, he said: 'It is in that spirit that I now reply. Personally I doubt very much whether the terrorists will take advantage of the Holy Week ceremonies to carry out a further attack on this town because they know full well that this would only serve to alienate them from the bulk of the population, and there is no evidence of their ever having done so in the central Andes where the Holy Week ceremonies draw large crowds. Besides, if the ceremonies are suspended in order to keep the *campesinos* out of the town, the logical conclusion would be to make the ban general and so close down the market and all local commerce.'

These remarks produced a lot of whispering and head shaking, and the priest saw that he had now had two groups on his side, the pious and the small business sector. With this support he came to the tricky part of what he wanted to say: 'Obviously to try to run this town as though it were a military encampment won't work, but what is more important is that nothing will work if the anti-terrorist strategy is based on prejudice instead of facts. Señor Núñez' proposals are rooted in the entirely unfounded assumption that all terrorists are *campesinos* and that all *campesinos* are potential terrorists.'

'That's precisely what they are!' shouted someone, and a fresh wave of murmurings round the room showed Father Alfonso that he was in danger of losing the support that he had gained. But he had to continue.

'The terrorists recruit wherever there is injustice and oppression, and for that reason I'm convinced that we aren't going to achieve anything positive if we impose more injustice on the *campesinos*. It is instructive that we held no meeting after the attack on Santa María del Valle, nor after the death of the district officer of Llangdén. In both cases the *campesinos* were the principal sufferers, so we weren't really all that upset. Now that the town has been attacked we are very upset.' With that a fresh wave of murmuring washed over the assembly. The priest continued: 'I am ready to collaborate with the colonel so that the Holy Week ceremonies be carefully monitored, but I suggest that we'd all be far better employed remedying the very obvious injustices that are rampant in this town and province. If justice were properly administered, if teaching posts were awarded on merit and not favouritism, and if the town's administration were carried out without bribes, the *terrucos* would have nothing to attack.'

The murmurings now rose in volume like a storm of angry wasps and Juan Ortiz, the education supervisor, shouted: 'Are you suggesting Father, that we are in some way responsible for the terrorist presence in this province?'

'Sí, Don Juan,' replied Alfonso quietly.

'This is outrageous!' hurled Otriz and the uproar became worse. Señor Lenin Izquierdo also leapt to his feet and shouted: 'The priest is right!' And this was followed by a barrage of insults and shouting until, with difficulty, the mayor brought the proceedings to a close, without any real agreement having been reached.

Captain Vargas looked over towards the priest and his cynical smile said: 'You poor bastard, you've really screwed yourself!'

IN THE DISTANT village of Llangodén, over the moors, Martha, the widow of Gilberto Llacta, stirred a pot of potatoes and then ladled them onto tin plates for her two small children. They hadn't stopped whimpering and crying since seeing their father killed by the hooded terrorists, whilst Martha herself had hardly spoken a word to anyone since hurling her curse at Humfri Becerra yesterday. She was convinced that he was the one to blame for all her troubles and there was a smouldering hatred in her eyes as she looked up at the poncho-clad stranger who suddenly presented himself in the kitchen doorway.

'Are you Martha León?' he asked abruptly.

'Sí. What do you want?' she hissed back defensively.

'To talk about your husband's death.'

'Why?'

'Don't you want revenge on those who did it?'

'Claro.'

'I can help you.'

'How?'

'Kill the bastards.'

'Who are you?'

'Does it matter?'

'Not if you really do kill them.'

'That's why I'm asking your help.'

'Come in then.'

She ushered him into the small kitchen and offered him a stool by the fire. Then she handed him a plate of boiled potatoes and he ate silently, watching her intently. Sánchez was wet and hungry. Following Captain Vargas's orders he had left Yanacancha yesterday whilst the storm was still raging and had reached Llangodén in the early hours of the morning. He had gone first to Gilberto's father's cottage. It had taken him some time to break free from the ramblings of the old man and come over to Martha's. He enjoyed the potatoes and quickly emptied the plate.

'More?' asked Martha.

'Sure, if you can spare them.'

'I'll give anything to the man who'll get the murderers of my Gilby, especially that Humfri Becerra bastard.'

'Tell me what happened.'

She described how the terrorists had broken into the house, found her husband hiding behind some sacks, and shot him whilst she pleaded for his life.

'Did you recognize any of the *terrucos*?'

'They all had their faces covered, but I'll swear that one of them was Becerra. He hated my Gilby.'

'Is he still around?'

'No, he pushed off with the other *terrucos*.'

'I'll have to find him.'

'And when you do, make him squeal like a pig does when we kill it. I want him to suffer. My Gilby never did anyone any harm, and then that bastard Becerra brings in the *terrucos* to kill him. What's going to happen to my kids? A woman by herself can't run a farm. Gilby was killed because he worked for the government. Does the government care what happens to us?' The sentences came out in short staccato bursts and Martha's whole body was heaving with emotion.

Sánchez knew all too well that the widow of a district officer wouldn't receive any pension, even though he had died in government service, and the only thing she could receive would be the satisfaction of knowing that her husband's murderers had been hunted down and killed.

'Tell me all you know about Humfri Becerra.'

'With pleasure.' And Martha smiled for the first time since her husband had been killed.

THE INTERROGATION cell in the barracks was bare. A radio was turned up loud so as to provide covering music over the screams of the girl who lay naked and spread-eagled on a bed in the centre of the room.

She had been roughly washed and the wound in her leg dressed. She also had a bandage round her head and a wad of lint covered her left eye. For over an hour they had tortured her, but she had revealed nothing, so tempers were rising. Earlier on, Captain Vargas had tried the kindness gambit. He had had some food brought in, poured a cup of coffee for her, offered a cigarette, and spoken gently. However, to none of these attentions had she deigned to make the slightest response. It was a though she were blind, deaf, and dumb, and totally indifferent to his existence. Finally he had become angry and shouted at her: 'Right you little bitch, you've got it coming to you!'

Now, and hour or so later, the only thing he had achieved was to make her scream each time he applied a lighted cigarette to her body.

'Talk, damn you, or I'll tear you limb from limb!'

She fixed a glazed expression on him. There wasn't even hate in her eyes, just a fishlike stare. He slapped her hard a number of times, but there was no reaction and all he could do was spew out a blasphemous torrent of abuse in his anger and frustration. The meeting in the municipality had shown him that his stock was high amongst the townsfolk and he wanted to have a good bargaining chip to maintain his position vis-à-vis the military, since he had no intention of being reduced to a cypher role. He desperately wanted to know the names of the subversives operating in the area, how many there were, where they met, what arms they had, and, above all, what were their plans. And the net result so far was precisely nothing. He began to fear that the military might be able to get information out of her that he couldn't, and he was very anxious to show those stuck-up officers and their conscript troops what a *sinchi* could do. Even the alligator clips applied to her genitals only produced screams and then she fainted.

'Throw a bucket of water over and bring in the two *campesinos*,' ordered Vargas.

'Sí, señor.'

After a few minutes Pablo and Eriberto were hauled into the room and then with a few kicks to shake them into life, were ordered to identify the girl.

'Dunno,' muttered Eriberto

'You little bastard, I'll teach you to bloody well know!' shouted Vargas and ordered a couple of policemen to punch him. At this Pablo immediately volunteered information, saying that he has seen the girl in Chugurmayo.

'What was she doing there?'

'She came with the comrades.'

'And?'

'They ordered us to go to the school.'

'Did you go?'

'Sí.'

'Why, you bloody little terrorist, to receive orders?'

'No, señor.'

'Why then?'

'They made us listen to their speeches.'

'What did they say?'

'I didn't understand much. They talked about injustice and oppression and told us that we should join the *Shining Path* led by some guy we'd never heard of.'

'So you became a *terruco*?'

'No!'

The interrogation went on, but they couldn't get anything really substantial out of Pablo. Nor did another go at the girl produce any result. Finally, Vargas had to admit defeat, but he couldn't hide his admiration for her: 'Bloody hell, with a platoon of girls like this one I could take on a whole sodding army of terrorists!'

It was then that a faint tinge of a smile lit up the girl's face.

WHEN THE MEETING at the municipality broke up Father Alfonso went straight back to the presbytery. He was angry with himself for having made a botch of things and was sure that Captain Vargas had lied about not having anyone under interrogation; but he had no way of proving it. Also he realized that the blindness and the prejudices of the Yanacanchinos would be almost more difficult to overcome than the terrorist threat to the province. He felt completely alone and when he looked up towards the mountain of Condorrumi where the great stone cross now lay shattered on the ground, he murmured to himself: 'It looks as though God too has abandoned us.'

'Oh there you are, Father!' came a bright metallic voice out of the damp misty morning. He recognized it and turned to face Doña Dagoberta Castillo de Robles, the leader of *The Ladies of Yanacancha*, an association concerned with preserving the traditions and values of the province. Well-dressed, educated and intelligent, these good ladies could move mountains when they so desired.

'We've been waiting to talk with your reverence.'

'Yes? About what?'

'The cross.'

'The cross?'

'Yes, Father, THE CROSS!'

'Of course, ladies. I'll have a word with the mayor to see if he can send some municipal workers to clean up the rubble before the Palm Procession tomorrow.'

'That's a very good idea, Father, but we haven't come to talk about cleaning up the rubble.'

'No?'

'No. What is far more important is the immediate formation of a committee for reconstruction of the cross.'

'Father, you must get the authorities to help at once!'

'Father, the central government must give a helping hand!'

'Father, you must get the *campesinos* to bring good stones and send workers!'

'Father, you must denounce the sacrilege committed by the atheist terrorists!'

'Father, how much help will the bishop give?'

'Father, why has this happened to us?'

'Father, what has God got against us?'

'Father, when do you think that we can start the reconstruction?'

'Father, don't you think that it would be a good idea to build a bigger and more elegant cross?

'Father, one can only offer the very best to God. We'll do everything we can, but He too must lend a hand, don't you think?

'Of course, of course!' replied the priest ritually to each phrase of this litany. He wasn't surprised that the ladies of the town should be so concerned about the reconstruction of the cross because it was such an important feature, along with the church —which dated from the middle of the eighteenth century— and the elegant Plaza de Armas with its gothic style bandstand in the middle. All this was far more important than properly paved streets or good drainage, since they can be found anywhere. What makes an Andean town special are its main square, its church, and such traditions as folk-dances and a band playing once a week as people stroll round the square. It's a question of cultural identity and local priorities. So the priest listened to the ladies and after a short discussion it was agreed that they must ask the mayor to preside over the cross reconstruction committee, whilst the priest accepted the post of treasurer.

'We'll go and see the mayor at once,' purred Doña Dagoberta. 'There's no point in wasting time.'

'Yes, do so by all means,' said Father Alfonso.

With that the ladies were well pleased and the priest smiled to himself for the first time that day.

THE MAYOR AND the supervisor of education had remained behind in the municipality after the meeting and they had opened a much needed bottle of rum.

'That priest is a bloody nuisance,' said Juan Ortiz as he poured himself a drink. 'Instead of throwing his weight behind a joint solution to our problem all he can do is create trouble and division.' He's got dangerous ideas and too much influence with the youth of this town. Can't we shut him up?

'We shouldn't worry too much,' replied the mayor calmly. 'Virtually no-one supported him in the meeting.'

'I don't agree Nicolás.'

'Who spoke-up in his favour?

'Publicly, no-one; but after the meeting was over I heard several people say that the priest was right.' He pushed the bottle of rum across the table to the mayor and continued: 'The man's got a genius for sticking his nose into what doesn't concern him. Just last week I had trouble with him myself.'

Don Nicolás poured himself a drink and downed it in one gulp. Then he asked: 'What did he do?'

'He came barging into my office and gave out about some wretched girl who's been contracted to teach in one of the village schools and wasn't paid last year. What the blazes does it matter to the parish priest which teachers get paid and which don't? He gets paid for the classes he gives, so why can't he keep his bleeding trap shut? In fact, why for Christ's sake can't he just do what priests are supposed to do, say Mass, hear confessions, and pray their rosaries, instead of charging round the countryside stirring up trouble. Politics, that's all bloody Father Alfonso preaches!'

'Did you take any notice of what he said about the girl's pay?'

'Well ...' blustered Ortiz.

'Well, what? I imagine that you didn't just tell him to piss off,' said Don Nicolás with a dry laugh.

'I certainly wanted to; but I said I'd look into it and added something about one's life being a valley of tears.'

'And?' prodded the mayor maliciously.

'Didn't buy it of course. I'll say this for him, he's down to earth. He told me very politely what I could do with the valley of tears and promised me that he'd pester the living daylights out of me until the girl got paid.'

'Has she been paid?'

'Of course.'

The mayor burst out laughing and served himself another drink, whilst Ortiz got up and walked over to the window. He stood there for a moment look over the square; then he turned and asked: 'What are you going to do about the cross that stood above the town?'

'Me? I'm not going to do anything,' replied the mayor petulantly. 'The municipality hasn't got any money and I've got heaps of problems without adding the cross to the list. It's the priest's job to worry about that.'

'Well, I reckon he won't. Do you remember how he reacted when we suggested that the old church be pulled down and replaced with a new one of stone and marble? He almost ate us alive!'

'Yes, I remember all too well. I wanted that to be the crowning work of my time as mayor, and the priest just chucked the whole project into the wastepaper basket.'

'And he'll probably say that there are more important things to do that build a cross as a sign of civic pride, or something of that nature.'

'Oh, shut up, Juan!'

'Well, I can see trouble on the horizon. *The Ladies of Yanacancha* are coming this way right how, and I'll bet that they want to see you about restoring the cross.'

'If they do, I'll insist that the priest see to it.'

'I wonder who'll win.'

And just as Ortiz was pouring himself another drink came the voice of Doña Dagoberta: 'Don Nicolás!'

'Bloody hell!'

Ortiz laughed cynically as he downed the glass of rum.

AFTER SEEING DOÑA Dagoberta and her ladies Father Alfonso went to the morgue on behalf of Alcides Sifuentes' family, but the red-tape surrounding the unfortunate deceased showed no sign of being unraveled for several days.

'You must understand Father, it's Saturday.'

'What's that got to do with it? Are you people Adventists.'

'Yes, the guy who deals with the necessary paper-work is an Adventist and doesn't come in on Saturdays.'

'Isn't there someone else who can deal with it?'

'No Father.'

'Why?'

'Because that's the way it is.'

'But the family wants to bury Don Alcides.'

'His body will be quite safe with us until the paper-work has been attended to.'

'What about the feelings of his widow?'

'That's a personal matter and has nothing to do with us.'

'How long will the paper-work take?'

'It depends.'

'Depends on what?'

'It's the first case of a death during a terrorist attack and difficulties could arise.'

'Frankly I don't understand,' sighed the priest with asperity and left the morgue to see the family.

They didn't understand either and Alfonso, who had never found it easy to comfort the bereaved, found it even more difficult in this case. The same incomprehension was to be found amongst Alcides Sifuentes' fellow-drinkers in Ma Vásquez' cantina which was doing a roaring trade. So, whilst the town's worthies were gathered in the municipality drinking rum, the not-so-worthies were slurping *chicha* and musing over their friend's death.

'The bastards killed old Sifuentes.'

'Yeah! The poor bugger didn't have a chance.'

'The people at the morgue won't release Sif's body.'

'Why?'

'Something about a post mortem, whatever that is.'

'It's an examination of the body to decide the cause of death.'

'Everyone knows that he was blown up by a grenade. Do they think he had a dose of flu or something?'

'I've been to the morgue and the guy there says that the law requires an examination of the corpse.'

'When I told him what he do with the law, the guy just laughed and told me to piss off.'

HARDLY HAD FATHER Alfonso returned to the parish house with the intention of shutting himself up in his study in order to prepare his homily for tomorrow, Palm Sunday, when there came a knock at the door and a head popped round.

'Father Alfonso!'

'Hello Manuel, what brings you back here?'

'I'd like a confidential word with you.'

'Come in then.' The homily would just have to wait. 'Cigarette?'

'Gracias.'

'Now, what's up?'

Manuel lit the cigarette and smoked silently for a minute, then he said: 'Father, this morning in the municipality you asked Captain Vargas whether he was holding any terrorist suspects, and he said no. Do you believe him?'

'No, but I can't prove that he's a liar.'

'He is though.'

'How do you know?'

'One of the police is a friend of mine, a guy called Francisco Luna, and he wants out of the force. He's trying to prepare himself to take the entrance exam to the university in San Roque and I've been helping him a bit. So occasionally he comes to the house and he told me this morning that the police are holding two *campesinos* and a girl.'

'Does he know who they are?'

'No, but he thinks that they're from Chugurmayo and he told me that they've been beaten-up.'

'That gives us a lead and we could try to get a writ of Habeas Corpus. I'll go and see Dr. Santillán.'

'He's useless.'

'I know, but there's no-one else.' The priest got up to leave and said: 'There's beer in the fridge in the kitchen. Help yourself, I probably won't be long.'

A few minutes later Father Alfonso had Manuel's opinion confirmed when he found the lawyer drinking rum in his office and announcing that he had no intention of getting involved: 'If the police have detained some *campesinos* suspected of being terrorists, then they know what they're doing and we must let matters take their normal course.'

'I don't see anything normal about this. You yourself heard Captain Vargas deny that he was holding people, and now I know for certain that he was lying. There's something behind all this.'

'Father, we live in difficult times and we must let the police do whatever they think is best. It doesn't do to interfere you know, or we'll find ourselves being accused of terrorism.'

'So you won't do anything?'

'No. Now I wish you a pleasant week-end,' smiled the lawyer felinely and took another swig at the bottle of rum on his desk.

The priest returned to his house and found Manuel waiting for him.

'No go?' asked the young man.

'Nada. Santillán's scared of getting involved.'

'I told you that he's useless.'

'He's typical of all our local authorities. For years I've been trying to get them to clean up their act, but they're so blind or perverse that they just can't see that the lack of justice, the favouritism, and the bribery have been building up a reservoir of resentment that must overflow one day. And now that the flood is beginning to descend they look terribly upset and surprised, and search desperately for some scapegoat to blame for what has happened.'

'You, by all accounts.'

'Looks like it. I just can't understand why people are so bloody stupid! There seems to be something in the human psyche that refuses to accept the unpalatable, and maybe that's necessary for our sanity and survival in some cases. Let's face it, when the Minister of the Interior says that the terrorist problem is under control, or the Minister of Finance tells us that the economy is picking up, we believe them because we want to, even though all the evidence is pointing in the opposite direction.'

'That's what a lot of people feel about religion, just a myth to keep us happy when in reality we're all screwed-up.'

'Do you believe that, Manuel?'

Before he could answer there came a knock at the door and Flor Delgado entered asking for a ladder: 'We need it in order to decorate the high altar with palms, Father.'

Father Alfonso grinned at Manuel and whispered: 'Thank God for people like Doña Flor.'

'The myth in the face of reality?'

'No, just goodness and sanity,' he said with a smile.

SEVERAL HOURS LATER the priest slipped into the church and sank down on his knees before the high altar, now decorated with palms. The church was old and he had an affection for it. Ever since this massive adobe building had been raised in the eighteenth century generations of the faithful had added their contributions to the interior adornment so that there was a miscellaneous collection of styles and tastes, some exquisite, some non-descript, and some frankly hideous. However, the net effect was one of happy harmony which always managed to have a soothing effect. Father Alfonso glanced at the different statues that would be carried in procession each night of Holy Week, figures of Christ during his passion, and then his gaze wandered over the high altar, a superb piece of gilded rococo carving, with barley-sugar pillars leaping and twisting their way like a crazy scaffolding to hold God and his court in heavenly bliss. Part of that court was San Agustín, the patron saint of the province. Alfonso looked intently at the figure, stiff in a gold embroidered cope and a pure silver mitre, seemingly remote and unfeeling. Yet this was the statue of that fiery tempered man from North Africa who had fathered an illegitimate child and then not only gone through a deep conversion, but had written passionately about it in his *Confessions*. After that, back in North Africa, Agustín had watched the world order of which he was a part fall into total chaos. What must it have been like to receive the news that Rome had fallen to the barbarians and been sacked? He reacted not by fleeing into some intimate spiritual communion, but by making a profound analysis of history and bequeathing us *The City of God.*

'What'll I manage to create in the midst of the chaos in which I'm living?' Alfonso wondered with a tired smile.

Three

Sunday dawned fine, as was traditional for Palm Sunday in Yanacancha. No matter how hard it rained in March, one could guarantee that the morning of Palm Sunday would be blazing hot. Condurrumi raised his glistening peak against the deep blue sky and it was difficult to believe that only two days ago the whole province had been awash under seemingly ceaseless rain. It was equally difficult to believe that there were any terrorists within a thousand kilometres, or that the broken bodies of tortured terrorist suspects lay in a cell in the police barracks.

The *campesinos* from the surrounding countryside flocked into the town as they did every Sunday because it was market day. The streets were choc-a-bloc with the bright red ponchos of the men, and multi-coloured flared skirts of the women under an endless sea of wide-brimmed straw hats; and it was around the market that the mass of people was to be found at its most dense. There was also a stream of people walking out towards the lower slopes of Condorrumi, where the great stone cross had stood, since it was from here that the Palm Sunday procession would start.

The crowds were thinnest in the Plaza de Armas where preparations were being made for the flag-raising ceremony. It is the custom in Peru for the national flag to be raised solemnly in the presence of the local authorities and with a march past by school kids. Since there were now troops in Yanacancha, the colonel hoped to impress the locals with a martial display by them and the police; and also he had ordered Major Cantuarias to prepare a patriotic discourse. However, there were very few people in the square to listen to it since the school year had not yet started and there were no school kids, nor a college band, the two elements guaranteed to draw a crowd.

The biggest group in the square, apart from the soldiers, was a gaggle of men hard at work building what looked like a scaffolding across one of the streets. On enquiry, this turned out to be the gates of Jerusalem being erected as part of the Palm Sunday proceedings.

'The people of Yanacancha don't seem very anxious to show their patriotism, señor alcalde,' remarked the colonel acidly to Don Nicolás as they waited for the flag to be brought to them.

'I myself spoke over the radio last night, colonel, urging people to be present at the flag-raising ceremony, but you know what it is in a provincial town like this, folk don't change their ways easily.'

'Do you mean to say that you don't usually raise the flag on Sundays?' asked the colonel with narrow eyes.

'Of course we do, colonel, but today is Palm Sunday and a lot of people will be in the procession.'

'Is that why the priest isn't here? Though, after listening to him yesterday, nothing would surprise me. I reckon he's got subversive ideas.'

'He's probably up on the hill where the procession starts,' murmured Don Nicolás as both he and the colonel watched an almost continual trickle of people walking by with branches and flowers in their hands.

Slightly apart from the military and civilian authorities stood Captain Vargas, officially a kind of third sex now, relegated to limbo. But he had no intention of letting this happen and he had put on his *sinchi* combat uniform, in preference to the more suit-like dress uniform, just to emphasize the fact that he was still very much a force to be reckoned with. By his side stood a police sergeant and they talked to each other in undertones.

'Still nothing?' asked Vargas.

'Not a bloody thing, sir. We haven't got a word out of her. I admire the bitch, I'll admit that.'

'So do I. We could do with a few like her on our side.'

The sergeant looked at the taught young officer. Prior to Vargas' arrival in Yanacancha a few months previously, the life of policemen had been relaxed and enjoyable. Occasionally they had had to beat-up an abusive drunk or a minor thief, but it had been nothing like what they had been doing to the terrorist suspects. Now, almost unconsciously, the sergeant found himself being drawn inexorably to the officer's way of doing things. He had become an accomplice torturer.

'Something bothering you, sergeant?' asked Vargas lightly.

'I was just wondering what we're going to do with the suspects, sir; hand them over to the military?'

'Not bloody likely! If we can't get anything else out of them ...,' the captain smiled and drew the edge of his hand across his throat.

'Kill them?'

'Yes, unless you can think of something better'

'In cold blood; just like that?'

'Exactly.'

'We've never done that before.'

'You haven't been dealing with terrorists either. I have. I've been in the centre of the country and know how to deal with terrorist scum; kill them like the rats they are!'

'And if those two *campesinos* aren't terrorists?'

'It's all the same; after all, you wouldn't like anyone to discover that you've been beating the shit out of them, would you?' sneered Vargas.

'What would we do with the corpses?' asked the sergeant desperately trying to find some way of not becoming further enmeshed.

'I've already thought about that. Old man Robles owes me a favour or two since I've been turning a blind-eye to his drug-running. He uses pack-animals and he can take the bodies and get rid of them out in the mountains where no-one will ever find them.'

The sergeant didn't reply, but thought to himself: 'What a mess I've got into! Here am I discussing the disposal of people who will simply be *eliminated* by engaging the help of a drug-runner, and all as though it were merely a matter of sending some perfectly ordinary packet through the post! What the bloody hell is happening to us!'

A light nervous twitching round the edge of the sergeant's eyes betrayed what was going through his mind and the captain found himself amused. Hudson Vargas had grown up in a hard school and he had no time for weaklings. Unlike many police officers he had not enjoyed a comfortable middle-class background where daddy went to work in an office each day and mummy supervised the servants in a house in one of the pleasanter suburbs of Lima. No, he'd grown up in a shanty-town on the outskirts of Chiclayo, one of several brothers and sisters who shared the same mother but had different fathers. Their mother supported them thanks to the visits of innumerable *uncles*, many of them little older than his eldest brother.

Hudson Vargas had not had an unhappy childhood, but it had been a rough-and-tumble one. He had learned to fight and to win in the dusty streets between the shacks that straggled out beyond the city into the desert; and ever since he had been a small boy he had wanted to join the police. Their smart green uniforms and their crisp air of authority, backed up by a prominent revolver at the waist, had always exercised a deep fascination over him. So, unlike his brothers and most of his friends, he didn't waste all his time playing football or loafing on the street corners, but found himself menial jobs of any kind to pay for his school uniform and books. He did well at school and, after a year in the ranks of the police, managed to get into the officer training college. Shortly after becoming a lieutenant he was selected for the *sinchi* training course and had really enjoyed the toughening experience which had turned him into an efficient killer and hastened his promotion to captain. Anyone who came near him could sense the energy in his lithe body, and even this morning, relegated as he was by the presence of the military, he knew that both the colonel and the civilian authorities were eyeing him warily as he balanced lightly on the balls of his feet.

An army corporal appeared with the flag in his hands and this was carefully unfolded so that the authorities present could take hold of it. They then walked slowly with this spread out emblem of the country round to the flag-pole, where it was solemnly raised and the national anthem was sung. Major Cantuarias' patriotic speech came over the loudspeakers of Radio San Agustín, and after that the army platoon and a squad of police did a goose-step march past.

For the colonel, this ceremony of the flag-raising meant more to him than any religious ritual; and as he watched the red and white flag wave gently in the morning breeze against the background of the deep blue sky he swelled with pride. This was the sacred emblem of Peru, and it was this that the terrorists besmirched, and so deserved to be crushed unmercifully.

Suddenly there was a burst of explosions.

'What the bloody hell's happening?'

'They're only rockets, colonel,' said Don Nicolás with a gentle smile. 'We always let off rockets during our processions. Nothing could be more normal. The Palm Sunday procession must be drawing near, so we'll await its arrival at the municipality.'

'Normal!' expostulated the colonel. 'Here we are with terrorists breathing down our necks and you talk of normality!'

PALM SUNDAY IN Yanacancha had always been a grand occasion. Once again, this year a group of *campesinos* had prepared the donkey and its foal in the patio of the Robles' house. Both animals had to be smothered in flowers and then led out to the hill for the start of the procession. Where once had stood the great stone cross a temporary altar had been placed and on it was enthroned the statue of Our Lord of the Palms waiting to be placed on the donkey.

By the time Father Alfonso arrived with a gaggle of altarboys there was already a big crowd, and members of the town band were blowing and puffing to warm up their instruments. Their repertoire was limited to a few huaynos, cashuas, and marineras* for dancing, and some rather nondescript religious music for processions or funerals. However, any lack of repertoire and musical skill was more than fully compensated by the enthusiasm of bandsmen.

The faithful who were waiting for the blessing of the palms were

---

* Huaynos and cashuas are Andean dances, whilst the marinera is a costal dance and probably the most representative dance of Peru. The city of Trujillo is the home of this extraordinarily beautiful dance.

milling around in a chaotic and disorganized fashion, in spite of the efforts of the members of the Palm Sunday Sodality to impose order. The basic problem was that whilst there were plenty of people shouting instructions, no-one seemed disposed to take any notice of them. However, with the arrival of the priest some semblance of order began to emerge. There was no question of trying to organize a stately procession; rather it would be a jostling river of people waving their branches, singing, chatting, and behaving very much as those who had accompanied Christ on his ride into Jerusalem two thousand years ago.

One of the reasons why Father Alfonso always enjoyed the Palm Sunday procession was because it produced a certain leveling of classes. Although the Robles family were the *mayordomos* responsible for ensuring that the band were paid, that there be a plentiful supply of rockets, and abundant food and drink, it was one of the indigenous communities of *campesinos* which provided the donkey and the flowers. Then, once the procession got moving, everyone would become thoroughly jumbled up as they pushed and shoved to get close to the figure of Christ on the donkey.

Using a megaphone, Father Alfonso blessed the palms and other branches which the people had brought, some of which were intricately adorned with flowers. Then the members of the sodality lifted the figure of Christ onto the reluctant donkey; the band blew a number of trumpet blasts and banged drums; and so everyone lurched forward for the hour-long procession down into the town.

As the procession drew closer to Yanacancha the numbers swelled, and once in the streets handfuls of flower petals were thrown from the balconies. On several occasions the donkey did its best to rid itself of the statue and the restraining hands surrounding it, whilst the foal was all for having a romp as it leapt from side to side. However, in spite of this, the procession moved along pretty well. Rockets were launched into the sky, the balconies of the houses were adorned with fine lace or silken counterpanes, and almost every hundred metres there was an arch of flowers. The crowd became thicker and more excited, and popular hymns were added to the overall enthusiasm. Father Alfonso felt happy, and here in the midst of his people was able to forget the tensions of the past few days, so he soon found himself singing as lustily as anyone else.

Eventually the procession neared the Plaza de Armas where the street was blocked by the massive trellis-like gates made out of bamboo and adorned with flowers, which the authorities had watched being constructed shortly before. They were the handiwork of the teachers of the school which had been taken over by the military; not known for showing much piety during most of the year they were very anxious that their school make a good showing every Palm Sunday. Slowly the gates were opened, the church bells were now ringing in a glorious clanging, and dozens of rockets were being let off to welcome Our Lord of the Palms. The whole joyous scene was accompanied by children running in the square and dogs leaping and barking. The one jarring note this year was the presence of young soldiers holding naked bayonets and wearing steel helmets; some of which had scrawled on them the slogan they'd seen in yanqui movies about Vietnam: *Nacido para matar—Born to Kill—*. Father Alfonso wondered what might be going through the minds of these youngsters from the coast sporting a tough guy stance.

From the balconies round the Plaza de Armas rose petals floated down in clouds, and the enthusiasm of the Yanacanchinos, determined to enjoy this Palm Sunday just like that of any other year, knew no bounds. Father Alfonso perspired under the heavy embroidered red cope and let his attention be drawn to the assembled authorities. The mayor and the town councilors were trying to look as though they were still the real power in the town, whilst Captain Vargas stood lightly to one side of them with an air of amused indifference, and the military stood disdainfully to the other. Beside the colonel stood the major who had given the patriotic speech, and suddenly Alfonso's heart missed a beat. He was sure that the officer was Telmo Cantuarias. They had been together in the first year in the seminary and had been quite close friends. Then, at the beginning of Holy Week in the second year Cantuarias had suddenly been expelled. After that they had lost touch, though Alfonso had heard rumours that Cantuarias had got into the army's officer training school. 'I wonder where he's been hiding himself,' mused the priest. 'I'd love to hear all his news.'

The procession had halted now and the donkey was being led forward with difficulty to where the authorities were standing. For his part, Father Alfonso held back. Although he was prepared to accept the town's custom that on Palm Sunday the mayor and the councilors pay homage to Christ, he was not ready to show much enthusiasm for the practice. He would have preferred that their homage be something more substantial and meaningful than a bouquet of flowers. Furthermore the priest was unhappy with any ceremony which suggested that Church and State still embraced each other in unholy matrimony since this had been scrapped in the Constitution of 1979.

Don Nicolás tried to place his bouquet of flowers in the outstretched arms of the Christ figure but, since the donkey insisted on bucking, this proved to be difficult. After a minute or two Captain Vargas stepped forward and grasped the bridle with such force that the animal decided to stop making itself a nuisance and cooperate. The brief ceremony over, the captain released the donkey and stepped back with a satisfied look on his face.

The procession continued round the square on its way to the church. Don Nicolás turned and touched the colonel's sleeve: 'I have a bottle of rum in my office; perhaps you'd like to join me in a drink.'

'With pleasure, señor alcalde.'

'The major too?'

Cantuarias accepted with a nod, whilst Captain Vargas knew himself to be excluded. He shrugged his shoulders and muttered an obscenity under his breath as he gave a formal handshake of good-bye. Of the civilian authorities, the only one favoured with an invitation was Juan Ortiz, and the rest drifted away, either to join the procession or go to their respective homes.

As the procession mounted the church steps, Captain Vargas crossed the gardens in the middle of the square and walked over to the hotel where he had a room. He'd seen an interesting girl there when he had breakfasted this morning and decided that she might be worth chatting up. He smiled to himself since, as far as he was concerned, the possibility of inveigling a girl into his bed would be a good step towards the world of normality.

THE CELL IN the police barracks where the two *campesinos* were being held was dirty, though they had largely got beyond concerning themselves about their physical surroundings. Both youths ached in every limb and Eriberto had been vomiting continually. They had broken teeth and their testicles were swollen. A small patch of sunlight fell through the high barred window and they could hear the rockets and the band of the procession in the distance. To be reminded of other people enjoying themselves only made the agony worse.

Pablo staggered to the door and gasped in a rough voice to the guard outside: 'Jefe, I need to piss.'

He was told to piss right there, so he did, and the stench of the urine mingled with that of Eriberto's vomit and the rest of the filth in the cell. They continued to loll listlessly in their own muck and Eriberto gurgled through his swollen mouth: 'Pablo, I can't take much more. I'm finished.'

'So am I.'

'I thought that if you were arrested you could have a lawyer, and look what happened when I asked for one: "Go screw yourself," said that Vargas.'

'The police don't want anyone to know we're here.'

'But your Dolores knows that the police took you. No-one saw me being arrested.'

As they continued to talk quietly the face of the guard appeared at the small window in the door: 'What are you talking about?'

'Nothing, jefe.'

'What do you mean, nothing? If you don't shut up we'll give you another working over.'

'No, please!'

'Then shut up!'

They lapsed into silence and then both fell into a tormented half-doze until the door was opened and the captured guerrilla girl was pushed in, falling almost on top of them, to the accompaniment of obscene comments and laughter. Then the door was shut. The two young men looked at the girl, but she took no notice of them and heaved herself into the opposite corner of the cell. Eriberto tried to give her a friendly smile, but she merely returned a cold disdainful stare.

'Alright miss stuck-up,' he muttered. 'Keep yourself to yourself if you like, but it's thanks to you and your bloody comrades that we're here.'

For all the interest she showed he might just as well have been talking to himself.

Pablo thought of his cottage and Dolores. He knew what the police had done to Luisa Quispe and he wondered with dull hate whether they'd done the same to Dolores. 'Christ, I hope not! She's eight months gone with my kid!' Would he ever see the child? He was only 22 and had lived all his life in Chugurmayo. He had gone to the primary school in the village where he learned to read and write. Then, a few years ago, he had started going to the courses that Father Alfonso organized in the parish. There he learned to think about the world he lived in and understand that it was one where the *campesinos* continued to suffer exploitation, even if there had been the Agrarian Reform and they owned their plots of land. Thus began the most interesting period of his life. He began to read a bit, to learn and discuss a lot, and then he became involved in the *ronda* —the vigilante group set up by the *campesinos* to protect their cattle and to resolve their differences without having to appeal to the official justice system—. Before long, Pablo and others members of the *ronda* became the targets for the hostility of the police and the lawyers because they had put an end to a lucrative system of exploitation. For the lawyers it wasn't remotely convenient to have the *campesinos* protect themselves and administer their own justice instead of having to pay through the nose for these services in a thoroughly corrupt legal system.

But the members of the *ronda* found that *Sendero Luminoso* was also against them. 'Why?' Pablo asked Father Alfonso one day. 'The *terrucos* say that they're fighting for people like us, so why don't they back us up when we try to run our own lives?'

'They don't want you to think for yourselves. They just want to impose their own ideas.'

'So no-one wants to let us do things our own way?'

'Exactly, Pablo. The poor and the underdogs of society are not supposed to have ideas, so be careful.'

'I haven't done anything against the law.'

'Maybe, but the law doesn't matter much around these parts.'

It had been a sobering conversation but Pablo had continued to be a member of the *ronda* and his name was on the police hit-list when they entered Churgurmayo. As far as they were concerned, he was a subversive element and as guilty as hell.

Pablo stole a glance at the girl and wondered what we going through her mind. She wasn't from Yanacancha, but she must have been pretty before the police had messed her up. She maintained her total reserve and didn't favour Pablo with the slightest attention; and he knew that if ever they regained their freedom he could expect little mercy from her and the *terrucos*. A tremor of fear ran through him.

'Scared?' asked Eriberto quietly.

'Shit scared.'

'So am I.'

'Will we ever get out of this bloody mess and back into normal life?'

'I doubt it.'

CAPTAIN VARGAS ENTERED the Hotel Velezmoro where he was lodging. It was nothing more than a typical Yanacanchina house with rooms opening onto a series of flower filled patios. If Hudson Vargas had had an eye for natural beauty he would have found the Velezmoro house particularly attractive with its masses of bougainvillea and jasmine giving the place an air of profound peace and tranquility. As it was, his eye ran little beyond feminine curves and he wanted to get back to the girl he had left sprawling in a wicker chair after his hasty breakfast this morning. He strode purposefully into an inner patio and was delighted to see that the girl was still there, glancing idly at a fashion magazine. He greeted her courteously and with a flourish of his kepi asked: 'Señorita, may I join you?'

'Of course, captain,' she replied as coquettishly as the three words would allow.

'Gracias.' He laid his kepi on a table and took the other chair available, drawing it closer to her. He smiled, liking everything that he could see and calculating what he couldn't. She returned the smile and re-crossed her legs. He then unbuttoned his combat jacket and let it fall open so that the girl could see the *sinchi* badge and motto on his sweat-shirt.

'A *sinchi*, captain?'

'Exactly, señorita.'

'Hmm,' she murmured reflectively.

'To your taste or not?' he asked quietly.

She looked at him for a few seconds and then said: 'Very much so I think.'

'May I pay you the same compliment?'

'Delighted,' she replied laughing.

'I haven't seen you around before.'

'I came in on the bus yesterday and found that the whole place was in utter confusion.'

'Yes, there was an attack by a group of *terrucos*, but fortunately we beat them off; but what brings a beautiful girl like you to a God-forsaken place like Yanacancha?'

'Here, hold on! Who are you to call my native town God-forsaken?'

'I'm very sorry,' he countered, with laughing contrition in his eyes. 'It's just that I've not seen such dazzling beauty here before.'

'We are full of compliments, captain.'

They eyed each other closely and then Vargas stood up and said: 'I'm going to get a beer; can I bring you something?'

'A Coca-Cola would do fine.'

He gave her a polite bow and walked across the patio to a small bar where he ordered the drinks. By the time he returned he had decided that he must sleep with her tonight, but he wanted to enjoy the experience fully and had every intention of playing with her like an angler with a juicy trout. He poured the drinks and handed her the glass of Coca-Cola: '¡Salud!' She replied and then said: 'So you're a *sinchi*, captain?'

'As you see.'

'Am I right in thinking that only the most macho police are chosen to become *sinchis*?'

'You flatter me with your question.'

'I'm genuinely interested, captain. One hears quite a lot about the *sinchis* and they always seem to be where the fighting is roughest.' Then she dropped her voice slightly and continued: 'A lot of the reports suggest that they act like savages.'

'Do I look like a savage?' he asked with a clean open smile.

'You look tough.'

'Sure, I am. But that doesn't mean that I'm a savage, does it?' The laughter continued to play provocatively across his face.

'Could you prove it?' her grin was equally provocative.

'Look, who's leading who?'

'Meaning, captain?'

'Come off it! I reckon that we're both very much on the same wavelength. I know what you want and you know what I want.'

She allowed a silence to fall between them and then said in a matter of fact tone: 'Okay, captain, but I'd like lunch first and also learn a bit more about you.'

'Bloody hell! You lead a guy on and then tell him you want lunch!'

He looked at her with frank amazement. He had never been submitted to a cross-examination before sleeping with a woman. Rather, he was used to women who just accepted him and weakly submitted, so this young lady was a very different proposition. She leaned over and looked at him more closely, saying: 'Well, before we jump into bed together I'd like to know who are you and what are the ideals a *sinchi* fights for?'

'Himself,' replied Vargas shortly.

'No great theories about the defence of democracy and all that?'

'Frankly, no.'

'A pity.'

'I disappoint you?'

'Yes, I think so.'

'I've never done much thinking in my life,' he replied. 'Too much of a bloody luxury. I just take things as they come'

'So you've never questioned the role of the police or asked yourself what you are doing?'

'I just accept that every State needs a police force and I've wanted to be a policeman ever since I was a kid.'

'But in a normal State you wouldn't be expected to fight a war like you're having to do now, and a war that the State seems to be losing.'

'What are you on about? Are you some kind of *terruco* fifth columnist out to lower police morale?'

'No captain,' she replied with a disarming smile. I'm just interested to know what goes on inside the head of the man I'll sleep with tonight.'

'I've got to wait until tonight?'

'I'm afraid so.'

'What about the lunch you want?'

'That's going to be with an old family friend.'

'No preview of tonight's show?'

'¡No, señor!' she said with an air of finality, and then stood up, smoothing her skirt. 'Until later, captain.'

He watched her leave. He'd slept with a number of women, but none had stirred his curiosity like this one. He finished his beer and decided to go down to the barracks to deal with the problem of the two *campesinos* and the girl. Then he intended to visit Jorge Robles and once that was over he could think about enjoying what promised to be the normal pleasure of sex this evening.

THE BOTTLE OF rum which the mayor had offered to share with the colonel, Major Cantuarias, and the supervisor of education, was quickly emptied and two more were sent for. The four men were sat in the mayor's office, with Don Nicolás himself behind his desk, however, it didn't take long for the leadership of the conversation to fall into the colonel's hands:

'Señor alcalde, I've got a difficult job to do here as you must realize. I've only got one battalion to cover hundreds of square kilometres of the Andes, plus orders to return this province to constitutional law and order as quickly as possible. This is as much in your interest as it is in mine, because once I and my men leave, you can reassume your full authority. So I'd be very interested to hear your analysis of the situation. Why do you think that the terrorists have struck here in Yanacancha?'

Don Nicolás shifted in his chair uncomfortably. He had never been asked a direct question like that before. Whenever Party officials arrived they always wanted to be told that everything was fine and then they'd let themselves be wined and dined before going back to Lima feeling very pleased with themselves. To have a deliberate searching question asked was really most disconcerting, especially when it came from a man with penetrating eyes and who obviously didn't suffer fools gladly. The mayor thought for a minute and then said: 'They're outsiders you know.'

The colonel grimaced visibly at this typical waffly attempt to deflect a question by giving an answer that had nothing to do with what had been asked. However, he was used to this from civilian authorities, and that's why he despised them.

'Señor alcalde, I asked *why* the terrorists had struck here, not where they're from. However, since you have been so kind as to volunteer the information that they are outsiders, could you substantiate that? I was under the impression that no terrorists had been captured so far, but perhaps I'm mistaken. Or maybe there's some source of information of which I'm not yet aware. You do understand that I'm anxious to become fully conversant with the situation as soon as possible.'

His calm precise tone was even more disconcerting to the mayor who stammered: 'Of course, of course, colonel. I'm ready to help in every way that I can.'

'So the terrorists are outsiders?' insisted the colonel.

'No-one in Yanacancha would join the *terrucos*. It's unthinkable.'

'Why? The terrorists are real enough. We're not imagining them.'

'I know we're not, colonel, but people here just aren't like that. We've never had any trouble before in this province,' stuttered Don Nicolás looking hard at Ortiz with a silent supplication that he come to his aid.

However, it was Major Cantuarias who intervened: 'Señor alcalde, we can quite understand that all this business of the terrorists has upset everyone, but there must be some reason for their fixing on Yanacancha, be they from here or be they from outside. At the moment we're not concerned where they are from, that'll come later. What interests us right now is to find out why they are here.' He then looked at the education supervisor and said: 'Perhaps Don Juan could give us his opinion.'

'I've no idea,' muttered Ortiz with an angry look.

'Is the terrain here more suitable for hit and run tactics?'

'I'm not a military man and I don't know anything about tactics.'

'Perhaps the *campesinos* are poorer here than in other parts of the country.'

'They're not poorer than those in the central and southern Andes,' intervened Don Nicolás emphatically.

'So, what's the additional factor?' insisted the colonel.

'Bloody hell! This is like a bleeding exam!' thought Ortiz, whilst the mayor could think of nothing better to do than get the bottle of rum circulating again. The two military men each took a drink, but they had no intention of being deflected from their purpose and waited patiently whilst the bottle passed from hand to hand.

Then the colonel took up the theme again: 'Don Nicolás, Don Juan, you must understand the importance of my question because I'll have to base my strategy on the answer. Has the problem been latent? Have you seen trouble brewing? Have the *campesinos* changed at all over the past few years?'

'Yes!' shouted Ortiz, surprised at the force of his own intervention.

'Could you explain?' persisted the colonel.

'For some time the *campesinos* have been getting above themselves. The bloody Indians think that they're our equals!'

'That's true,' intervened the mayor, anxious to show that he too had something to contribute to the proceedings. 'What with the *ronda* the Indians think that they can run things their own way without any reference to the authorities here in the town. Just a few days ago Dr. Santillán told me that his legal business has been falling off drastically and that soon it'll be impossible for a lawyer to make a living here because the Indians say the justice administered by the *ronda* is quicker, cheaper, and better. They don't give a damn for the official judicial system. Worse still, the district officers appointed by the prefect in San Roque are now less important than the president of the local *ronda*.

'How is he appointed?' asked Cantuarias.

'He's elected by the members of the *ronda*.'

'They've become bloody impossible!' spat out Ortiz. 'They even think that they can stick their noses into the education system. Last year in two different villages they closed the schools and told the teachers to bugger off.'

'Why did they do that?' asked Cantuarias.

'Because they said that the teachers were ignorant and lazy! The impertinence of it! So now I have to find teachers who pass muster before a bunch of dirty Indians! As far as I'm concerned the *ronderos* are no different from the *terrucos*!'

'Would you agree with that, Don Nicolás?' asked the colonel.

'More or less, yes; and it's time that the *campesinos* were made to realize that they can't just run things their own way as though they lived in a different country.'

'What you are saying is very interesting,' observed the colonel. Now perhaps you can help me with a question that is puzzling me. Surely the *campesinos* haven't got the *ronda* movement going on their own initiative?'

'Of course not!' snapped Ortiz. 'They're too bloody ignorant to do that!'

'So how did the *ronda*s start here in Yanacancha?'

'The priest is to blame! He's been running courses in the parish and putting ideas into the Indians' heads: a whole load of crap about their being equal and having the same rights as everyone else.'

'What do you say about that, Don Nicolás?' Asked Cantuarias.

The mayor stammered nervously: 'Father Alfonso says strange

things and has some uncomfortable and radical ideas which he's been teaching ever since he took over the parish some ten years ago. In the old days, when Father Rengifo ran things, we authorities knew that we could always rely on his support. But not with the present man! Father Alfonso spends a lot of his time out in the campo visiting the villages instead of being here in the town and you yourself, colonel, heard him speak during the meeting yesterday.'

'Yes, he virtually said that you and the other authorities in this town are responsible for the terrorist presence in the province.'

'Bloody terrorist himself!' spat Ortiz again.

'If you want to know what he preaches,' said the mayor, 'why don't you go over to the church and listen to him. He's got a big crowd there today.'

'Good idea, Don Nicolás!' approved the colonel.

The mayor's face lit up now that he had managed to say something to satisfy the military, whilst the colonel leant over to Cantuarias and said: 'Cut over to the church and listen to what the priest is saying. I'd like to know if he really is an agitator.'

'Very good, sir,' replied the major getting up and taking his leave.

Don Nicolás now relaxed and passed the bottle of rum to the colonel saying: 'Another drink?'

'Gracias.'

The bottle continued to circulate and the conversation turned to more general topics until the colonel stood up to leave. 'We'll be keeping in touch, señor alcalde,' he said as he shook hands. Then he descended to the Plaza de Armas and strolled out into the mid-morning sunshine. The air was gloriously fresh and the gleaming peak of Condorrumi sparkled like a crown of diamonds. However, deep black clouds were boiling up again behind the mountain and anyone who could read the signs knew that the afternoon would bring another heavy rain storm.

In the mayor's office the two friends broached another bottle of rum, and, after saying '¡Salud!' Don Nicolás asked Ortiz: 'What do you think the colonel will do?'

'I've no idea. But if gets that blasted priest to shut up and keep his nose out of what doesn't concern him, he'll be doing us all a favour.'

'And normally one favour expects another in return. So what will he ask of us.'

'God only knows.'

MAJOR CANTUARIAS CLIMBED the steps up from the Plaza de Armas to the forecourt of the church, pushing his way through the crowds of people, and then up a further flight of steps into the church itself. No-one paid any attention to his uniform as he went inside. The place was packed and there was a sea of branches waving back and forth. Cantuarias took in the scene at a quick glance, his precise military mind being accustomed to a rapid sizing-up of people and situations. Then he let his gaze focus on the priest, resplendent in red vestments and standing beside the figure of Christ which had been taken from the donkey at the end of the procession and placed on a special throne near the altar. 'Alfonso hasn't changed,' thought the major. Their eyes had met briefly during the homage ceremony in front of the municipality, but both had been too surprised and enmeshed in their respective roles to be able to do more than smile a greeting. Now Cantuarias had time to study the priest: the same angular face with its black flashing eyes, and his hair flopping across his forehead as it had always done.

Father Alfonso was speaking in a low earnest voice and the burden of what he said was that Christ had come with a message of liberation from sin: 'Not only from personal sins like stealing and fornication, but from the sinful structures of society. We live in a province where every effort is made to exploit the humblest and the weakest, to subject people to a system that guarantees that they remain poor. The terrorists have come to try to impose their ideas on us, and kill us if we don't agree; now the military have arrived and we find ourselves squeezed between them and the terrorists. As Christians we must reject anything that means destruction, slavery, or death, no matter who propagates them. Christ is the symbol of creation, of freedom and of life! He tells us that truth will set us free and that he has come in order that we may have life, and life in abundance!'

Canuarias listened carefully. As far as he could gather his old class-mate was insisting that genuine Christianity meant liberation from the established order. He had said nothing about obeying legitimate authority or rendering Caesar his due.

The priest continued for a while longer in the same vein, insisting on his hearers' right to struggle for a more just society, 'because, as the psalmist says, without justice there can be no peace.'

Whilst Alfonso spoke Cantuarias was also concerned with watching the reactions of the people, and, to his surprise, they seemed to be paying considerable attention. He had enough experience of crowds to know that they often don't really listen to what their leaders have to say; however, here there was an obvious empathy between the priest and his people. There was no doubting the sincerity underlying his words, a rapport which had been created by years of hard work and personal testimony.

The homily came to an end and, as Alfonso led the people in reciting the creed, Cantuarias let his mind drift back into the past. Fifteen years ago he too had participated in the Palm Sunday ceremonies in the seminary. He had been a handsome young man, dressed in flowing white like all the other students, and it had been the last time that he had taken part fervently in the official ceremonies of the Church, because that evening he had been expelled, and with that had lost all faith. The army had offered a place of refuge and, thanks to a bit of string-pulling, he had got into the officer training school.

Cantuarias hauled himself back into the present. Bread and wine had been offered and incense was clouding round the altar as Alfonso walked with the smoking censer in his hands and the gaggle of altar-boys came behind him like a flock of chirruping birds. The prayers and the hymns continued. The bell was rung for the elevation of the Host and Chalice, and then everyone burst into a spontaneous hymn of praise. Cantuarias didn't really know why he remained. His orders had been to listen to what the priest had to say; nothing more. But somehow he found himself rooted to the spot and he knew that once the Mass was over he'd have to go and talk with his one-time classmate. The old ritual of the Church still exercised its fascination even though he had stopped believing fifteen years ago, and he found himself pleased to see that Alfonso had had the sense not to strip down the rites and ceremonies as so many priests had done. Here there were splendid vestments, candles, incense, and bells in all their glory, and not some cold cerebral prayer-meeting.

The people were pushing forward to communion now; branches waving and swaying, and everyone was finding it difficult to move in the tight crush. Cantuarias suddenly envied these people their faith and their simplicity of vision, and he watched them milling round until the last prayer and blessing, with the priest saying: 'You may go in the peace of the Lord.'

There was a surge of people towards the doors, but also many of those present pushed their way forward to the statue of Christ so as to leave their votive candles. Then, as the numbers thinned, Cantuarias walked towards the sacristy and entered. Father Alfonso was now free of the heavy vestments and when he saw his old class-mate enter he sprang forward eagerly: 'Telmo, it's great to see you! I wanted to go over to you when I saw you in front of the municipality, but what with the donkey and everything else it was impossible. How many years has it been?'

'Fifteen, Alfonso.'

'Well, I'm delighted to see you,' said the priest as he gave his old friend a tight embrace.

'Gracias, Alfonso. Me too!'

'Look, just give me a few minute to clear up things here and then we'll go into the house for some lunch. Agreed?'

'Agreed.'

'Fine.'

Father Alfonso turned to Flor Delgado who was occupied tidying up, and Cantuarias let them talk. People came into the sacristy with requests for this and that: a rosary to be blessed, a prayer to be said over a sick child, a Mass intention to be written down, and so forth. As Cantuarias watched Alfonso deal with each request he wondered how he would have made out as a priest. Would he have had the patience that Alfonso was showing: the kind word, the smile, the gentle embrace for a widow, and a hearty one for the youngsters who formed the choir. Finally the sacristy emptied and the priest pulled on a denim jacket, leading Cantuarias into the patio of the house. They crossed over to a small table where Alfonso invited his friend to take a seat.

'Beer? Sorry I've got nothing more sophisticated.'

'That'll do fine.'

Alfonso went into the kitchen and returned with a couple of bottles and a glass. '¡Salud! And welcome to Yanacancha!'

'Gracias.'

After taking a long drink Alfonso said: 'I needed that. These lengthy ceremonies are thirsty work.' Then he settled back into his chair with an expression of contentment. The flower-filled patio with its small fountain in the centre always soothed him when he felt tired and nervous, and this morning he had been especially keyed up. After yesterday's meeting in the municipality he had wondered how things would go today. Had he been right in assuring the colonel that the terrorists wouldn't take advantage of the religious ceremonies in order to commit some further atrocity? Would there be an outcry in the church if he spoke clearly in the homily? Perhaps no-one would turn up out of fear. Well, in the event, everything had gone off as well as he could hope for. Now, enjoying this quiet drink, he looked intently at Telmo Cantuarias and said: 'Tell me about yourself.'

The major paused and then asked: 'Were you told why I was expelled from the seminary?'

'No. There were just rumours that you'd got a girl pregnant.'

'I slipped out one night without permission, got sloshed and slept with a girl. She became pregnant and denounced me to the rector, however, it turned out that the kid wasn't mine but that of a university student. By that time I'd been thrown out without a word of sympathy, and I lost all faith in the Church and God. In fact, I was to find more solidarity in the army than I ever did in the Church. I became an officer and married a girl, but it didn't work out. We separated and since then I've found a marvellous girl with whom I'm going to have a child.

'Congratulations!'

'Don't be too hasty! My wife is doing everything she can to prevent me getting a divorce and has informed the parents of the girl about the pregnancy.'

'And?'

'The father of the girl is Carlos Miranda....'

'Bloody hell! THE Carlos Miranda?'

'Yes. Miranda wants to crucify me, my family has turned its back, my padrino who helped me get into the officer training school has died, I've long since lost my faith, I've no idea what to do except try to distinguish myself in action against the *terrucos*. So, as the Yankees say, the shit has hit the fan.'

'Or, a Sword of Damocles is hanging over you.'

'And over you too, by the way. You're not trusted by the local authorities.'

'I know. They think that I favour the *terrucos*. It's absolute rubbish of course, but there seems to be no way of getting them to understand that they represent a fundamentally flawed system. What the *terrucos* have to offer is no better; worse probably. So I don't know whether it's the Sword of Damocles or finding oneself between the Devil and the deep blue sea,' concluded Alfonso with a forced laugh.

They continued to talk and both of them found their tensions lessening as they released their fears and doubts.

'Life is like a search for the Holy Grail,' said Alfonso.

'At least you've found yours.'

'Don't you believe it! We're both still searching. We both want peace and security, but what have we got as we struggle along our dark paths? You're between your estranged wife and Carlos Miranda, with both wanting to crucify you, and I'm between the pig-headed authorities of this town and the *terrucos*, both of whom would like to crucify me.'

Suddenly there was a flash of lightning and the threatening rain came crashing down, obliging the two men to run for shelter in the kitchen where Flor Delgado had a meal ready. As they ate they continued to talk, but when Alfonso insisted: 'Telmo, no-one is going to get me to sprinkle holy water over the social and political status quo,' a strained atmosphere settled over them. Then he added: 'I hope that there is no conflict between you and me whilst you're here.'

'So do I, but if there is, you must remember that I'm a major in the army before anything else.'

'And I'm a Catholic priest. So, under the circumstances, is there any possibility of our maintaining a normal friendship?

'No sé, Alfonso. I just don't know.'

They carried on eating, but the taste had gone out of the meal and the storm over the town underlined their tension.

AFTER THE PROCESSION and the Mass, many of the participants went to Jorge Roble's house, and there, in the front patio were able to consume great piles of food and litres of *chicha.* Meanwhile, in a small back room, Robles himself was now closeted with Captain Vargas. Robles was a paunchy individual of some 60 years, with a thick crop of grey hair and an unshaven double-chin, looking more like a decrepit failure in life instead of the richest man in Yanacancha. There was nothing either in his dress or immediate surroundings which suggested wealth. However, none of this was of any interest to the young captain who had come for a serious talk after the girl in the hotel had left. So far he had not managed to broach the subject for which he had come because Don Jorge insisted on regaling him with plates piled high with food and several glasses of strong *cañazo.*

'Me and the wife always play host to the folk who participate in the procession on Palm Sunday,' said Don Jorge as the laden plates were brought in. 'Eat all you like. There's plenty for everyone, especially for an honoured member of the police force,' he added with a sly grin.

After they had eaten and chatted about this and that, and before the *cañazo* took a severe hold, Vargas decided to come to the point and said: 'We've been good friends so far, Don Jorge.'

'As you say, captain,' Robles replied warily as he thought: 'What does the bastard want? He's probably going to ask for a rise in hush-money and I'll have to show this jumped-up *sinchi* who runs things around here. There'll be no rise, and if sonny-boy doesn't behave himself, well, there's always an unfortunate accident that could occur.'

'I've come to ask a small favour, Don Jorge.'

'Sí?' murmured the older man unhelpfully.

'Your mules leave this evening for the Marañón I believe.'

'Could be.'

'Sod you! Yes or no?'

'Come, come, captain! Those aren't the terms that friends use, especially when the one using them is asking a favour,' returned Don Jorge with a glint of menace in his eyes.

'Okay, no offence meant,' replied Vargas with unaccustomed humility. 'It's just that it's very important for me to know whether the mules are leaving tonight or not.'

'And why would that be?'

'That is precisely the favour I've come to ask.'

'Tell me what the favour is and then we'll see about the mules.'

The police officer took another drink to drown his anger. He'd willingly plant a boot in the bastard's paunch; however, he said evenly: 'I want the animals to carry something for me. I believe that they always go to the Marañón unloaded.'

'I see. What do you want them to carry?'

'Some sacks.'

'Just sacks?'

'Three *full* sacks,' replied the lieutenant emphasizing the word full.

'Full of...?' The question hung in the air.

'Don Jorge, I don't ask what your mules bring into Yanacancha, nor what you do with the goods.'

'True, but they're my animals and my goods.'

'And you could find yourself in prison for a very long time if I were to show any interest in those goods,' snapped Vargas.

'I doubt it, captain,' countered Robles with a smile. 'Because you could find excessive curiosity extremely dangerous, you know.'

Although Vargas continued to look his adversary straight in the eye he knew that he was slipping into disadvantage; so he said in as a matter of fact tone as he could summon up: 'Don Jorge, all I'm asking you to do is to transport three sacks and get rid of them en route to the Marañón.'

'Get rid of them?'

'Sí.'

'I'm sorry, captain, I don't quite understand.'

'If I remember rightly, there's a very deep ravine just beyond the pass called San Andrés.'

'Yes, it's a drop of well over a thousand metres.'

'Good. I'd like the sacks to be hurled into that ravine.'

'Nothing more?'

'Nothing more, Don Jorge.'

'Just a favour?'

'I hope so

Another silence followed whilst Robles weighed up the pros and cons of the request. A favour done for the police was always a good entry on the credit side of a delicate relationship. On the other hand what would the *terrucos* —or *compañeros,* as he preferred to call them — have to say about it? Life for a decent hard-working drug-runner like himself was really becoming very complicated these days! On the one hand there were the police who had to be kept sweet and on the other there were the *compañeros* who were very nasty people to offend. What was so annoying was the injustice of it all! If it weren't for the drug-dollars the already fragile economy of the country would just fall apart, so why on earth should the police make life difficult for patriots who were keeping the national show on the road? And if it weren't for those same dollars, how would the *compañeros* be able to buy arms? There really ought to be a bit more consideration from both sides towards the only people who were really pumping money into the economy! 'Well, that's the injustice of life I suppose' Robles thought to himself as he pushed the bottle of *cañazo* over towards Vargas.

'¡Salud, capitán!'

'¡Salud, Don Jorge!'

'Do you send the sacks round here, or do you want my men to pick them up at the police barracks?'

'At the barracks.'

'Time?'

'Just after midnight'

'Fine.'

'You promise that the sacks will go into the ravine and that nobody will know anything about them?'

'Of course, captain.'

'And no prying into the contents.'

'Send a couple of your men to accompany the muleteers to the ravine.'

'I'll do that.'

They drank again, the captain eyeing the older man suspiciously until Don Jorge said with a laugh: 'Cheer up! When I have ever failed you in one of our little agreements?'

Outside, as was only to be expected, it was pouring with rain again.

ON THE ROAD that comes from San Roque there was an accident involving one of the trucks bringing more soldiers to Yanacancha.

'Sodding mud!' cried the driver when they pulled him out of the vehicle which had fallen on its side into a river. 'Never seen a road like this in all my bloody life.'

Nearly all the soldiers had escaped serious injury, but one had been badly crushed and was now lying in the road with a tarpaulin over him. The sub-lieutenant in charge ordered the troops to lift the wounded man into one of the other trucks so as to be protected from the rain, then he sent a sergeant in a jeep ahead to Yanacancha to bring a doctor, but he had no luck. When the sergeant reached the doctor's house his wife said: 'My husband is with Dr. Santillán, the lawyer. It's Sunday,' she announced in a tone that she presumed explained everything.

'What's so special about Sunday?' asked the sergeant.

'My husband and Dr. Santillán always drink over the week-end.'

'So he's drunk?'

'Of course.'

'Bloody hell! Now what do we do?'

'There's a medical student here on holiday, Manuel Verástegui.'

'Where do we find him?'

'He's probably enjoying the party at Don Jorge Robles' house.'

'Which is where?'

The woman gave the sergeant directions and he found Manuel who had gone down to the Robles house with several friends after the procession and Mass. One of them said: 'You've got to give it to old Dagoberta, she may be a bitch but she knows how to provide food and drink.' Another member of the group was Lucio Benites who now lay comatose on the floor, and before getting completely drunk he had had a furious argument with Manuel, ending up by shouting: 'It's alright for you, you've got a future, but what have I got? Just sweet bugger all!' With that he heeled over and fell on the floor.

'What'll we do with him?' asked Manuel.

'Leave him there,' said one of the others. '¡Salud!'

When the sergeant entered the house a shiver of fright ran through everyone who was enjoying the Robles' hospitality. 'Is Manuel Verástegui here?' he asked.

'Yes, that's me,' answered Manuel cautiously.

The sergeant explained about the accident and then asked: 'Will you come with us to attend to the soldier who has been wounded?'

'Haven't you asked the doctor?'

'He's pissed.'

'As per usual at the weekend,' said Manuel nonchalantly. Then he added almost jocularly: 'One's not supposed to get sick or have an accident in Yanacancha at weekends, but you're a stranger so didn't know that.'

'Young man, stop buggering about! Will you come?'

'Yes, I'll do what I can. What happened?'

'The road is so bad that the truck fell on its side and then slithered down to a river.'

'That'll be the Yanamayo.'

'Everything here is *yana* this and *yana* that. What the bloody hell does it mean?'

'*Yana* is the Quechua for black.'

'That's just about it. We're in the bloody black arsehole of the Andes.'

'Funny you should think that. We call it "the Pearl of the Andes".'

'Some fucking pearl for Christ's sake!'

When Manuel reached the soldier he found that the man had fainted from loss of blood, but he managed to stem the flow and patch him up temporally.

'He'll have to be seen by the doctor tomorrow.'

'Will he be sober?'

'Of course; he only drinks at weekends and tomorrow he'll be fine.' By the way, what's the soldier's name?'

'Lázaro Gómez.'

After attending to the soldier, Manuel felt tense and was happy to stand in the road and let the rain pour over him. It was a kind of cleansing that helped him feel as though nothing untoward were happening in the province; just life as usual.

FOR THE REST of the day the rain washed over Yanacancha and a gloomy evening settled in. There's not much to do in a small Andean town on a wet night except drink or, if the electricity supply is working, see an indifferent film.

Don Nicolás Leal had walked home after Juan Ortiz had left his office and he now sat slumped in a wicker chair under the wide eaves of the corridor that ran round the patio of his house. The rain dripped monotonously, a dreary accompaniment to his own dreary thoughts. Since the military had arrived it was clear that he was no-one. They would run Yanacancha as they pleased and would merely parade him as a puppet. He felt humiliated and bitter at the abnormality of his situation.

IN SPITE OF the accident with one of the military trucks the main body of troops reached the town, and once the colonel was satisfied that they had been billeted and that food was being prepared he sat down to talk to Cantuarias.

'Well, what did the priest have to say? Is he an agitator or is he on our side?'

'Difficult to say, sir. I don't think he's on either side.'

'Typical bloody Church!' returned the colonel. 'Playing her own power game. I don't trust her and I don't trust this priest. Every man in this life is out to get what he can from it for himself, and I don't believe that your friend Father Alfonso is any different. If he preaches brotherly love and all that crap, it'll be for some private gain, and I have every intention of finding out what it is.'

'Are you suggesting that he's some kind of fraud, sir?'

'All priests are frauds. They can't possibly believe what they preach, especially if they claim to be on the side of the poor.'

'I don't think he's a fraud, sir. On the contrary, I reckon that he's very sincere.'

'Have it your own way, Cantuarias, but fraud or sincere he doesn't fit into our scheme of things. He's independent and that means he's a bloody nuisance, so we'll have to shut him up.'

'How, sir?'

'I'll think of something. And by the way....'

'Yes, sir?'

'Even if he is your friend, remember that you're an army officer first.'

'I've already told him that.'

'Good.'

After that the two men parted.

Now, as he lay on his bed and listened to the rain hammering on the corrugated iron roof, the colonel realized that he felt a deep dislike for this town tucked away in its remote Andean valley. There was something primitive and sinister about the place, for all its display of Christian piety. There was a dark brooding atmosphere, so not without reason was it called Yanacancha —The Black Field—. Its Andean culture and its lack of fervent patriotism, as he understood it, irked him.

The colonel himself was from Tacna, the southernmost city on the coast of Peru, and which had remained in the hands of the Chileans after the disastrous War of the Pacific in the 1880's. In accordance with the Treaty of Ancón, signed after Peru's defeat, Tacna was given back in 1929, and ever since, every 7th June, Flag Day, the city has been the scene of deep emotional patriotism. The heroes of the War of the Pacific were the colonel's saints and he had never questioned the version of Peruvian history that he had been taught as a child. Now, in this Andean town, he felt that somehow it was questioned. He couldn't quite fathom it, but he sensed that his heroes and his vision of Peru were not shared up here. This was a different country, with a different history and different heroes, unrecorded in writing, unsung, but tucked away deep in the Andean conscience. Here the official, and for the colonel the normal, view of history just didn't exist.

FOR HIS PART, Cantuarias had gone to join the officers who had arrived with the rest of the troops. Young Sub-Lieutenant Álvarez who had sent for Manuel to attend to the wounded soldier, described the journey from Piura in the far north as though it were one marvellous adventure. 'Even before you cross the Yanamayo, or whatever the bloody river is called, the whole place is just one shagging quagmire. How the hell are we going to be able to manoeuvre in this shit?'

'We probably aren't,' replied Cantuarias drily.

'So what are going to do, just sit on our arses and get shot at by the *terrucos*?'

'Something like that.'

'Christ! What I have I let myself in for?' exclaimed the young officer with an infectious grin, as though the whole business were some kind of normal boy scout adventure.

Cantuarias envied him and went out into the rain.

THE RAIN LASHED down even harder as Captain Vargas supervised the loading of the three large heavy sacks onto the mules.

'You know where to throw them?' he asked the leading muleteer.

'About half a kilometre beyond the San Andrés pass.'

'Hurl them well out so that they fall into the ravine.'

'Nothing else, jefe?'

'Nothing.' Then Vargas turned to the corporal and policeman who were to accompany the mule train. 'Rojas, Luna, make sure that these sacks and their contents are disposed of and then cut back here at once.'

'Yessir!' they replied in unison.

The mule train went slowly out of the barracks into the rain-drenched night and the captain turned up the street, walking slowly to his hotel. His problems were behind him and life seemed normal again as he looked forward to sex with the girl.

FATHER ALFONSO KNELT before the high altar of the church and tried to pray. He felt an increasing sense of loneliness. Initially it had been great to meet up again with Telmo Cantuarias and talk together until he realized that between them there stretched a wide gulf. They both wore uniforms and each had a role to play in life, and somehow these had served to obliterate the common humanity that they shared.

The small flame in the sanctuary lamp flickered in the draughty building, almost going out at times, then it recovered and cast its normal glow of comfort; whilst outside the rain crashed down with ever increasing force.

Four

MONDAY DAWNED WITH a cold light throwing the mountains into sharp relief. The rain had stopped around four-thirty, and since then a steady wind had blown the clouds away, enabling the first fingers of the sun's rays to touch the mountain tops and making them glow gold. The sweet rich scent of the countryside soon became mingled with the eucalyptus wood smoke which rose from the hundreds of kitchen fires in Yanacancha over which breakfasts were bubbling and sizzling.

Father Alfonso found the early Mass with a few pious old ladies soothing after the dry, almost dead prayers of the previous evening. Hardly was the Mass over than a number of people began to arrive with candles, flowers, bundles of twine, and a business like air to start transforming one of the *andas* —the heavy platforms used for carrying statues in procession— into the Garden of Gethsemane, since local devotion prescribed that the day be devoted to Our Lord of the Agony in the Garden.

Next came several youths with ropes and ladders to lower the statue of Christ leaning on a rock and with outstretched arms from its altar to be placed on the *andas*. Others arrived, dragging branches. Since olive trees did not grow around Yanacancha the custom had grown up that the Garden of Gethsemane be an orange grove.

Father Alfonso wandered over to see how these early preparations were going and was greeted by a chorus of 'Morning, Father!'

'Morning, everyone! How are things going?'

'Fine!'

'Oh, by the way, Father….' The tone and the trailing off of the voice meant that something was coming that should have been discussed days ago, but was being slipped in now in such a way that it would be virtually impossible for the priest to say 'no' without causing ill feeling. 'We've got a lovely idea to make the Garden of Gethsemane much prettier this year.'

The priest blanched at the idea of making Gethsemane 'pretty', but he braced himself and asked: 'Yes, what is it?'

'We're going to put fairy lights in the trees,' came the bright reply.

'Fairy lights!' He couldn't keep the incredulity out of his voice.

'That's right, Father. Don't you think they'll make a big improvement?'

The comment that sprang to his mind was not for the ears of well-meaning pious folk, so he merely muttered: 'Hmmm,' and went back to the parish house for a quick breakfast. He hadn't finished before there came an imperious knock at the door and he found himself confronted by Doña Dagoberta Castillo de Robles and *The Ladies of Yanacancha*. Doña Dagoberta had a determined expression on her face, however, her greeting was all honey: 'Father Alfonso, a very good morning to you. I hope that the procession and the Mass yesterday weren't too tiring. We missed you afterwards you know.'

The priest muttered an apology for having failed to show up at the Robles' house after the Palm Sunday Mass, and then said: 'It's a pleasure to see you all; now what can I do for you?'

'We've come about the cross, Father.'

'Oh,' he murmured. 'How did how your meeting go with Don Nicolás on Saturday?'

'Everything went splendidly, Father. Dear Don Nicolás is such a patriot and he's ready to do everything in his power to help push ahead with the rebuilding project.'

'I'm very glad to hear it.'

'However, a problem has arisen.'

'Yes?' he replied monosyllabically, wondering what grenade Doña Dagoberta was about to bring out of her handbag.

'We aren't all agreed as to exactly how the cross should be rebuilt.'

Immediately there came a cataract of voices: some were in favour rebuilding the cross exactly as it had been; others were in favour of concrete rather than stone; there were those who wanted elaborate lighting installed, and others in favour of a crucifix.

'Since there are different opinions and the cross is part of the Yanacancha identity, perhaps the best thing to do would be to call a town meeting and so give everyone a chance to have their say.'

'Oh, Father, you know what a town meeting is like. One person says one thing, and then someone else says another, and we end up with a terrible confusion. It would be far better if you made the decision. You know that everyone will accept whatever you say. After all, you are the spiritual father of this town,' she added emphatically.

'Rather, everyone will have a good reason to criticize me,' thought Father Alfonso, and then again insisted on the calling of a town meeting.

'You must remember Father that we're now in a state of emergency, so I'm sure that the colonel won't allow any kind of public meeting.'

'Well, I'll get hold of the mayor and together we'll talk to him about it.'

And with that the ladies had to be satisfied. They bade him good-bye and as he watched them descend the steps to the square he felt a certain affection for them. It was true that they could be a bloody nuisance at times and often made him angry, but *The Ladies of Yanacancha* worked hard for what they felt the town needed. 'Women are the real back-bone of this country,' he thought to himself. 'We men strut and bluster, but it's the women who so often carry the load. It's a pity that Dagoberta hasn't got a more useful target to which to direct her energies, but whatever happens she'll get the cross up, in spite of terrorists, in spite of inflation, in spite of hostility or apathy. It's difficult to like her, but I certainly admire her — a barmy mix-up to say the least.'

Captain Vargas stretched himself and looked at the girl beside him. She had been as good as she had promised. He slipped out of bed and gazed at himself in the full-length mirror of the wardrobe. His body was compact and tough, and he was proud of it. No matter how much boozing and whoring he might indulge in, he had no intention of letting himself run to seed. He exercised hard each day and could run any of his men into the ground. He was every inch a *sinchi*, and he was going to stay that way. He turned when he heard a movement in the bed and saw that the girl was looking at him.

'You look very pleased with yourself,' she commented.

'I feel it,' he said. He walked over to a table, took a cigarette from a packet, lit it and smoked contentedly for a moment. 'You know, a man finds life good at times, and this is one of them for me.'

'I wonder how many other people here in Yanacancha are finding life good this morning. I reckon that this town is running scared.'

'As far as I'm concerned a bit of danger is like spice in the food.' He grinned like a contented schoolboy. Then he added: 'You still haven't told me what you're doing here. Alright, you were born here, so what? I can promise you that I don't want to go back to the crap-heap where I was born.'

'Yanacancha isn't a crap-heap!'

'Sorry, señorita,' he replied with mock contrition.

'I've come …,' she stopped, as though searching for the right words.

'You've come for what?'

'Oh nothing really,' she prevaricated with eyes flickering nervously. Then came a forced smile.

'You intrigue me.'

'Why do you say that?'

'I sense that you feel strongly about me, but I'm not sure whether its love or hate.'

'Captain, we've hardly known each other for 24 hours, so how am I going to feel strongly about you?' Once again her eyes flickered nervously.

'I'm not totally insensible and I think that you're the first woman to fascinate me.'

'Have there been many?' she asked quickly so as to change the subject.

'What do you reckon?'

'I imagine that there have quite a number. You're attractive.'

'Many thanks,' he laughed mockingly. Then he said in a more serious tone: 'Remember I've worked in terrorist dominated parts of the country and a man has to take advantage of what he can out of life. Some of my comrades in arms have passed a really good night with a girl and been killed the following day. Life's like that, so one has to live in the present because that's the only thing that exists. Why worry about tomorrow, which perhaps won't come, or cry about yesterday, which has now passed?'

'So that's the way you see me, just a passing moment of pleasure and nothing else?'

'And you?' Once again Vargas observed a nervous flicker in her eyes. There was no doubt that she intrigued him. He stubbed out the cigarette and began to dress. 'I hope that we'll get to know each other better.'

'I hope so too.'

After dressing rapidly, Vargas left her and she remained in the bed, gazing at the ceiling and thinking. Yes the sex had been good even though she knew that she had to hate him. Somehow she admired the handsome captain, but she was barred from liking him, and love was completely out of the question. In this strange mixture of emotions she had no idea what she was going to do.

MAJOR TELMO CANTUARIAS awoke in what had been the headmaster's office in the school which the military had taken over and gazed abstractedly at a large portrait on the wall of Juan Carlos Losada Aguilar, a minor poet who had lived in this house and had written during the 1920s and 30s. A volume of his poems lay on small table beside the bed, and Cantuarias had been reading some of them since he had awoken early. They all belonged to the romantic school. It was Losada who had first called Yanacancha 'the Pearl of the Andes', and his poems also spoke of *'Yawarrumi lit with carmesí'*, of *'The Red Stone Eagle, diamond crowned'*, of the skies, the birds, the superb views over the mountains and lakes, but never of the *campesinos*, of the toil in the fields, or of the suffering and misery of the province under the sway of the hacienda owners. Losada offered a vision of another history, almost at the opposite end of the spectrum from the official one, but just as warped and just as inadequate as a frame of reference to understand Yanacancha.

Outside, a bugle was calling the men to breakfast, and Cantuarias knew that he'd have to brace himself for a strategic planning conference with the colonel and the other officers in order to decide how they were going to handle this *'Pearl of the Andes'*. He dragged himself out of bed, shaved in cold water, and then went bad temperedly towards the classroom where the meeting was going to be held. When he entered the classroom Cantuarias crammed himself into one of the rickety desks next to Sub-Lieutenant Álvarez who was keen and raring to a get a crack at the 'bastard *terrucos.*'

'You'll be lucky,' said Cantuarias morosely. 'The *terrucos* are like bloody mosquitos. They buzz in, suck your blood and then bugger off before you know what's happened. The only difference between them is that the *terrucos* buzz with sophisticated arms. They hold the initiative and know exactly what they're on about, whilst we fart around like drunks.'

'You're bloody pessimistic, major. We've now got modern techniques with which to fight the *terrucos.*'

The conversation was cut short with the colonel's entry. He was accompanied by Captain Vargas, who was duly presented to the army officers. The colonel made a number of introductory remarks about the nature and difficulty of their task. However, he expressed confidence that the army would be able to meet the challenge, adding that to help in planning operations 'I've invited Captain Vargas to share with us his experience.'

Vargas smiled good humouredly, and expressed his pleasure at being invited to collaborate with the military. 'Señores, there aren't many terrorists in the province as far as we know, but they are highly mobile and the local population offers them protection. We can't barge around blindly trying to search every village and isolated farmhouse; what we've got to do is select a few well-chosen targets to attack, and attack hard!'

'What's the danger of making innocent people suffer in these attacks, captain,' asked Cantuarias.

'Major, in a war innocent people suffer and die; collateral damage, as the Yanquis say. That's the way it is. We didn't start this war, but now we're involved in it we're bloody well going to win it! And you can't win a war by pussy-footing. We've got to be prepared to fight hard and to kill. If there's a village or a family which gives protection to the terrorists they are our enemies and we've got to strike at them without pity.'

'Captain,' said the colonel, 'on Saturday, in the municipality, you mentioned a village....'

'Chugurmayo perhaps.'

'Yes, that was it. You mentioned that the police had entered and not done more than ask a few questions and make a routine search after the place had suffered a terrorist assault. But was it really like that? Perhaps you knew of a terrorist presence in the village, and in that case your incursion would have been punitive perhaps. Am I right?'

Vargas smiled and nodded in agreement.

'Well, since we're all involved in fighting the terrorists could you give us a franker version of what you did there?'

'Thank you, colonel for your confidence. Civilians know nothing about the reality of war and I couldn't tell them that we gave the people of Chugurmayo a lesson that they'll never forget. We had information that they favoured the *terrucos* and they had to be punished.'

'What did you do?'

'We beat the shit out of them!'

'Aren't you concerned that some Human Rights Commission might investigate and denounce you?'

'One of my men was killed by a booby-trap when he went to pull down the *terrucos*' filthy bloody flag in the Santa María del Valle cooperative. The bomb destroyed his legs and opened his stomach. He died slowly and screaming with pain. We had no anesthetics. Señores, just don't talk to me about human rights where terrorists and their supporters are concerned! As I've said to me own men, fuck Human Rights!'

There was a hearty round of applause, and the colonel thanked Vargas for his clarity and frankness. 'We'll be bloody stupid if we don't take into account what the captain has said. We'll find out who are the people protecting the terrorists and we'll strike hard at them. Maybe you already have some targets in mind, captain?'

'Yes, where villages are concerned, there's one called Llangodén and I've already sent an undercover agent to sass it out. That's some distance away; but if you want a target right here in the town I reckon that you couldn't do better than gun for the priest.'

'Normally it's not advisable to tangle with the clergy, captain.'

By way of reply Vargas laughed cynically and said: 'I'll admit that I admire the guy. He's got balls; but I still hate his guts.'

A FEW HOURS after dawn, the mule carrying the sack which contained the remains of the girl, began the sharp descent to the Marañón, and it would still take several hours before reaching the bottom of the vast gorge separating two cordilleras of the Andes. The two muleteers who accompanied the animal had no idea of the contents of the sack, nor of the other two which had been sent back towards Yanacancha with a couple of their companions.

Last night four of them had been walking for several hours before being intercepted by a group of heavily armed masked men. At first they had thought that it was the local *ronda*, but soon discovered that they were *compañeros*. Normally these never took much interest in the mule train whenever it passed between Yanacancha and the Marañón, so their sudden appearance and detention of the mules came as a complete surprise, whilst the accompanying police had no chance of defending themselves. They were seized and disarmed. After that, the four muleteers had been led aside and were questioned behind some rocks. Then they were taken back to the mules which were still loaded and received orders from their captors: 'Two of you take this one and its sack to the Marañón; the other two mules go back.

Leave their sacks and contents at the ruined cottage at the top of *La Quebradita* —*The Little Ravine*—. After that you can return with the mules and carry on to the Marañón.'

'And the police who were with us?'

'Don't ask questions.'

Now, as the two muleteers descended to the Marañón with the mule still laden with its sack they said nothing to each other though both wondered why the other mules had been sent back. One of the muleteers was a man of about 40 and the other his 16 year old son. The older man chewed *coca* leaves and the youth amused himself by flinging stones at the occasional bird. They were so used to making this trip that neither of them took any interest in the landscape which was one of the most impressive that the Andes have to offer. The descent from the moorlands that stretch out between the mountain tops to the river below is one of over 3,000 metres, and it goes from bitter cold to boiling heat. In the upper reaches there is a certain amount of agriculture with small parcels of maize and wheat, plus a few fruit trees but further down the landscape becomes lunar, totally arid and devoid of any kind of shelter from the sun.

Down and down walked the man and his son, giving the mule an occasional thwack on its flanks. It was getting on for midday when they finally reached the bottom of the gorge and the cable car which crossed the swift flowing river, swollen with the rains and ochre with the silt it was bringing down, twisting sinuously between the huge precipices like the Golden Serpent as it has been called by Ciro Alegría, one of Peru's best known authors.

As the man and his son approached the cable car they walked through desert scrub, but on the far side of the river there was a totally different world containing luxuriant plantations of fruit and *coca* whilst the noise of the parakeets was louder even than that of the river. They crossed and found that they were expected.

'Untie the sack and bring it over here carefully,' ordered one of the armed men who waiting for them. They did as they were told. 'Now take the mules and leave us.'

Several young men, each armed with a light machine-gun, came forward, laid aside their weapons and undid the sack. Then they pulled out the girl's corpse reverently. It was wrapped in swathes of plastic and, as they unwound it, the extent of her suffering before she was killed became apparent. They hissed obscenities against the men who had done this to her.

'Bloody bastards!' screamed one as he threw himself onto the corpse to embrace it.

'We know how you feel, *compañero*,' said another, lifting him gently by the shoulder. 'You can be proud of her. We know that she never uttered a word of betrayal. La *compañera* Lucha has been an example to us all.'

Once they had cleaned the corpse they buried it with a brief ceremony. All those present were subdued, even though their leader gave a short rousing discourse which exalted the dead girl's commitment to the ideal of a socialist society based on Marxist-Leninism.

Throughout the proceedings Humfri Becerra remained in the background. Then he was called forward.

'Now you see what it means to be one of us.'

'Sí,' he answered in a low strangled tone.

'We're not a group of idealists who rob the rich to pay the poor, or any of that kind of crap. We're fighters for a new social order.'

'Sí.'

'You won't question your orders and you'll carry them out to the letter.'

'Of course.'

'You understand that only after you've complied with a number of tasks in order to test your loyalty and effectiveness will you be fully admitted as a *compañero*?

'Sí,' came the dry response once again.

'If you fail, you know what to expect.'

'I believe so.'

'Death!'

Humfri blanched. He knew that they were all watching him closely.

'We have your first task.'

'¿Sí?' He managed to turn the word into a question this time.

'You will kill Captain Vargas.'

'No!' shouted the youth who had lived with *compañera* Lucha. 'That should be my privilege!'

'You've got a wounded leg and can't go to Yanacancha.'

'Bring the bastard here. He killed Lucha, so let me torture him to death slowly. We all know that Lucha screamed under torture, though she never revealed anything. I want to hear Vargas scream!'

'I can understand your feelings, *compañero*, but this is not the time to give way to bourgeois emotionalism. The death of Vargas will be an official execution, not a matter of personal revenge.' Then he turned to Humfri Becerra: 'We want you to kill Vargas in the middle of Yanacancha and in the most public way possible, so that his death will be a lesson to everyone.'

After a short silence, Humfri said: 'I'm not questioning my orders, *compañero*, but I'm surprised that you give such a responsibility to someone as untried as myself. I will, of course, do my utmost to be worthy of your trust.'

'As I said, we want this execution to take place as publicly as possible, and to do that we need an agent whom no-one suspects. All of us are known to the police, but you aren't. You're just one more *campesino*, and that's the most normal thing in the world. You can walk with impunity in the streets of Yanacancha and even give the impression that you admire what the police are doing. That'll quell any suspicion and will enable you to draw a gun on that bastard Vargas. That's what we want. Fell him in the Plaza de Armas if you can so that even people who don't agree with us can admire what *Sendero Luminoso* is capable of.

As ALWAYS, Ma Vásquez' cantina was open and business was booming. Indeed it would be difficult to say whether it ever closed or whether Ma herself ever took a minute off from dispensing liquor to her clients to engage in such mundane affairs as eat, sleep and go the toilet.

Alcides Sifuentes' old cronies were gathered at their usual table, but sad this morning. There had been another hitch over his funeral and his drinking companions were upset. Not content with the civilian autopsy, the military were insisting on doing their own. So, all in all, Alcides was proving as unlucky in death as he had been in life. Why did the stupid bastard get himself blown to bits on a Friday night, was the basic question. No-one with any sense dies on a Friday when doctors and lawyers are starting up their week-end boozing, just as you wouldn't think of starting any other business at the end of the week. Besides, most people have enough intelligence to die in their beds or from some ordinary accident, like falling drunk into the river on the way back from the cantina. But to get blown to bits on a Friday night was just asking for trouble.

First the bits had to be found, with the judge present and all that. Since Dr. Santillán was standing in for the judge that meant he had to be hauled up to the ruins of the municipal depot. Well, that had happened on Saturday, after the meeting in the municipality. Then the police had intervened and now it was the military who were delaying things.

'We can't even give the guy a wake, let alone a funeral,' muttered Antenor Chilón.

The calabash was passed round again and each drank greedily, but glumly. Not only had their little world suffered a severe disruption with the death of their friend but the empty seat of the night-watchman seemed to look reproachfully at them as though each of them was partially to blame for his death. Why hadn't they stopped Sifuentes from going up to the depot? Why hadn't they got him so drunk that he couldn't walk? However, natives of the Andes as they were, they were fatalists and now could do little more than shrug their shoulders, take another drink and say: 'His time was up.'

They continued to drink as though they were in a substitute wake in honour of the late Alcides Sifuentes, conjouring up anecdotes of pretended admiration for a poor guy whom no-one had really liked: 'Not even his bleeding missis!'

In Chugurmayo the people were still suffering from the shock of the police incursion the previous week, and as there was no news of either Pablo Huamán or Eriberto Huaripata, Pablo's partner, Dolores Vergara, decided that she would accompany Eriberto's mother down to Yanacancha to see whether she could find out something. Since she'd only been to the town twice before in her life she was nervous. So this Monday morning both women had been up long before dawn attending to their animals and then, when the black velvety sky began to soften, they set off at the swift strange half-walk, half-run, of Andean *campesina* women. They didn't waste their energy on talk as they knew that they would need all their wits about them once they reached the town: two more women searching for their menfolk, as mothers and wives had been doing in their hundreds over most of the past decade in many provinces of the Andes.

They arrived at Dr. Santillán's office in the middle of the morning and found several other people waiting. However, the lawyer himself was not in evidence. A young girl secretary was at work on a battered typewriter, or rather was banging away at it and making a lot of mistakes in whatever it was she was typing, so she had to keep stopping and erasing them. This operation was accompanied by much popping and blowing of pink bubblegum.

Eriberto's mother enquired timidly of the secretary how long it would be before the lawyer turned up and was informed indifferently that he'd be along shortly — one of those vague phrases which mean anything from five minutes to five hours. The two women resigned themselves to waiting patiently and went outside to sit on the pavement. There they occupied themselves with spinning wool on hand distaffs. They were oblivious to the comings and goings of people along this side of the Plaza de Armas and to the remarks made by some of the passers-by about 'Bloody Indians who take over the town every time they set foot in the place. If they want to sit down, why can't they go and sit on a bench like normal people, instead of sprawling themselves all over the pavement?'

The morning was wearing on when a rumour began to circulate in the town to the effect that some bodies had been found and, like a scrub fire on the moors during the dry season, word leapt from mouth to mouth with every variation imaginable:

'Bodies of *terrucos* killed the other night.'

'Bloody great mass grave with hundreds of bodies.'

'Poor bastards were killed by the *terrucos*.'

'The police are responsible, you mark my words.'

'More likely the military.'

'Whoever it was they've really massacred the poor buggers!'

'I wonder who they are.'

'How many?'

'Twenty you say?'

'Tortured?'

'Yes, quite unrecognizable of course.'

'Fortunately they're only *campesinos*.'

'Uchurrucay*!'

'Accomarca*!'

'The prison massacre in Lima!'*

---

* In 1981, Uchurracay, a small Quechua speaking community in the central Perúvian Andes at over 4000 metres above sea level, suffered severely at the hands of the *Shining Path*. The inhabitants took their revenge and brutally killed a number of the *Shining Path* leaders. Then, on the 26th of January 1983, the people mistook a group of eight journalists for *Shining Path* terrorists and lynched them.

* Accomarca, another small Andean community, was wiped out by the army on August 14th, 1985, after the systematic torture and violation of the population that was suspected of being a base for terrorist formation, though in fact this was completely untrue. Of the 69 people who died, 30 were children, 27 were women and 12 were men.

* In June 1986 a series of riots took place in the prisons of Lima and Callao whilst a Congress of the Socialist International was taking place in Lima. The army, the navy and the police assaulted the prisons. At least 224 people lost their lives, many of them in summary executions after they had surrendered.

'Cayara*, and now this!'

'San Agustín de Yanacancha will go down in history!'

'Bloody marvelous historical memory!'

'We must be running up a world record for unidentified bodies and mass graves!'

'There'll be another commission, investigations, and then nothing; just like the others.'

'At least they've got the bodies this time, not like Cayara where they simply disappeared.'

'Let's go and see what's been found.'

In ones and twos, men alone and groups of youths, also the more intrepid girls and a few women, started out towards *La Quebradita* —*The Little Ravine*. However, the two *campesinas* from Chugurmayo remained oblivious to the rumours and scrambled to their feet in a flurry of skirts when Dr. Santillán turned up at last with an imperial hang-over and a foul temper. No sooner did he enter his office than all his waiting clients crowded round him demanding to know about 'the papers you promised to look into.'

'My old man's will!'

'The case that went to court weeks ago and I've not heard a thing.'

'My Eriberto!'

The lawyer took his seat behind his desk and imposed some semblance of order, insisting that he could only deal with one person at a time.

'The secretary is attending to the papers, so if you'll just have a little patience, señora, everything will be ready shortly.'

'Yes, I've filed a suit with respect to the will.'

'It isn't my fault if the judge hasn't dealt with the case yet, and now he's away, so you'll just have to wait.'

---

* On May 13th, 1988, the *Shining Path* ambushed a military convoy in the District of Cayara. The following day 180 soldiers entered the small town and carried out a brutal massacre, using knives and machetes, and then finishing off their victims with bullets. Subsequently the military impeded a judicial investigation and every effort was made to obliterate the evidence.

'But you're standing in for him aren't you?'

'Sí.'

'Can't you push the case through quickly?'

'You must understand that the law doesn't allow me to be both judge and defence lawyer, so there's nothing for it but wait until the judge returns.'

'Bugger the law!'

'Quite so, my friend,' sighed the lawyer, rubbing his throbbing temples.

'And my Eriberto?'

'What about him?'

'Haven't you looked for him?'

Dr. Santillán suddenly recognized the woman who had come to pester him the previous Friday and now said: 'I've done what I can, and it seems most likely that he's run off with some girl to the coast. Happens every day you know.'

'And my Pablo?' asked Dolores aggressively in her nervousness.

'Who is your Pablo? I've never seen you before my girl.'

'The police took him in.'

'Well, go down to the police barracks and ask there instead of wasting my valuable time.'

'I paid you to find my boy,' wailed Eriberto's mother.

'Señora, you paid me a paltry sum to investigate his disappearance, and I've done my best. However, I'm not a magician and I can't pull rabbits out of a hat.'

The old lady looked at him uncomprehendingly. She had never heard the word 'magician' and added: 'It was the pig that he took to sell, not a rabbit.'

'For Christ's sake, I've looked for your bloody son and he can't be found!'

'Then I want my money back!'

'Oh go to the Devil!' He snapped just as a messenger boy from the court arrived to inform him about the finding of the two bodies, and that his presence was urgently required in *La Quebradita*.

'Bloody hell, what a life!'

However, there was nothing for it but to go. And so, with much muttering and swearing, the lawyer assumed an air of importance and pushed his way through the people in his office and out into the Plaza de Armas, whilst his clients aired their dislike in general 'for the bloody legal profession.'

WHEN SERGEANT CHÁVEZ saw the bodies of the two young men he had helped to torture he felt his stomach tighten. 'There's been a right balls-up!' He gasped in an undertone, and then ordered the two policemen who accompanied him to keep people away from the bodies whilst he reported to Captain Vargas.

'What do you mean, sergeant?'

'The two we had here, captain.'

'It's impossible, man!' retorted Vargas going pale and narrowing his eyes.

'I've seen them myself, sir.'

'That bastard Robles has double-crossed me. We've got to get rid of the bodies immediately.'

'Impossible, sir, there's hoards of people out at *La Quebradita.*'

For a few moments Vargas tapped his teeth with a pencil. Then he said forcefully: 'It's easy. We haven't admitted to having detained anyone here, so we've got nothing to do with these bodies. When the autopsy reveals that they've been beaten-up, we'll say that it was *terrucos* who did it.'

'Let's hope that people believe us.'

'Yeah, let's hope so. Now stop shitting bricks and go and find Robles. I want to see him at once. Apart from that, keep your bleeding mouth shut.'

'¡Sí, mi capitán!'

The sergeant saluted smartly and left Vargas to his own thoughts. He took out a cigarette and smoked thoughtfully for half an hour; cigarette after cigarette. Nothing had been said about the girl. Where were Rojas and Luna? He'd flay them alive once he got his hands on them. What the bloody hell is going on? The world is standing on its head!

Don Jorge Robles entered Vargas' office:

'Bloody traitor! What have you done?' snarled the police captain.

IT TOOK DR. Santillán all of an hour to do the short walk to *La Quebradita* because he was neither suitably dressed for walking more than a few metres along the streets of the town, nor was he accustomed to doing so. After ten minutes he handed his jacket to the messenger from the court, who was anxious to accompany the lawyer and see the bodies for himself. Then off came the waistcoat. A bit later he removed his tie, and by this time he was sweating profusely. However, eventually he made it and found himself standing at the edge of a small cliff that descended to the stream below. By the side of the stream there was a meadow on which were tumbled the two bodies. With a lot of help, and even more difficulty, the fat little lawyer clambered down to the spot beside the bodies, which, as the remains of their clothing indicated, were obviously of young *campesinos*.

'Any documents on them?' Santillán asked the policeman who was standing watch.

'No, señor.'

'Life would be so much easier,' sighed the lawyer fussily, 'if only people would abide by the law and carry their identity documents on them at all times.'

'Sí, señor.'

'Is there nothing by which we can identify them?'

'No, señor. It looks to me as though they've been in a fight. *Campesinos* are great for getting drunk and fighting.'

'Quite so, quite so,' replied the lawyer with an abstracted look on his face. Then he said abruptly: 'Give me my jacket!'

He found the photo of Eriberto Huaripata in one of the pockets. He compared it with the disfigured faces of the two young men and was just able to recognize that one of them was indeed Eriberto.

'So it looks as though I've found the old woman's boy and she can stop pestering me for her money back.'

'Sorry, sir?' said the policeman questioningly.

'Oh, nothing.' Then he turned and said in an authoritative voice: 'These two must be taken at once to the morgue for an autopsy. Everything must be done in accordance with normal judicial processes.'

THE CONVERSATION BETWEEN Vargas and Robles had just reached the point where the captain was convinced the drug-runner hadn't double-crossed him and was genuinely ignorant as to what had occurred to the mule train when there came a knock at the door.

'¿Sí? called Vargas irritably.

The door opened and the corporal on duty entered with a rough bundle of clothes in his hands. 'Sorry to interrupt, sir, but I thought you ought to see these at once. They were thrown by someone who passed the barracks on a motorbike,

'What are they?'

'Uniforms, sir.'

'What!'

The corporal placed the clothing on the desk and Vargas found himself staring at two bloodstained uniforms. He went deathly pale as the corporal also handed him a piece of dirty paper on which was scrawled: '*Death to the enemies of the people!*'

'Bloody hell!'

'The paper was with the clothes, sir.'

Vargas opened the pockets of the jackets and the police identity documents fell out. 'Oh Christ, Rojas y Luna!'

During this exchange Robles' fleshy stubbly face had sagged and turned grey. Now it began to recover as he rubbed his chin thoughtfully and then said: 'Captain, we don't want this business to get out of hand and turn nasty for both of us since we could become the centre of a national scandal; so you'd better persuade the military to clamp down at once and get rid of the corpses.'

'Fine, Don Jorge, but everyone now knows that there are a couple of corpses. How do we explain that?'

'There's no need to explain anything. All we need is a squad of soldiers to march into the morgue and carry off the corpses. Explanations can come later.'

'How the bloody hell do I get the military to intervene? Do you think that I can breeze into the colonel's office and say: 'Sir, I've made a balls-up, so could you please send some of your men to clean up the shit?' Damn it, Robles, the army won't want to get involved.'

'You don't go the colonel, you go to Major Cantuarias,' smiled Robles as narrowly as his pudgy face would allow.

'Why on earth do I go to him?'

'Shall we say that I know a thing or two about the major that he wouldn't like to be generally known.'

'He's only been here a couple of days, so what do you know about him?'

'A man in my business has to keep his wits about him, captain, otherwise he'll soon find himself in trouble. Now, don't go asking a lot of unnecessary questions, but just go and see friend Cantuarias, and let him know that either I can help him where Carlos Miranda is concerned or drop him further in the shit than he is already.'

'Are you talking about the famous Carlos Miranda?'

'Yes.'

'What's Cantuarias got to do with him?'

'Captain, I suggested that you don't ask unnecessary questions. Just go and see him. All you have to say is that I won't split and let Miranda know about some unfortunate details concerning Cantuarias.'

'What details?'

'As I've just said, don´t ask questions, captain.'

With that, Robles got up and began to take his leave, saying: 'And by the way, I'll get to the bottom of what happened last night with the mule train. I don't like to have my normal routine upset any more than you do.'

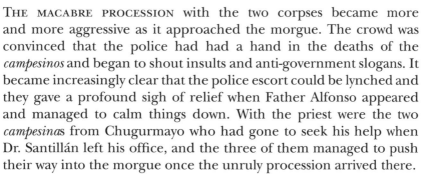

THE MACABRE PROCESSION with the two corpses became more and more aggressive as it approached the morgue. The crowd was convinced that the police had had a hand in the deaths of the *campesinos* and began to shout insults and anti-government slogans. It became increasingly clear that the police escort could be lynched and they gave a profound sigh of relief when Father Alfonso appeared and managed to calm things down. With the priest were the two *campesinas* from Chugurmayo who had gone to seek his help when Dr. Santillán left his office, and the three of them managed to push their way into the morgue once the unruly procession arrived there.

'I'm afraid you're too late to give them the last sacraments, Father,' bantered Dr. Santillán at the back of the morgue as he slowly recovered from the speed, jostling, pushing, and general disorder of the mob which had propelled him there. Father Alfonso gave him a withering look and then said: 'I've brought these two ladies along on the off-chance that they might be able to recognize the bodies since they are looking for two young men who have gone missing.'

The lawyer looked at the two women and turned over in his mind whether he was going to play the role of majestic authority or subtle accomplice. He opted for the latter and drew the priest to one side. He showed Father Alfonso the photo of Eriberto Huaripata and said: 'I'm certain that this is one of them, the old woman's son, so probably the other is the fellow the young girl is looking for. We'll let the doctor make the autopsy and then we can have a good look.'

'Thank you,' said Father Alfonso, thinking: 'If you'd shown a bit more interest and energy on Saturday, these two young men would probably be still alive.' Then he said: 'It looks as though they've been beaten-up. Do you suspect anyone?'

'That's a very delicate question, Father. I'll have to order an investigation.'

The mob outside continued to shout and yell, creating a tense atmosphere in the morgue, whilst the doctor, assisted by Manuel, went about the autopsy with meticulous deliberation. When this was concluded the doctor walked over to where the priest and lawyer were standing and said: 'I reckon that they've been tortured. I'll have my official report ready within an hour.'

Whilst they were talking the two *campesinas* slipped forward to the tables where the corpses lay and no sooner did they recognize Pablo and Eriberto than they erupted in ear-splitting lamentations. Then, before anyone could drag them away there was a disturbance at the entrance of the morgue and Major Cantuarias, Captain Vargas, and a number of soldiers entered. The major walked straight over to Dr. Santillán and said imperiously: 'The colonel has ordered that these two bodies be transferred at once to our encampment so that an official enquiry can be held as to what has happened.'

'That's preposterous!' stuttered the lawyer. 'The colonel has no right to give such an order. I'm the judge here.'

'The colonel is the supreme authority here in Yanacancha now that a state of emergency has been declared,' barked Captain Vargas.

'A state of emergency does not suspend the judiciary from its functions,' intervened Father Alfonso.

The major and the captain turned their backs and, ignoring both the priest and the lawyer, ordered the soldiers to cover the corpses and remove them. The two *campesinas* who were wailing over the remains of their loved ones were dragged aside roughly and told to stop that 'bloody row.'

'These women have come to identify the bodies,' expostulated the priest.

'An official enquiry will be held to establish their identity, Father,' replied Cantuarias without looking him in the eye. Then he turned to the doctor and, holding out his hand, said: 'Your report on the autopsy, please.'

The doctor handed it over without a murmur.

'Gracias.'

As the two bodies were borne out of the morgue by the soldiers the mob in the street yelled and jeered louder than ever, but didn't dare attack the well-armed escort. The lawyer and the priest followed the crowd and the former said: 'No doubt this sees the end of the matter. The bodies will disappear and after a few days fuss the dust will settle. Then everything will carry on as normal.'

'Dr. Santillán, you can't let that happen!' protested the priest.

'And what would you have me do, Reverend Father? The military are all powerful now in Yanacancha, and we civilians count for nothing.'

'So you're just going to take this lying down?'

'It would be the most prudent thing, Father. After all, the two dead youths were only *campesinos*, and I'm not going to complicate my life further just for them.

'If I weren't a priest, I'd tell you what you can do with your bloody prudence!'

Then he left, muttering to himself about 'sodding lawyers; the most unrespectable professional brood imaginable.'

DURING THE AFTERNOON, the rain deluged down again over Yanacancha, as was usual for this time of year, and it was this, rather than the police or the military, which finally drove the slogan-shouting youths off the streets.

In the church some 20 people continued to work hard on the creation of the Garden of Gethsemane. The fairy-lights duly appeared in the orange trees and batteries to produce electricity were hidden beneath the undergrowth of the garden. In addition to the few oranges which were on the branches which had been cut to create the scene, several basket loads more were being wired onto them because it was a tradition for the children present to be given an orange apiece when the procession was over. The whole elaborate confection, with the figure of Christ in the centre, was ready just before darkness began to settle over the town and it was transferred to the side of the altar, ready for the Mass which would begin at eight o'clock.

Meanwhile, Father Alfonso had installed himself in the confessional and had begun to hear a stream of petty faults. It was not for nothing that someone described hearing confessions as 'being pecked to death by ducks,' thought the priest as the peck, peck, of gossip, smutty thoughts, swearing, and other peccadilloes, interspersed with fornication, adultery, drunkenness, and minor robbery, assaulted his ears.

Then, as the hour for the Mass approached, the priest could hear a clanking, shuffling sound, and he knew that the *penitentes* were arriving. This was a custom which had come from southern Spain along with the conquistadores, and had taken on its own peculiarities here in Yanacancha. During Lent the parish priest would make a secret list of the names of the 16 men and youths who wished to be *penitentes* during Holy Week. It was they who would carry the heavy *andas* during the processions on Monday, Tuesday, Wednesday and Friday. For this, they had to be dressed in a white shirt and knee-britches, walk barefoot and with a tall white hood over their heads. In the hood there'd be two slits for the eyes and one for the nose, and round the waist of each a thick rope, wound to prevent a rupture when they raised the heavy *andas* onto their shoulders. Attached to their ankles there'd be heavy chains, accounting for the clanking as they shuffled along. Prior to the Monday evening Mass they'd go to confession and then be the first to receive communion during each Mass of the week.

Now, this Monday, they arrived in a slow and solemn procession, with everyone present in the church standing back respectfully to let them pass. Their confessions were not the minor faults of the pious ladies, but sins far more serious, however they had in common with the peccadilloes the fact that they were boring and unimaginative on the whole.

The last *penitente* came and went through the routine ritual of starting a confession, asking the priest's blessing and placing himself in the presence of God under the protection of the Blessed Virgin Mary. Then Father Alfonso asked him how long it had been since his last confession:

'Quite a long time, Father.'

'That's rather vague, but we'll let it pass.' He recognized Manuel's voice and hoped that the young man would not have much to say because he was feeling tired after a nerve-wracking day. 'Do you have any particular problem?'

'Yes, several. In the first place, I don't think I believe any more.'

'But you've offered yourself as a *penitente*. Isn't that a contradiction if you don't believe?

'It isn't that I don't want to believe, I do. So I thought that if I were a *penitente* I might find faith again. Yes, I do want to believe. I want my life to have meaning and purpose. Although I've been brought up in a profoundly Christian family I just can't accept now that God, if he exists, would allow what is happening in this province: the killing, the violence, the hatred. So I find myself wondering whether life does have any meaning. Perhaps everything is chance or, if there is any explanation, it is better given by science, philosophy, or the arts. Perhaps nothing really matters and it is just a question of everyone for himself to get the most out of our few years on this planet, or, as I said the other day, perhaps religion is just a myth that pretends to give meaning to a meaningless existence.'

'Or it could be that you are being led to a deeper plane of faith. When I raise the Host at the consecration and say 'This is the mystery of faith', mystery isn't myth, nor does it mean something we don't understand, but is a fact that goes deeper than purely rational understanding, like falling in love. To reduce love to the purely rational or scientific is to destroy it; and as I understand it, faith and love go hand in hand.'

They conversed a while longer until Father Alfonso said: 'Manuel, time is running on and I must start the celebration of Mass. I'll give you absolution now and then later on, after Holy Week and when things have calmed down, we'll have another talk.'

'Fine, I'd like that.'

Father Alfonso gave Manuel his blessing and then stepped out of the confessional to face the crowded church and begin the normal Mass for the Monday of Holy Week.

MAJOR CANTUARIAS KNOCKED at the door of the colonel's room.

'Come in!' came the peremptory voice of his superior officer.

Cantuarias entered and found the colonel standing with the some papers in his hand and trying to read them by the murky light of a fly-blown bulb that hung from the ceiling in the middle of the room. The colonel led the major to a chair, pulled out a packet of cigarettes and offered him one. Once they had it lit up he asked: 'Anything to report?'

'Operation body has been carried out, sir.'

'Good, though I must admit that I'm still at loss to know why you were so keen to get us involved.'

Cantuarias hesitated for a moment and then said: 'I know that the police made a complete balls-up and we could have left them to carry the can; but we have to realize that the civilian population doesn't make any distinction between us and the police. As far they are concerned, we're more or less the same outfit…'

'God help us!' interrupted the colonel.

'We had to intervene quickly so as to be able to concoct a story about the two youths being *terrucos*. We've fired some bullets into the corpses.'

'But the doctor knows that isn't true.'

'He's collaborating. He'll give us a new report on the autopsy and he understands how things have to be because he's got a son in the marines. The report and the state of the bodies will coincide so that any journalist who sticks his nose in will be satisfied.'

'Or your bloody priest friend. Now, to change the subject, I reckon that Vargas is right about hitting hard at one or two key people or places, so I'm thinking up a plan in which I want him to be involved. In spite of the balls-up over the corpses I reckon he's just the man I need, tough, fairly intelligent, and not screwed-up by a moral conscience. Furthermore, should my plan fail, he'll have to carry the can, not us.'

'Sounds interesting, sir,' replied Cantuarias with as much indifference as he could muster. Personally he wanted as little as possible to do with the police captain. 'Once you tell me what your plan is, I'll get in touch with Vargas.'

'Good. Now what about a drink?'

'Fine by me.'

'There's rum and pisco in that cupboard in the corner. Which do you prefer?

'I'm a pisco man when I get the chance.'

'Admirable, so am I! That's the only really decent drink for people like ourselves.'

IN THE CHURCH the celebration of Mass advanced as was customary and now Father Alfonso had launched into the homily, emphasizing that today, Monday of Holy Week, local tradition led them all to reflect on the agony of Christ in the Garden: 'One of the great meditations that has been made on this incident speaks of Christ being able to see all the evil that ever was, or ever will be, rising like a foul tide to engulf him. And that it is what is happening to us,' he almost shouted. 'We are being engulfed by evil!'

Alfonso knew that all eyes were upon him, and however fidgety his people were normally, this evening he sensed that they were absolutely intent on listening to what he was saying.

'None of us here needs to have it rubbed in any further that we have become surrounded by violence and evil. Last Friday the town was attacked by those who preach that justice can only be brought about through bloodshed, and today the tortured bodies of two young men have been found in *La Quebradita*. You know that the judicial and medical authorities went about their lawful business to begin to establish what had happened and who was responsible for this crime. However, the normal processes of law were rudely interrupted by the military authorities who have told us that they are here to protect us from violence!'

There was a deathly silence in the church.

'Why?' he shouted. 'Are we to believe that this has been done so as to favour justice? No my friends! This has been done to cover up a crime! The Pilates, the Caiaphases, and the Judases of our time continue to crucify Christ in their abuse of the poor and the defenceless, and they are doing it right here in our midst. I make a public denunciation of what has happened today and, in the name of the families of the deceased, demand that the bodies be returned to the judicial authorities forthwith!'

In a lower tone the priest urged everyone to tackle the violence in their own hearts and concluded almost in a whisper: 'My friends, we are all in this together. We cannot delude ourselves by thinking that we can save our own skins by means of a pious withdrawal from what is happening. We live here in Yanacancha. Christ suffers his agony here, and each of us is involved in that agony.' He stopped and looked earnestly at his people. The silence was beginning to fragment under coughing and a shuffling of feet, and he realized that he had said enough. Those who had ears to hear and understand what he had said had heard sufficient, whilst the rest would understand nothing no matter how long he talked.

Once the Mass was over, Father Alfonso returned to the sacristy to remove his vestments and put on a cloak so as to accompany the procession. Señorita Flor Delgado was there to help him.

'Was that prudent, Father?' she asked.

'What I said during the homily?'

'Sí.'

'I doubt it,' he replied with a slight grin. 'But then I don't subscribe to the theory that prudence is always a virtue, and especially not when it involves silencing the truth. I think I was right to say what I did. Remember the saying: 'silence is approval', and I can't possibly let anyone in this town think that I approve of what has happened here today. I couldn't have kept silent. Oh I know that there'll be some who don't agree with me and who will accuse me of preaching politics. I can't help that,' he added with a shrug.'

'You must be careful, Father, we are living in strange times.'

'I agree with you there,' he said, giving her a broad grin and a friendly pat on the shoulder.

He hastened back into the church just as the 16 *penitentes* were lifting the massive *andas* sustaining the *Garden of Gethsemane* onto their shoulders and so began the steady, slow, and almost mournful pace of a Holy Week procession in San Agustín de Yanacancha. They moved down the main body of the church towards the doors, and then the *penitentes* shuffled and clanked out into the star-studded night, since every sign of the afternoon's rain had disappeared and there was not a cloud to be seen. From the top of the church steps, Alfonso could see the river of candles and the glint of the occasional rosary.

As the procession started to wend its way through the streets of the town, the participants sang a penitential hymn before starting the Sorrowful Mysteries of the Rosary that would alternate with the town band and other hymns. Just when the procession reached the police barracks, Father Alfonso announced the first mystery: *The Agony of Our Lord in the Garden.* He paused for a moment and then continued: 'As we think of Christ sweating bloody and knowing that shortly his body will be lacerated by the lash of the Roman soldiers, and his mind will be crushed by their insults and jeers, let us pray for the repose of the souls of the two young men whose corpses were found today. They too were tortured by men who have forgotten that we are all made in the image and likeness of God, however humble, however poor, and however insignificant many of us may seem. Our Father who art in heaven ...'

The people took up the prayers and the procession continued slowly on its way, claank, claank, claank, swiissh! And so the *penitentes* bore the figure of *Christ of the Agony.*

Inside the police barracks Captain Vargas lay sprawled in a chair in a half drunken stupor. He'd started punishing a bottle of rum as soon as he got back from the morgue. Now he was well into a second one. The sight of the two bodies had jolted him and he knew just how close to personal disaster he was sailing. Alright, if Cantuarias suspected that he was personally responsible for the death of the two youths, he hadn't said anything and had acted promptly and efficiently when told about Roble's promise concerning Miranda. 'I wonder what's behind that,' he asked himself drunkenly. Then he dismissed the question. Well, he had escaped, 'thanks to the bloody military, and at the cost of being very much in Robles' debt, damn it!'

But worse now than the thought of his own narrow escape from dismissal and disgrace were the deaths of Rojas and Luna. Their blood-stained uniforms still lay on the desk and the faces of the two men haunted him. Quique Rojas had been so much like himself, a lecher, a boozer, a guy who enjoyed life and had not shirked when it came to beating the hell out of any suspected *terruco*. And Francisco Luna? Luna had been known by his comrades as the Quiet Man. He was always studying whenever he had a spare moment, and Vargas knew that he planned to leave the police and go to the university. Now they were both dead.

The rum did nothing to assuage his grief or calm his anger. In fact it only served to concentrate this thought on all those whom he saw as enemies: the *terrucos* and the priest. Father Alfonso Calderón was becoming an obsession with him. The bastard had attacked him publicly at the meeting in the municipality on Saturday; he knew too much, and was very ready to defend any *terrucos* like the two *campesinos*.

Now Vargas could hear the procession pass outside the barracks, claank, claank, claank, swiissh! And Alfonso's voice came over the megaphone: '…Their bodies were tortured by men who have forgotten that we are all made in the image and likeness of God, however humble, however poor, and however insignificant many of us may seem. Our Father who art in heaven …'

'You defend the *terrucos de mierda*!' shouted Vargas in the priest's direction. But what have you got to say for the guys of my force who died last night? I tell you I'll get you, you son of a bitch, and I'll screw you into the fucking ground, carajo!'

THE COLD ANDEAN night lit by the paschal moon suited Alfonso's mood as he closed the doors of the church just after midnight. The last of the faithful had left and the *Garden of Gethsemane* looked a sorry mess now that its trees had been rudely stripped of their oranges. He walked slowly towards the high altar and sat down. He had turned off the electric chandeliers and the old building was illuminated only by a few candles that flickered uncertainly on several of the side-altars. The priest found himself questioning the stand that he had made. Why had he launched into the attack he had made against the violence in the province? Was it because he was a man of God and a man of peace? Or was it a cover-up for his own interior emptiness; an external trumpeting to give his ego the centre of the stage, the spotlights and the applause. Whom did he really love and serve, God or himself?

Five

$\mathcal{T}$UESDAY MORNING FOUND Father Alfonso discussing earnestly with Dr. Santillán the events of the previous day and he was insisting that the lawyer not take lying down the removal of the two corpses from his jurisdiction.

'It's not merely completely illegal, it's an affront to the people of this province! You yourself told me that in all probability one of the bodies is that of Eriberto Huaripata, and in fact the two *campesinas* recognized their menfolk at once. So we know who they are, Huaripata and Pablo Huamán, and their families have every right to give their loved ones Christian burial.'

The lawyer shifted uncomfortably in his seat. He had never in his life been in a situation which called upon him to act with courage, and he had long since forgotten how to do so with dignity.

'Isn't there just the possibility that the police are right?'

'Right about what?'

'There's a rumour going round that they were *terrucos*.'

'I've known Pablo Huamán pretty well and I'd stake my life on his not being a terrorist. However, let's presume that both of them were, their families still have a right to the bodies for burial.'

'Yes, of course, Father,' said the lawyer, rubbing his hands nervously. 'I expect that the military will hand over the bodies to the families in due course.'

'I very much doubt it unless you take some action.' Then the priest added more insistently: 'What do you propose to do?'

'Do?' thought the lawyer. 'If I have my way I shan't do anything.' Aloud he found himself saying: 'Father, you must understand that I'm in a very difficult position. In the first place, I'm not the titular

147

judge of this province. Dr. Marco De la Puente is really the person who ought to decide what the judiciary should do in a case like this.'

Father Alfonso had no intention of being put off so easily and, apart from thinking that the judiciary could stuff itself, said swiftly: 'Dr. De la Puente handed over full, and I repeat full, powers to you. So it's up to you to make the decision.'

'Of course, of course, Father, I take your point; but you must understand that I have no experience in these matters and I would like to consult a higher authority.'

The priest boxed back: 'I wouldn't have thought that it were necessary to consult anyone, since a judge has power to act, and the Constitution doesn't allow the military, or anyone else, to limit that power. One of the problems in this country at the moment is that the judiciary lets itself be shat on by the military.'

'Come, come, Father!' puffed the lawyer, swelling like an offended turkey. 'Your remarks lack the consideration and respect I would have expected from a man of the cloth towards the legal profession.'

'Dr. Santillán, I have no wish to fail in respect for your profession. What worries me is that the legal profession is lacking in respect for itself.'

The lawyer's discomfort was manifest in the way he continued to shift in his chair and drum his fingers on the desk, until eventually he said: 'I will consult the president of the court in San Roque.'

'Fine! You'll have to do it by telephone, otherwise you won't receive a reply until the corpses have disappeared off the face of the earth.'

Dr. Santillán shot the priest a malevolent look and was about to say that legality would require something in writing, but he thought better of it and sighed: 'Oh, very well, if you insist.'

With that the two men left the office and walked together to the telephone exchange, complete with the only telephones the town possessed and the middle-aged lady responsible for operating them. Until recently, the making of a telephone call had been a lengthy business of much cranking of handles, shouting, and little hearing. However, now new equipment had been installed and the citizens of Yanacancha could make calls with relative ease.

'Buenos días, mi estimado Dr. Santillán,' offered the lady operator with a predatory smile as she looked up from her knitting. Although she was a relatively humble and low-paid public servant, she occupied a position that made her the town's number one fount of information, and she knew how to take advantage of this for her own considerable benefit. The lawyer replied abruptly, whilst Father Alfonso offered a more fulsome salutation. Then Dr. Santillán said officiously: 'I want to make an urgent call to the president of the court in San Roque.'

'It would be a pleasure to serve you, señor, but ever since the storm the other day the line hasn't been working, and what with *terrucos* roaming all over the place and the police proving themselves to be useless ....'

'Yes, yes, señorita,' the lawyer interrupted. 'The *terrucos* are a nightmare for all of us, but if you can't help us we can't stand here all day gossiping. We have urgent business to attend to.'

'Of course, I understand; and you know that if you think that I can be of any help, you only have to ask. No-one in this town has ever been able to say that Nélida Marquina isn't one to help. No, señor; I'm always at your service!'

'Gracias, gracias.'

The two men left the telephone exchange and the lawyer muttered aggrievedly: 'Bloody useless telephone company. Now what do we do?'

'We confront the military.'

'Just a moment. Let's get the mayor to accompany us.'

The priest frowned and suspected that this would be another delaying tactic with the lawyer hoping that the mayor would prove an ally for not confronting the military. However, he accepted and the two walked over to the municipality. They found Don Nicolás in a thoroughly bad mood. He had just finished reading a report on the extent of the damage caused by the storm and the terrorists. The worst part of this was the fact that the machinery needed for clearing the road to San Roque of several landslides had been destroyed by the fire at the municipal depot. 'Bloody tempest, bloody terrorists!' muttered the mayor as he looked up to see the lawyer and the priest entering his office.

Dr. Santillán coughed and looked at the priest, so Father Alfonso kicked off: 'Don Nicolás, muy buenos días. Sorry to trouble you but we've come to ask your help with regards to the military.'

'The military?' replied the mayor as though he were oblivious to their presence in the town.

'Yes. There's the problem of the two bodies they seized yesterday.'

'Oh yes, I heard something about that,' replied Don Nicolás warily. 'Quite scandalous, of course, but that's the military for you. There's nothing that we can do about it. Whilst the army is here the colonel will no doubt play at being God, and we'll just have to put up with it; however ....'

'Don Nicolás,' interrupted Father Alfonso. 'That is where you are mistaken. We musn't put up with either the colonel, or anyone else, playing at being God. I insist that we protest and reclaim the bodies that the military seized.'

Don Nicolás produced every temporizing argument he could think of, but Father Alfonso didn't hesitate to slam hard in order to defeat him. Finally, the mayor gave way and said resignedly: 'Oh well, if you think that my presence will be of any help, I'll accompany you to see the colonel.'

'Let's go then and avoid further delay,' replied the priest as he propelled the two reluctant men out of the office.

IN THE VELEZMORO Hotel the girl woke alone in her bed. For a moment she wondered where she was and then, when she realized that she was in Yanacancha, she didn't understand why she was alone. She sat up in bed scratching her head, remembering. The captain hadn't come last night. She didn't know whether she was glad or sorry because she had never felt so ambivalent towards anyone in her whole life. She had heard of love-hate relationships and had never understood how they could work, but now she had fallen into one herself. She glanced at the photograph she had put on the table beside her bed once she was sure that the captain wouldn't come. It was of Lucha, her best friend; Lucha, who had meant everything to her and who had suddenly disappeared from home two years ago. For months there had been no news, and then, a few weeks ago, word reached her that Lucha was with the guerillas, and near San Agustín de Yanacancha. So, on the spur of the moment, she had decided to make the journey and try to contact her friend, because Lucha's mother in Lima was dying of cancer. On arrival, and thanks to the strange underground telegraph that operated between the *terrucos* and their supporters, a youth came up to her and said: 'They got her early this morning. Lucha was a great girl and led the attack on the barracks.' Later on, when the girl booked into the Velezmoro Hotel, she discovered that the captain in command of the barracks lived there and she decided to seduce him and try to intervene on Lucha's behalf.

On Sunday everything had gone to perfection and by lunch time she was feeling very pleased with herself. The captain had fallen into her trap with incredible ease and she even found him attractive. Then during the evening, came the bombshell: Lucha tortured and killed! And she was committed to sleeping with the man who had ordered it!

After crying her grief, she decided to go ahead with her plan; but now she would sleep with Vargas in order to find out how to take her revenge. But things hadn't turned out quite as she had planned; the captain had managed to fascinate her. So, when he didn't turn up last night, she was horrified to realize that the deep disappointment she felt was not because her prey seemed to have escaped, but because she yearned for him physically. She was appalled to discover that she actually wanted to sleep with the man who had tortured and killed Lucha; but she did.

Now she sat up in bed wondering what to do next. She was caught in her own net. Reluctantly she found her body hungering for the man whom her mind wanted to destroy.

Captain Vargas' office in the police barracks was typically institutional, painted a non-descript colour with a desk that was brash and metallic, chairs with plastic coverings, and a low-powered light-bulb dangling on a fly-blown flex. It probably hadn't been deliberately designed to make any visitor ill at ease, but it certainly managed to have that effect. This Tuesday morning the room exuded an air of tension whilst Vargas himself listened to the report that Corporal Sánchez had to offer concerning Humfri Becerra.

'So Becerra was in Llangodén when Llacta was murdered?' asked the captain.

'Definitely, sir. He went to the wake.'

'In that case, he's not likely to have been a party to Llacta's death.'

'The widow insists that he was and she charged him with it in front of everyone at the wake.'

'Did she, by Christ!'

'Seems that she flew at him in a rage and swore to revenge her husband's death.'

'A formidable lady!'

'She is,' replied Sánchez with a grin. Then he continued to tell Vargas about Don Nasho's attempt to defend Llacta's memory and being shot for it.

'Bloody fool!'

'Yes sir. After that, it seems that Becerra left with the *terrucos*.'

'And?'

'As far as I can gather, the *terrucos* went to their hide-out on the Marañón. San Pedro's the place, sir, and I presume that Becerra went with them.'

'San Pedro is where Jorge Robles processes his *coca*.'

'Así es, señor.'

'Bloody marvelous isn't it?' said Vargas cynically. 'The radical Maoists, the biggest capitalist in Yanacancha, and ourselves in some kind of twisted triple marriage. We protect Robles, so do the *terrucos*, whilst we and the *terrucos* hate each other's guts.'

'What a bloody mess, sir!'

'Exactly!' Vargas got up and walked over to Sánchez. 'Now listen! I want you to find out all you can about Becerra. We know that he's been adopted by one of the pious bags that hang around the parish….'

'Flor Delgado, sir?'

'Yes. And of course, we all know who the guy is who spews left-wing crap there.'

'Father Alfonso.'

'Yes, and he's the bugger I want to crush!'

The interview was interrupted by the news that Major Cantuarias had arrived from the military encampment and wished to speak to the captain at once; so Vargas dismissed the corporal and the major was ushered into his presence. The two men shook hands and Vargas motioned his visitor to take a seat. Cantuarias sat down and dropped his kepi nonchalantly onto the captain's desk saying: 'All fixed.'

'The bodies?'

'The bodies.'

'Thank God for that!'

'They were *terrucos* who died in the attack on your barracks the other night. We've duffed them up a bit and they look pretty authentic. Died of bullet wounds of course.'

'And the autopsy?'

'Confirms exactly what I've just said.'

A smile of satisfaction spread over Vargas' face, and then he said: 'May I offer you a drink, major?'

'With pleasure.'

The captain pulled a bottle of rum out of his desk and poured a generous measure into the glass which was still there from last night, saying: '¡Salud, mi mayor!' With that he threw the liquor down his throat and handed the glass to Cantuarias. Whilst the major poured himself a drink Vargas wondered what might be the purpose of his visit. The bloody high and mighty army didn't normally send a major to inform a lowly captain of police that they have cleaned up his shit; so something was in the wind. Maybe it had to do with Carlos Miranda since Vargas realized that yesterday Cantuarias had

had no interest in the bodies until he mentioned Miranda, and that had galvanized the major into action. The captain drank slowly and then took out a packet of cigarettes. He offered one to the major. They lit up and smoked for a few moments in silence, sizing each other up. Cantuarias was tall, almost willowy in Vargas' eyes, and the light brown colouring of his hair and moustache contrasted with the captain's jet black. Both had clean-cut faces, but Vargas had the more aggressive look and harder jaw.

'One good turn deserves another, captain,' said Cantuarias quietly.

'Of course, major,' replied Vargas, narrowing his eyes.

'The colonel thinks that you could be of service for a task he has in mind.'

'Anything I can do for the colonel will be a pleasure,' replied Vargas unemotionally.

'The colonel has thought about what you told us about how you think supporters of the *terrucos* ought to be treated, and he's in full agreement.'

'You mean kick the shit out of them?'

'Precisely'

'And you have some place in mind?'

'Someone.'

'It wouldn't be the priest by any chance?'

'Him.'

'And the colonel wants me to do something about him?' asked Vargas with a feline smile.

'He wants you to destroy his authority; but do it subtly. We don't want a scandal like the death of Archbishop Romero in El Salvador; just a total undermining of his standing in this town.'

'With pleasure.'

'Do it your own way, but understand that if you balls things up we won't come to the rescue this time.'

'And if I succeed?'

'I believe that there's another favour you would like of us; help your promotion?'

Vargas looked intently at the major and then asked: 'You know that my promotion has been blocked for the time being?'

'Yes. It seems that you were involved in some incidents in Ayacucho.'

'Look major, I'm a *sinchi*, not a bleeding boy-scout. I was involved in some hard actions in Ayacucho and you know what I think about human rights when it comes to fighting *terrucos*. Well, we had to do one or two things that have upset some of the politicians in Lima, and just to please those bastards my further promotion has been put on hold.'

'So perhaps we could help your promotion to go ahead?'

'I hope so.'

'Well, do first what the colonel wants and then we'll see what we can do.'

With that the interview came to an end and Major Cantuarias bade Vargas good-bye. He left the police barracks feeling sick inside. 'Bloody hell, I'm Judas!' he muttered to himself.

THE INTERVIEW BETWEEN the colonel and the civil authorities of Yanacancha began with all the correct formalities and courtesies.

'To what do I owe the pleasant surprise of your visit?' asked the colonel.

As Father Alfonso had feared, there was a marked silence during which both the mayor and Dr. Santillán looked at him for a lead. However, the priest decided that the lawyer must play his part and merely said: 'Colonel, our stand-in judge has a matter to raise with you.'

The colonel looked at the lawyer with a malicious smile whilst the latter cleared his throat nervously: 'Colonel, we've come about the two corpses you ordered to be transferred here yesterday.'

'Ah yes,' replied the colonel calmly. 'I presume that you are referring to the two terrorists.'

'The two *campesinos* who were found in *La Quebradita*,' countered Father Alfonso., emphasizing the word *campesinos*.

'Exactly, the terrorists.'

'What makes you say that they were terrorists, colonel?'

'You knew them, Father?'

'I have reason to believe that one is Pablo Huamán and the other Eriberto Huaripata.'

'Well, Father, no matter what their names are, without a doubt they were terrorists.'

'I'm sorry to have to disagree with you. Their names do matter, because not only am I certain that Pablo Huamán was no terrorist, but I also know that he had every good reason to be afraid of the terrorists.'

The colonel replied with a shrug of the shoulders and then handed the priest a copy of the autopsy which stated that the two men had died of bullet wounds. 'Furthermore, Father, we found copies of terrorist propaganda on them.'

The priest looked at Dr. Santillán. Hadn't the bodies been searched in his presence? There had been no mention of subversive propaganda; nor had there been any sign of bullet wounds. However, since the lawyer made not the slightest effort to question what the colonel had said, he knew that the battle was well on the way to being lost and history, as usual, was being written by the victors. His mind spun and he thought that should the truth ever be revealed some time in the future, no doubt there would be much breast-beating about the unfortunate collateral damage that the *campesinos* had suffered, and that would be the end of the matter.

After that the meeting slowly dissolved and the civilians were left with no choice but to accept the military version of the deaths.

'The military will see to the burial of the corpses,' announced the colonel drily.

'And the wishes of their families?' asked Father Alfonso.

'Since there were no identity documents found, officially the burial will be of persons unknown.'

'But the *campesinas* recognized them, colonel.'

'The hysterical screaming of a couple of Indian women means bugger all.'

And with that a reluctant Father Alfonso knew that there was nothing further that he could do.

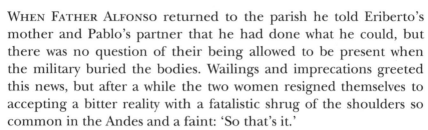

WHEN FATHER ALFONSO returned to the parish he told Eriberto's mother and Pablo's partner that he had done what he could, but there was no question of their being allowed to be present when the military buried the bodies. Wailings and imprecations greeted this news, but after a while the two women resigned themselves to accepting a bitter reality with a fatalistic shrug of the shoulders so common in the Andes and a faint: 'So that's it.'

With a heavy heart the priest went into the church where he found the Verástegui family hard at work creating another scene of Christ's passion to be carried this evening in procession; it was the scene of The Scourging at the Pillar. The centre-piece of this was a statue of Christ bound to a pillar, with a Roman soldier behind him, whip in hand. These figures dated back to the eighteenth century and were fine examples of polychrome art. The skin of Christ's body was almost translucent, and the look in his eyes captured something way beyond transient human suffering. Somehow the sculptor had managed to infuse them with a spark of divinity. By contrast, the Roman soldier was an epitome of brutality and his uniform was that of the colonial Spanish troops of the period in which the sculptures were made. Since then, two and a half centuries of devotion had added incongruous elements: the rope binding Christ to the pillar was a silken cord with a weave of silver thread, whilst the whip and its thongs were of pure local silver. Christ's loins were covered with a velvet cloth decorated with gold embroidery.

The whole Verástegui family seemed to be happily employed creating the scene and Father Alfonso enjoyed conversing with them, in marked contrast to the bitter exchange in the colonel's office. He couldn't resist asking mischievously: 'You aren't thinking of giving Christ a flashing halo by any chance?'

'Father, what on earth would we do that for? It would be horrendous!' exclaimed Doña Leonor.

'Well, since yesterday we had fairy lights in the Garden of

Gethsemane I wondered what bright idea would disfigure today's scene.'

'So you think a flashing neon halo would be a good idea?'

The priest laughed and assured them that he was only teasing.

'Fortunately for you, Father, otherwise we'd have to use the Roman soldier's whip on you!' said 15 year-old Beto.

'Beto!' said his mother. 'Don't be so disrespectful!' However, her admonition fell on deaf ears since everyone, including the priest and herself, was laughing.

'I think I'd better take myself off,' said Father Alfonso, 'and stop interrupting the good work. See you all later.' With that he turned away and made as to leave the church, but Doña Leonor came up behind him and said: 'Father, a word with you.'

'Certainly,' he replied, turning towards her.

'Father, I'm very worried about what's going on here and I'm afraid of the damaging effect it could have on my children. Up until now they've lived happy, un-preoccupied lives, but the attacks last Friday, the killing of old Sifuentes, yesterday's discoveries of the bodies in *La Quebradita* and the disturbances that followed, plus the rumours about what's happening in the countryside, are already beginning to shake them seriously. Yanacancha was such a lovely tranquil place, but now....' Her words hung in the air and she made a helpless gesture with her hands.

'I can understand only too well what you must feel,' replied Father Alfonso.

'Do you think that things will quieten down again?'

'I'd very much like to be able to say yes, but honesty compels me to doubt it. Today we are scandalized by the death of an old night-watchman and the finding of two bodies, and I fear that in six months' time such deaths will pass unnoticed; we'll only be scandalized by scores of deaths. And so it will go on. In the old days, before the *terrucos* arrived on the scene, not enough people got upset about, or even noticed, the scandal of *campesino* children dying from ridiculous things like diarrhoea and whooping cough. It never bothered us much that most of the kids in this country don't receive a decent education, even though it's a scandal crying to heaven. You're a mother and are rightly concerned for your children. I just wish that everyone could be more concerned about all the children in this country; the children who go hungry the whole time, the children who have to work from a very early age in order to live.'

'Father, I came looking for bread and you've given me a stone.'

'Doña Leonor, I'm sorry; I have no bread.'

The sound of quiet sobbing reached them and they turned to see the two *campesina* women from Chugurmayo sitting on the church floor in front of the statue of Christ being scourged at the pillar. Both women were praying in low voices, rocking gently back and forth pouring out their wretched misery. Father Alfonso commented: 'I don't think I've got even a stone to offer them, Doña Leonor. Not only are their men-folk dead, but they've been denied the simplest of human decencies with regard to the burial of the bodies. Their lives have been ruined, and for what? There are no ideals involved, no great aspirations; just a spewing out of meaningless violence.'

'That's what terrifies me, Father. If the anger and bitterness which has burst over this country has destroyed the lives of those two women, why shouldn't it soon do the same for me and mine?' She looked over to where her children were working happily and added: 'I've seen photos of sorrowing mothers in the central Andes and I'm terrified that one day I might join the list.'

'Doña Leonor, as I see it, useless death has stalked this country for centuries. It used only to affect the poorest and most despised sectors of the population, but now unfortunately it's affecting us all.'

THE REST OF Tuesday slipped by uneventfully, except for the simple burial service of Alcides Sifuentes. This took place during the afternoon, in the presence of his few relatives and friends, and under continuous rain. When night fell, once again the church filled for the evening Mass and just before this began there came the swishing and clanking of the 16 barefoot *penitentes*. They took up their stations near the *andas*, now decorated with the figure of Christ bound to the pillar within a framework of tall Roman columns. As on every night during Holy Week the number of candles on the side altars and in front of the *andas* multiplied, and soon the church was stiflingly hot in spite of the cold mountain air.

Prior to the Mass Father Alfonso spent some time giving careful thought about what he was going to say. When the time came for him to speak, after the reading of the Gospel, he began in a gentle tone, taking up the theme of the Suffering Servant to be found in the Book of Isaiah, where the Man of Sorrows, disfigured and abandoned, is presented. 'Last night I suggested that we are all, in some measure, responsible for the violence afflicting this province. We each of us have something of the Roman soldier we see on the *andas* this evening. If we are honest with ourselves, we will find facets of our lives reflected in this man; but, more important, can we identify with the figure of Christ? Of course, we all have experiences of suffering, but does this open us up to our fellow men, or does it have an embittering and hardening effect on us?'

Alfonso was aware that this rhetorical dialogue was aimed as much at himself as anyone else, and he knew that before Holy Week was over he would have to come up with some personal answers. His words slipped out in a lucid stream, and penetratingly; and the nub of his theme was compassion: 'Over the years, since the emergency started, I doubt whether we've really been compassionate. We've allowed ourselves to be shocked, to be fearful, to be morbidly curious, but I honestly don't think that we've been compassionate. We haven't been able to chip away at the dross which encumbers our capacity to love.'

There were no denunciations this evening; nothing overtly dramatic, and Father Alfonso maintained a very even tone. Once the Mass was over the procession assembled, and slowly the figure of the scourged Christ set on the *andas* was raised onto the shoulders of the 16 *penitentes*, to be followed by the claank, claank, swiissh of their rhythmical steps as the tableau swayed above the heads of the faithful, and the crowd moved towards the doors and then out into the cold night.

Christ was illuminated in a sharp white light from four cleverly disguised spot-lights, and as Father Alfonso gazed at the figure he had to give it to Doña Leonor and her boys that they had done a superb job in creating a dramatic focus for the walkers in the procession. Tonight, everyone was quieter when the band played slightly off-key funereal music and the prayers were more fervent during the recital of the Sorrowful Mysteries of the Rosary. Even the cinema owner, who was not averse to showing pornographic films, crossed himself piously.

The procession had to pass the school where the troops were quartered and in other years a special ceremony of homage would have taken place in front of the main entrance, but this year it had been transferred to one of the street corners nearby. As the procession passed the walkers could just hear the bawdy singing of the off-duty soldiers in the cantina, whilst two sentries stood at the entrance, their feet apart, weapons cradled in their arms, and gazed uncomprehendingly. They were coastal lads and had never been in the Andes before this. One of them turned to his companion and said: 'Those bloody hooded creeps would put the shits up anyone.'

'You're dead right man. Put the evil eye on you if you ask me.' And reluctantly he crossed himself.'

The procession turned out of sight, but they could hear the sad music and the blood-chilling claank, claank, swiissh of the *penitentes*.

ON WEDNESDAY MORNING, Captain Vargas arrived at his office in a perplexed mood. He had slept with the girl again, but it hadn't been the same as the first night. A barrier had come between them which he couldn't understand. However, once in his office he put the girl out of his mind and settled down to thinking about a plan to fix the priest. He had hardly managed to get his thoughts concentrated when Don Jorge Robles was shown in.

'Sorry to disturb you, captain,' said Robles as he rolled confidently into the room and took a seat.

'Something urgent?' asked Vargas irritably, noting that the drug-runner hadn't waited to be asked to sit down or even bothered to offer any formal pleasantries.

'I think so.'

'What's the problem now?'

'Yours rather than mine.'

'Well, get on with it for Christ's sake!'

Robles crossed his fat legs, clasped his hands over his paunch and said quietly: 'I've got some unpleasant news. My men are back and they've told me what happened the other night. It was a group of *terrucos* that waylaid them.'

'We'd already presumed that,' said Vargas, narrowing his eyes and looking grim. 'What about Rojas and Luna?'

'Their throats were cut and their naked bodies were flung into the ravine in place of the sacks that you'd ordered to be thrown there.'

'Bloody savages!'

A silence fell between them and Vargas buried his head in hands for a few seconds. When he looked up Robles murmured: 'My condolences, captain.'

'Gracias.'

'Do you want me to tell you about the third sack?'

Vargas nodded affirmatively.

'They took it down to the Marañón and buried the girl there.'

The captain started and then almost snarled: 'What girl, Robles?'

'Captain,' replied Robles evenly. 'I don't want to know more than is necessary for my good health. A piece of information comes my way; sometimes I file it away; sometimes I put it to immediate use, and sometimes I just forget about it. Now, if you ask a lot of unpleasant questions I'll make myself scarce. I've come here with friendly intentions, and if you want to hear what I have to say, I'll stay.'

'Carry on then,' said Vargas ungraciously.

'There's a *terruco* on his way to this town and he's got a special mission.'

'What mission?'

'Before I answer that we'll have to strike a little bargain, captain.'

'You bloody bastard!'

'Let's keep it polite, please, captain,' replied Robles with the same imperturbable look that he had maintained since entering the office. 'If I'm not mistaken, you're already in my debt, and in my code debtors should be polite to their creditors.' He watched with mild amusement as the expletives formed on Vargas' lips and then got choked down.

'Alright, alright,' replied Vargas wearily. 'What are your terms?'

'As you know very well, captain, I'm respected in this town even though everyone, with the possible exception of my dear wife, knows full well the nature of my business. Whilst there are no clear proofs as to what I do my fellow citizens receive me in their homes, are very attentive and appreciative, and life in general goes ahead smoothly and pleasantly for yours truly. However, it seems that our worthy judge, Dr. Marco De la Puente....'

'Who is not here.'

'Exactly! He's not here because he's looking into my little business. It's most inconvenient to say the least, so I hope that you will see to it that an end is put to the investigations.'

Vargas paled and then said: 'You're asking me to...?' and he pulled the edge of his hand across his throat.

'No, of course not, captain! I'm not that crude. All I want you do is to ensure that the investigation stops.'

The captain didn't reply and stared at his desk.

'You're not going to tell me that you have some moral scruples?' asked Robles.

'Bloody hell, no!' replied Vargas with a slight smile.

'You had me worried for a moment. You know as well as I do that the only reason why drugs are illegal is because they are produced in the Third World. The industrialized countries produce arms that kill people, but that's alright; it's the clean and respectable business of whites! But there's nothing clean and respectable when a dark-skinned fellow like me in the Third World also makes a living from something that kills!'

'You don't have to justify yourself to me, Robles,' said Vargas evenly. 'I don't give a damn how you make your money. The only thing that interests me is that I'm not going to find myself involved in some dirty business that could not only screw up De la Puente, but me also. I too have to think of my career!'

'I admire you!' countered Robles cynically. 'All I want you to do is to ensure that documents get lost, enquiries run into brick walls, and everything just gets bogged down in a never ending bureaucratic mess so that nothing will be discovered about my business.'

'Okay, I do that for you; now what do you tell me about a *terruco* and his mission?'

'The mission is to kill one of the town's authorities'

'Which one?'

'That I don't know, but the *terruco* himself is Humfri Becerra.'

'We know quite a lot about him. He's on our list of suspects. Was born in Llangodén....'

'Sí,' interrupted Robles. 'And strangely enough his godmother is Señorita Flor Delgado.'

'Isn't she one of the women always helping the priest?'

'Yes.'

'Probably a bloody *terruca* herself then!'

'I very much doubt it, but yes, Becerra always stays at the presbytery when he comes to Yanacancha.'

'That's interesting and could help me.'

'Help you?'

'Sí, para joder* al cura. I've got to screw-up the priest somehow.'

'What have you got against him?'

'That's my business, Robles,' muttered Vargas, reluctant to elaborate further.

'Have it your own way,' replied the drug-runner moving towards the door. 'And be careful, captain. I'm an old hand in the game of survival, and for all that you're a *sinchi* and have fought in Ayacucho, you've still got quite a lot to learn.'

'Bugger off!'

'Encantado,' replied Robles laughing.

---

* Joder, prounced with a guttural j, a common expletive meaning to fuck.

THE FIRST MOVE that Captain Vargas made was to dispatch Sánchez to Llangodén again: 'Find out every bloody thing you can about Humfri Becerra, and if you come across him, I want him brought down here, dead or alive.'

'Very good, sir.'

After that, the captain left the police barracks and went in search of Flor Delgado. He had no difficulty in finding the house because the old lady was known to everyone in Yanacancha. Typical of the older houses in the town the main door opened onto a patio filled with flowers. Since the door was open, Vargas merely gave a peremptory knock and walked straight in, finding Señorita Flor feeding some birds with bread crumbs.

'Oh my goodness, captain, what a surprise!' she said brightly. 'Do come in!'

'Gracias, señorita,' he replied; his heavy manly presence striking a marked contrast to this little world of femininity.

'Please sit down,' she said, indicating a padded bench covered with lacework. He sat and the revolver clasped to his hip immediately tangled itself in the lace. He pulled it free roughly: 'Fu...!' He just managed to swallow the expletive.

'To what do I owe the honour of your visit, captain? May I bring you a little refreshment? I've nothing very strong, of course, but I do make quite an acceptable liqueur from nísperos; though I say it myself,' she added with a twittery laugh.

Señorita Flor hopped away and was soon back with a small silver tray, two glasses filled with liqueur and a plate of home-made biscuits. After an exchange of pleasantries and downing the liqueur, Vargas said: 'Señorita, I've come to ask you a few questions about your godson....'

'Which one? Humfri?' she intervened.

'Yes. Do you know where he is at present?'

'No, Captain. He dropped by a week ago and told me that since the university in San Roque was on strike he'd like to visit Llangodén. That's where he's from, you know.'

'Yes, I do know.'

'Why do you want to know where he is?'

'He's in trouble.'

'What kind of trouble?' asked Flor going pale.

'We think that he's probably involved in an attempt to commit a crime that we want to prevent.'

'A crime!' uttered the old lady and burst into tears.

'Bloody hell!' Thought Vargas. 'Blubbering old women aren't part of my experience of the fair sex.'

Without going into many details, Vargas explained to the old lady that he believed that Humfri was connected with the *terrucos*.

'Humfri, a terrorist? Oh no!' The old lady's crying increased and it took a considerable effort on Vargas' part to bring her tears to an end. As she dried her eyes he embraced her gently and then asked: 'Do you have a recent photo of your godson?'

'Sí.'

'Please be good enough to let me have it.'

'You're going to arrest Humfri?'

'Possibly.'

'And?' The word hung in the air.

'Should he show up here, you must collaborate with us and not try to hide him from us.'

'You won't hurt him, will you?'

Vargas did his best to conceal any expression of wanting to beat the shit out of the youth and replied hypocritically: 'Of course not, señorita.'

Flor Delgado went in search of the photo and as he watched her, for once, Vargas felt that he had been brutal and was surprised at his own reluctance to hurt her further. The bright bird-like old lady had just crumpled into a non-descript and shapeless heap. The captain left her whilst she collapsed on the lace-covered bench and sobbed.

HAVING SEEN FLOR Delgado, Captain Vargas turned his steps towards the priest's house with a different mission. Two of his men had died and they must be honoured with a religious ceremony. The dull grey day coincided with his mood, but he relished the idea of intruding on the priest and, hopefully, engaging in a sparring match that could land a few blows just to soften up his intended victim. He strode into the priest's office and found Father Alfonso conversing with Manuel.

'Sorry to interrupt you, Father,' he said formally.

'Not at all, please come in and take a seat.' The captain took a chair and sat with a commanding air. Father Alfonso asked: 'What can I do for you?'

'Two of my men were ambushed and killed a couple of nights ago whilst escorting some valuable goods of Don Jorge Robles.'

'My sincere condolences, captain.'

'Gracias.'

'You want to arrange their funeral?'

'The *terrucos* who killed them hurled their bodies into an impenetrable ravine; so we can't bury them.'

'What on earth did they do that for?'

'Because they are barbarians and will do anything against a guy in a police uniform.'

The priest didn't know what to say and remained silent. The captain watched him, trying to see what this man really thought. Was he shaken by the deaths of the two policemen, or was he pleased? After a few seconds, Father Alfonso said: 'That's awful.'

'At the very least,' returned Vargas drily.

'Even if there can't be a funeral, at least in this evening's Mass we'll pray especially for your men and for the repose of their souls.'

'Very good, Father. Of course, I and my men will be present, and I'll extend invitations to all the authorities here, both civil and military.'

'As you wish, captain. And perhaps you would be kind enough to give me a few details about the two policemen who have been killed.'

Whilst he spoke, Manuel tried to tell him something with his eyes, but the priest didn't understand. Meanwhile Vargas felt irritated that the priest had not given him the slightest opening for any kind of disagreement. He wrote down the information that Father Alfonso had asked for and the meeting came to an end.

'Gracias, padre.'

'De nada, capitán.'

The two men shook hands and Father Alfonso accompanied the captain to the door. When he returned, Manuel said: 'You're in a right fix now, Father.'

'Why do you say that?'

'Did you know the two men?'

'Not really. Members of the police force aren't very assiduous Mass-goers on the whole,' he said with a wry smile.

'Luna was a pretty decent guy, but Rojas was a right bastard!'

The priest made a gesture of surprise at the young man's vehemence and asked: 'Why do you say that?'

'As a priest, Father, you're not much acquainted with what guys in the cantinas say so you don't know what a lot of people feel about the late Corporal Enrique Rojas; Quique, as they always called him.'

'Tell me.'

'He was a good friend of Captain Vargas. He enjoyed beating the shit out of people. He took part in the raid on Chugurmayo, and I wouldn't mind betting that he was involved in the rape of Luisa Quispe. So for Christ's sake, don't preach during the Mass some panegyric about his dying for the honour of the flag or for democracy, because you'll make yourself a laughingstock. If the *terrucos* killed Rojas, I reckon that they had a pretty good reason for doing so.'

'Just a minute, Manuel! I've heard it said too often that the *terrucos* kill people for a good reason. What good reason could they have had for killing poor old Alcides Sifuentes, or young Valdivia when he hauled down their flag in Santa María del Valle? Even your friend Francisco Luna didn't deserve to have his throat cut and his naked body to be hurled into a ravine so as to be devoured by birds of prey.'

'I suppose that the *terrucos* would say that the fact that Valdivia and Luna wore police uniforms was enough justification for killing them.'

'It bloody well wasn't!'

'Okay, we won't argue about that now. All I want you to realize is that you will not just be praying for Luna tonight, but also for Rojas, and he was always bad news here in Yanacancha.'

'Gracias, Manuel; I'll have to work out carefully what I'm going to say.'

'I hope you don't sit on the fence and do the smooth-arse clerical act. When the Church does that she loses all credibility, as we know from what has happened in Argentina. You spoke out clearly enough on Monday night, so now, however much you might be reluctant to do so, I hope that you do the same tonight.'

'I hope so too, Manuel, but you'd better pray that I make a good job of it.'

'I will.'

BY THE TIME the Mass was due to start, not only was the church absolutely packed, but there was a large crowd outside in the forecourt. The civilian and military authorities were lined up at the foot of the steps waiting for the arrival of the police. They arrived shortly before eight o'clock, with Captain Vargas leading his men smartly. When they reached the waiting authorities the national flag was handed to the captain and was duly raised to half-mast to the funeral strains of a military bugle. At the conclusion of this simple ceremony, all the authorities entered the church.

The first part of the Mass ran its course. Then Father Alfonso, wearing ample purple vestments, stepped forward to address the congregation: 'My friends, tonight our local custom dictates that the central figure for our attention be Christ the Nazarene, or Christ, Our Lord of the Fall, as we often call him.' The priest pointed to the *andas* beside the altar, on which the statue of Christ was alone and majestic, without any adornments to distract attention. The Christ figure was dressed in a superb purple robe of velvet, embroidered with gold and silver threat; he was stooped forward, carrying a cross with ferrules of silver and semi-precious stones which sparkled in the light of the candles.

Father Alfonso continued: 'On his way to Calvary Christ fell, and there could be no clearer symbol of our human condition. We are a fallen race.' He looked at Vargas and the colonel. They sat impassively, and he suspected that his words flowed over them without making the slightest impression. The priest continued: 'Tonight we also turn our thoughts to two young men from the police force who died the other night at the hands of the terrorists. We must pray for them; pray that God will forgive their sins and receive their souls. At the same time we see these deaths as a result of the senseless violence which is wracking our province, and most of our country. We all have a duty to root out the causes of this violence and search for a solution to the conflict which intensifies each day like the storms which so often batter us here in Yanacancha.'

Then the priest looked directly at the colonel and Captain Vargas and said: 'I beg you gentlemen of the army and the police not to send a punitive expedition against any village unless you are a hundred percent certain where guilt lies, and then only to bring the culprits to face trial. Your temptation will be to take the law into your own hands and carry extra-judicial sentences dictated by anger and passion. I plead with you not to do this because it will only make the situation worse, and the Christ in all of us will be down on his face in the mud under the weight of collective sin. At the same time, I plead with the guerrilla forces to halt their campaign of violence which is bringing nothing but misery on the heads of all of us.'

He paused and then asked everyone to pray for the souls of Francisco Luna and Enrique Rojas.

After that the Mass continued as normal, and then came the procession. The *andas* with the stooped figure of Christ were hoisted onto the shoulders of the 16 *penitentes* and began its journey through the streets of the town to the sound of the claank, claank, swiissh of their feet. Once they were outside, Father Alfonso glanced behind him and saw in the distance that the statue of *La Dolorosa*, dark-clad above a pyramid of candles. She was receding in the opposite direction since the custom was for two processions to take place this evening, the men following Christ and the women the Virgin Mary.

The hours went by, with Christ falling at every major street junction, to the accompaniment of an eerie lament. It was nearly two in the morning when both processions entered the Plaza de Armas from opposite sides and began to converge on the church. Finally, as the two statues came face to face, Christ fell for the last time and *La Dolorosa* made a graceful inclination. In the cold Andean night there was a beauty in the scene which every year moved Father Alfonso, but this year even more so. He always chose this moment to say a few words, and now he made an extra effort to move the hearts of his people.

A deep hush hung over the dense mass as he spoke of the sorrowing mothers of Peru seeking their sons, just as *La Dolorosa* tonight had sought Christ and found him fallen under the weight of his cross. Alfonso made no distinction between the mothers of the police, of the military, of the *terrucos*, of the *campesinos*, of the students, and of all the ordinary citizens who had fallen in the years of strife.

Alfonso had never been an emotional preacher, but tonight he moved many to tears and he caught sight of Flor Delgado weeping bitterly. He was surprised, but let it pass. He also noticed that by this time neither the military nor the police were present. The flag had been taken down from the large pole in the square, which stood like some reluctant accusatory finger pointing to heaven.

IT WAS THREE in the morning by the time Father Alfonso at last found time to sit in front of the high altar where a lamp flickered, indicating the presence of Christ in the Reserved Sacrament. Somehow he felt calmer than he had on previous nights. The dryness had receded and he sensed that he must be reaching the end of the tunnel of the dark night of the soul, because the blackness was so intense that surely it could get no blacker.

Six

WHEN FATHER ALFONSO woke early on Holy Thursday morning he refreshed himself with a quick cold shower, dressed, and then threw open the windows to enjoy the biting Andean air. At once, all his feeling of well-being was shattered. On the flag-pole where last night the national flag had hung at half-mast, there was now the guerrilla red flag with its hammer and sickle whipping boldly in the breeze. For a couple of minutes the priest gazed at this obscene reply to his appeal during Mass the previous evening.

The priest went out of the house to see what else the *terrucos* had done during the night. Several walls were painted with their slogans, but there seemed to be no more. He gave a sigh of relief at not finding any bodies with crude messages left on them, but still he was under no illusion. The mocking challenge of the flag would almost certainly be met by a bitter and harsh response from the military since the guerrillas had made their intentions abundantly clear — there was to be no peace in Yanacancha.

Sadly Father Alfonso returned to the parish to prepare to visit the sick and the old, as was his custom every Holy Thursday.

HUMFRI BECERRA ARRIVED in Yanacancha early on Thursday morning and he slipped into the market in order to buy himself some breakfast. As always, there were plenty of people eating hasty helpings of rice and fried eggs, or plates of *caldo verde*—a typical soup in the northern Andes made from herbs, potatoes, eggs and cream-cheese. Since four-thirty there had been people hard at work in the market, and by six o'clock the food stalls were doing a roaring trade. Over the hubbub of voices there were the inevitable loud-speakers blaring out music; not international pop or rock, but Andean cashuas, huaynos and yaravís.

Humfri was busy shoveling rice and eggs into his mouth when he felt a sharp slap on the back: 'Becerra you old bugger! Great to see you!' He whipped round and saw a thoroughly unkempt Lucio Benites.

'Where the hell have you sprung from?' spluttered Humfri through a mouthful of food. 'Have you eaten?'

'No, man, I'm skint. Drank all my remaining cash last night.'

'I'll treat you to a plate of something.'

'Thanks. Where've you suddenly got money from?'

'I could say that I've sold a cow, or that I've robbed a bank,' replied Humfri with a harsh grin. 'Anyway, what does it matter? Just for once I've got some cash and you're welcome to join me.'

'Gracias.' He asked for a plate of soup.

'Did you get pissed last night?'

'Only half. I didn't have enough cash to do the job properly,' said Lucio as he ran a dirty hand through his mat of hair. Then he asked: 'By the way, have you seen the flag in the square.

'No. What flag?'

'The *terruco* rag. They must be in town.'

Humfri went pale but said nothing. Lucio didn't notice anything and wolfed down his plate of soup when it was brought to him, slurping spoonfulls as though he hadn't eaten in a week. Between slurp and slurp he looked up for a moment and said: 'I heard that the *terrucos* finished off the district officer in your village.'

'Yeah,' replied Humfri.

'Why?'

'Don't ask me. Why do the *terrucos* kill anyone? Maybe Llacta was denounced to them, or maybe they just didn't like his mug,' said Humfri with studied indifference. He'd known Benites when he'd come to Llangodén last year as a teacher and on several occasions they'd had a few drinks together. As far as he could tell, Lucio Benites was quite a good guy, though a bit of a creep, but he wasn't trusting anyone at the moment and was irritated when Benites said: 'Come off it, Becerra! Llacta was a bloody shit and you know it.'

'Perhaps.'

'Don't want to talk about him?'

'Not really.' Then, so as to change the subject, he commented: 'You look a right mess.'

'Enjoyed a few piss-ups this week.'

'Lucky you!'

'I wasn't celebrating; just trying to forget.'

'Forget what?'

'That bastard Juan Ortiz won't give me a job this year.'

'And?'

'And nothing! I'm on the bloody scrap heap!' snarled Lucio. 'And to be quite honest, if the *terrucos* had strung him up last night instead of a flag, I'd be delighted.'

'Shut you bleeding mouth, Lucio! If you go around shouting things like that you'll be picked up as a *terruco* yourself.'

'Frankly, I reckon I'd like to join them. Nothing is ever going to get sorted out in this country until we get rid of bastards like Ortiz. And there's only one way to do it, shoot the buggers or hang them!'

Humfri looked at Lucio straight in the face and smiled. The only shooting that Lucio Benites would ever be capable of was with his mouth.

'By the way, Hunfi, what brings you into town?'

'The university is on strike, so I'm at a bit of a loose end. There's nothing much to do in Llangodén, so I thought I'd come down here.'

'Nothing to do here either, unless you've suddenly gone all religious. There are processions and God-knows what every night.'

'No fear of that, Lucio my friend,' replied Humfri with a laugh.

They continued to eat and chat for over an hour, and then Humfri said: 'Well, Lucio, I must be on my way. Perhaps we'll see a bit more of each other and enjoy a few drinks together.'

'I'll look forward to that, Humfri.'

'Maybe I'll have something to celebrate.'

'A secret?'

'Unfortunately, for the time-being, yes.'
With that they parted.

As far as Captain Vargas was concerned, each night that he spent with the girl was more intriguing than the previous one, and he sensed that a subtle change in their relationship was taking place. A long time ago he had lost count of the girls he had slept with, some just for one night, others on a more regular basis. Initially he had taken it that his relationship with this girl would be equally ephemeral —a few nights of fun and then good-bye. However, things weren't turning out that way. Now, still early on Thursday morning, the two lay awake in bed, she with her head cradled in his left arm and he smoking pensively.

'What are you thinking about?' she asked.

'You.'

'Good heavens! Do I merit so much attention?' she mocked lightly. 'Or am I being catalogued in your list of conquests, somewhere below Ana, but better perhaps than Rosa?'

'Why do you want to spoil our fun with your mockery?'

'I was only joking.'

'No, young lady, there was mockery in your voice, and behind that must lie something else — bitterness perhaps?'

'We are deep today.'

'Maybe. You know, there's something about you that I don't quite fathom.' He saw her eyes flicker nervously. 'Why did you want to sleep with me in the first place?'

'Come on, captain! You seduced me!'

'Rot! We seduced each other.' Then he grabbed her roughly: 'Spit it out! Tell me why you wanted me!' He released her, stubbed out the cigarette, and waited for her reply.

She didn't say anything whilst looking at the handsome man at her side. Reason and decent sentiment told her that she had to hate him, but their relationship had taken a strange turn. She found him incredibly attractive in spite of all the things she knew about him. He had tortured her best friend and had probably ordered that she be killed; and in spite of this she seemed to be falling in love with him — this just couldn't be happening!

'How long are you going to lie there thinking?'

She struggled to find a suitable reply, but eventually blurted out: 'The best thing for both of us is to terminate this liaison here and now.'

'What the bloody hell's the matter?' he whipped out. 'Don't I screw good?' She squirmed and muttered: 'Please, just leave me.'

'So now we're going to play the virtuous virgin are we?'

'You don't understand.'

'You're right there! I don't understand a bloody thing! And let me tell you that I'm not accustomed to being summoned to a girl's bed and then being given a kick up the arse and told to bugger off. But before I go ....' He threw himself on top of her and took her violently. When he had finished with her he leapt out of bed and hurled: 'You wanted to tangle with a *sinchi*, and now you know a *sinchi* is like.' After that he sprang out of the bed, flung on his clothes and stormed out of the room in a whip-lash of obscenities.

She lay there for a long time, crying sadly to herself and murmuring his name for the first time.

ACCOMPANIED BY FLOR Delgado, Father Alfonso walked the streets of the town on his round of Communion calls to the sick and old. Together they climbed narrow staircases, penetrated into dark back patios and into tiny crowded rooms. The priest felt a deep compassion for these people all too often tucked away so as to be as far out of sight and mind as possible. He always hoped that when his turn came for terminal illness he would be given a room full of light, with big windows looking out towards the mountains. To be treated like so much useless lumber is the final indignity heaped on so many people, and at least Alfonso had the joy of knowing that his visits were brief spots of light in an otherwise gloomy existence; and often he was told: 'Gracias, padre. It's good to know that I won't die like an animal, unshriven and unblessed.'

Whilst they walked along together, Father Alfonso refrained from mentioning the red flag, but he soon realized that something was troubling Señorita Flor. Normally she hopped along, full of bright chatter, but today she was very subdued, and eventually the priest asked: 'Señorita, is something troubling you?' She didn't answer. For a while, he respected silence, but he could see that she was holding back tears, so he tried again: 'Are you sure that I can't help?'

'Oh Father!' she wailed. 'I don't know what to do! Something terrible has happened!'

'Perhaps it would help if you told me about it.'

Again she hesitated, and then she told him about the visit she had received from Captain Vargas the day before. 'He told me that Humfri was in trouble, could be linked to the terrorists, and that I must inform the police if I learn of his whereabouts. I can't imagine what the trouble is. He's so studious and serious; always a model of politeness. And then I wonder what the police will do to him should they arrest him.'

'Would you like me to talk to the captain? I'll admit that there's no love lost between us, but if you think that would help I'll go right away.'

'Oh gracias, padre!'

'Well, you go along back to the parish and I'll drop by the police barracks to see Captain Vargas.'

Father Alfonso found the captain smoking furiously in his office. He was still livid about the way the girl had terminated their relationship, and just to add to his bitterness was the fact that the red flag had been raised in the Plaza de Armas, a mere stone's throw from where he had slept with her. Under any circumstances, the hoisting of the red flag on the town's principal flagpole would be a deliberate challenge, but on this occasion it had been a real kick in the groin against the police who had been honouring their dead. He looked bitterly at the priest and said: 'A surprise that you should visit us, Father. Can I do something for you?' He didn't invite the priest to sit or offer him a cigarette, but held up the flag that had been brought to him. 'Do you know anything about this bloody rag?'

'Is it the flag that was flying in the square?'

'Yes, and what do you think about it?'

'It's deeply upsetting.'

'Is that all?'

'Captain, I fully understand how you must feel, particularly since you are mourning the loss of your men, but still I urge you not to react violently. It will only make matters worse.'

'Father, these murdering bastards have thrown out a challenge. By hoisting this flag they're saying: "Fuck peace!" I'm going to take up that challenge. I'm going to wage war!'

'I think that the war started some time ago and I regret it.'

A silence followed until Father Alfonso said: 'I understand that you have plenty to worry about at the moment, but the purpose of my visit was to ask about Humfri Becerra.'

'What about him?'

'Yesterday you visited Señorita Flor Delgado and told her that you suspect Becerra of being involved in some criminal or even terrorist activity. Do you really think he's a *terruco*?'

The captain looked hard at the priest and wondered: 'Has this guy come to get some intelligence out of me?'

'Do you think that he is?'

'I don't know him all that well, but I presume he's got nothing to do with the *terrucos*.'

'He stays in the presbytery when he comes to Yanacancha. Don't you know what class of people you receive?'

'He stays at the presbytery at the request of his godmother, Señorita Flor. She helps a lot in the parish and the least I can do is to accede to her petition.'

'Well, whether Becerra is a *terruco* or not, I've reason to believe that he is planning to commit some crime, so if he turns up at your house you are bound to let me know, or be considered an accessory to a criminal act.'

'I understand,' replied Alfonso sadly.

'I hope so,' smiled Vargas malevolently.

WHILST FATHER ALFONSO had been visiting the sick and then gone to the police barracks, the members of the Fraternity of the Blessed Sacrament, were hard at work building the Altar of Repose. An elaborate scaffolding had been erected in a side-chapel, and onto this large swathes of tulle and satin were being draped, whilst another group arranged vases full of flowers and as many candles as they could cram into the space available. Way back in the 1950s, when Pius XII had been Pope, it was decreed that the Altar of Repose, where the Blessed Sacrament would be placed after the Holy Thursday evening Mass, should be a simple affair with just a few candles and flowers, and that the faithful should only remain in prayer there until midnight. None of this had made the slightest impression on the good people of Yanacancha. Ever since the parish had been founded centuries before, a vast Altar of Repose had been erected every Holy Thursday and people had prayed there throughout the night. Furthermore, a Fraternity had been founded with the explicit mission of seeing that all this were carried out. So it had been, and so this was the way that things would carry on, orders from Rome not withstanding. In the face of local determination, Father Alfonso had allowed the old customs to continue, and he now surveyed the handiwork of the Fraternity. And, to be honest, everything was looking as beautiful and well designed as in any other year.

Señorita Flor Delgado had joined the group and when she saw Father Alfonso enter the church she went over to him and asked anxiously: 'Any news of Humfri, Father?'

'No more than what the captain told you yesterday. Like you, I was severely warned to inform the police should he turn up.'

'I'm worried about what they'll do to him if they arrest him.'

'When the police are aware that we know that they are holding someone in custody they are more careful about they do. The real danger is when the police get hold of someone and nobody outside the barracks is aware of it. So it'll be better for Humfri if we spot him before the police do.'

With that he gave the old lady a friendly pat of the back and turned to see Major Cantuarias a few feet away: 'Nice to see you, Telmo. What brings you to the House of the Lord?'

'Official business,' replied Cantuarias stiffly and handed over a white envelope.

Father Alfonso opened it and found a letter couched in formal terms, informing him that the colonel and his officers, plus a contingent of troops would be assisting at this evening's ceremonies, so a special place of honour should be reserved. Furthermore, since the colonel was now the maximum authority in the town, he must be given the key to the Tabernacle on the Altar of Repose after the Sacrament had been placed there. All this would be in accordance with Peru's ancestral Catholic tradition and as a public manifestation of the solidarity between the Church and the military in the face of the challenge that had been thrown down by the terrorists.

Father Alfonso blanched at this. Here was an attempt to highjack the Church as an ally of the military no matter what they might decide to do. He knew that the colonel was basing his demands on old customs, but these had been abolished officially when the new Constitution was written in 1979, explicitly separating Church and State. He also knew that they weren't really all that separate; that some members of the Church were only too happy to be seen to have power as an ally of the State, and that the State used the Church as a moral prop. If he turned down the colonel's demand he'd be seen as a supporter of the terrorists, and if he accepted it he would be seen as a lackey of the military.

'I'm sorry, Telmo, there's no way I can accept this. If the colonel, his officers and his troops wish to attend this evening's ceremonies, they'll be most welcome, but now we don't do more than reserve a few seats without creating any special places of honour; and as for handing over the key of the Tabernacle, that is out of the question.'

'You wish to be seen as someone supporting the *terrucos*, Alfonso?'

'Of course not!' Then he added: 'Telmo, does it really have to be this way?'

'I warned you the other day that if we found ourselves on opposite sides, then I'm an army officer first,' replied Cantuarias.

'I'm sorry that you now see me as an opponent.'

'You have chosen to be so.'

'It's not a question of choosing but of acting in accordance with my conscience.'

'Have it your own way, but I warn you, Alfonso, the noose is closing round your neck,' he said in a tone that managed to combine sadness with an air of military authority.

DON NICOLÁS LEAL had planned to enjoy a quiet day before assisting at the Holy Thursday ceremonies in the evening in his role as mayor of Yanacancha. He was not a religious man but felt, like Napoleon, that religion, if properly employed could be a good thing —it helps in the maintenance of law and order. For this reason he always assisted at the Holy Thursday and Good Friday ceremonies, as had been the custom for the civil and military authorities down the centuries; even though this was no longer required officially. Apart from those days, Don Nicolás would be present in the church for the Feast Day of San Agustín, the Anniversary of the Province, and July 28th, Independence Day. So now, having a leisurely breakfast, he was surprised by the sudden arrival of Captain Vargas.

'Sorry to interrupt you, Don Nicolás,' said Vargas abruptly.

'Not at all, captain. May I offer you a cup of coffee?'

'Gracias.'

The mayor handed him a cup and the coffee urn. 'Milk and sugar?'

'Just sugar.'

'Now tell me, captain, what brings you here this morning?'

'I presume that you know all about the flag.'

'Yes, a bad business.'

'As you say,' responded Vargas drily. 'Well, apart from the flag being hoisted as a challenge to us, we know that there is a *terruco* loose in the town on some terrorist mission. He probably aims to kill at least one of the authorities and you are the most obvious target.

Goodness knows how many mayors have been killed over the past few years; so you must take every precaution.'

'Thank you, captain; it's very good of you to warn me. And in view of what you have just told me perhaps I ought to show you what was found under the door this morning.' He got up and walked stiffly into one of the rooms, returning with a piece of crumpled paper which he placed on the table in front of Vargas. The paper was dirty, and at the top there was a crude drawing of a hammer and sickle. Below, written very badly was the following message: *'Nicolas Leal Urteaga, arse-likker and guvunment lakky!!! We give yu fortiate howers to resine as mayer and pay a undred dollars!! Leive the muny in a box under the bush by the cemetery gate. If yu du not, yu will be eliminated as an enemi of the peepul. Long liv the armed struggul!!'*

'As you say, Don Nicolás, it's very badly written, but that could be because whoever wrote it wanted to disguise himself.'

'The spelling is so bad that it could be by some child in primary school.'

'The ideas aren't those of a child in primary school. More like those of a university student linked with the *terrucos*.'

'And you say that there is a *terruco* loose in the town?'

'We believe so; and the person we have in mind is a university student.'

'As far as I know no student has anything against me.'

'The motive for killing you won't be personal. The fact that you are a member of the governing APRA party and mayor is reason enough as far as the *terrucos* are concerned.'

'To be perfectly honest, captain, I don't understand what the *terrucos* are on about. Alright, I'm a member of APRA and have been all my adult life. Also I'm mayor and I reckon that everyone knows I've tried to do my best for Yanacancha. I haven't just given jobs to members of the Party, and I've been pretty honest. I may not be perfect, but I'm not so bad as to merit being shot in cold blood. Besides,' he added petulantly, 'the citizens of this town have voted for me in several elections; free and open elections I might add. So who the hell do these terrorists think they are? Why do they think that they've got a God-given right to overturn what the people have decided?'

Vargas stopped this flow of indignation with a wave of the hand and said: 'I agree with all that you've just said, but what either you or I think doesn't matter a damn to the terrorists. Anyway, the important thing at the moment is to get the *terruco* on the loose before he gets you.'

'Or you.'

'Why do you say that; because I'm a policeman?'

'Because you're *sinchi*, and known to be hard on *terrucos*.'

'A reputation I have every intention of retaining,' replied Vargas, patting the revolver at his hip. 'Now I'd be grateful if you would collaborate fully with us and not leave this house.'

'Captain,' said Don Nicolás calmly, 'of course I don't want to do anything that will make your job more difficult, but, whatever other faults I may have, I'm not a coward. According to this note I have 48 hours grace, and I have every intention of fulfilling my accustomed public duties both today and tomorrow.'

'You'll be a sitting target if you attend the church ceremonies,' snapped the captain irritably. 'For all we know there could be no connection between the note and the threat I'm talking about; and if you insist on appearing publicly, then I must ask you to sign a document to the effect that you do so at your own risk and against my advice.'

'Fair enough! I quite understand that you have to cover yourself, captain; but we must each do what we think is right.'

'This house will be watched day and night, and when you leave it one of my men will be there to accompany you. I'll also send over a bullet-proof vest.'

'Very kind of you, captain.'

Vargas swallowed a hasty cup of coffee saying, as he banged the cup on the saucer: 'Well, Don Nicolás, let's hope that everything goes alright. Of course, your best chance of safety lies in resigning at once.'

'Obviously. However, captain, as I've already said, I'm not a coward.'

'Just one more thing.'

'Sí?'

'Please don't tell anyone about this conversation or the note until we've had a chance to investigate further.'

'As you wish.'

'Gracias.'

The mayor then accompanied Captain Vargas to the door and watched his guest depart. They made an incongruous pair: the white-haired mayor, an almost sad figure in his late 60s, and in a dressing-gown and slippers; the captain, tough and in his late 20s, in combat uniform and a prominent revolver in a hip-holster.

IT WAS NEARLY mid-morning when Captain Vargas presented himself in the colonel's office at the military encampment and he hardly had time to offer more than a perfunctory greeting when the colonel shouted at him: 'That bloody priest has denied me the right to have a special place of honour reserved at this evening's Mass and to receive the key of the Tabernacle! Who the hell does he think he is! In effect he's told me to piss off!'

Although Vargas didn't follow all the details of the upset between the priest and colonel he smiled grimly at the thought that whatever Father Alfonso had done it would make his own task of discrediting him all the easier.

'Well, man, don't just stand there grinning like some bleeding hyena! Tell me what you have in mind to discredit this bastard.'

'Don Nicolás Leal has just shown me a note threatening him with death if he doesn't resign within 48 hours.'

'Are you going to say that the priest sent it?'

'More or less.'

'You'll give me the order to search the parish house a bit later on and we'll *find* some more notes threatening the authorities.'

'The priest is hardly likely to write them.'

'Of course not, but the *terruco* we suspect to be on the loose in this town is a certain Humfri Becerra, and he lodges at the presbytery. He'll have written the notes, and the priest becomes an accessory for giving him lodgings.'

'That sounds better.'

'Should we be able to get hold of Becerra in the house, then we'll be home and dry.'

'Do we know what Becerra looks like?'

'His godmother gave me a photo yesterday.'

'Who's she?'

'One of the pious bags who's always up at the church.'

'So the parish is behind the *terrucos*?'

'That's what we've got to get people to believe.'

'Well, just to make sure, you'll need to find more than a few fabricated notes.'

'Claro. We'll produce some *terruco* propaganda and maybe even a copy of Mao-Tse-Tung's Little Red Book.'

'The only thing lacking will be to find machine-guns under the altar,' laughed the colonel.

After that they enjoyed a drink of rum whilst going over the details of the plan, and also talking about the general security measures to be taken in the town: document checks and body searches. As they concluded, Vargas asked: 'Colonel, after what the priest has said about no official seating, do you and your officers intend to be present at tonight's ceremonies. If you do, I'll show up as well, if not, I'll stay clear.'

'We'll be there,' replied the colonel with a hard smile. 'I intend to keep my men sober and away from the whores for a couple of days, and show the people of this town that whatever their priest may be like, we men of Caesar know how to respect the laws of God. Besides, people like you and me have our allies in the Church. A lot of bishops and priests, and even plenty of people in this town, can't stand types like bloody Father Alfonso Calderón. It's important that the people of Yanacancha understand that our quarrel is not with the Church, but with this particular *terruco* priest.

Then they both eagerly downed a last drink: 'To happy hunting! ¡Salud!'

WITHIN AN HOUR or so of Captain Vargas leaving the colonel's office, rumours that the priest was definitely in favour of the *terrucos* began to circulate round the town like some mysterious plague and before long everyone had their own twist to give the tale. Down at Ma Vásquez' cantina the *chicha* flowed as it had always done and the companions of the late Alcides Sifuentes had plenty to say on the matter and, like so many other people in the town, they turned the rumour over and over, like cows chewing the cud, and the more they chewed, the more convinced they became of its truth.

Another scene of similar cud-chewing was Dr. Santillán's office. He had decided to open up for business this morning because he was a long way behind in his work — the burden of being the temporary judge had thrown the normal low-gear process of cases through his office into an even slower pace, and some of the cases were out of gear altogether. So he had immersed himself in a pile of papers and was surprised when Captain Vargas entered his office: 'Well, well, captain, to what do I owe this honour?'

'I'll be brief and not take up more than a few minutes of your time. All I want to know is whether you'll be good enough to accompany me if I have to make a raid on a building where there may well be subversive propaganda and even arms.'

'Since the province is under a state of emergency, that won't be necessary, captain. You don't need a warrant, or anything like that.'

'I'm well aware of that, but the place I plan to search is very prominent, so I think that it would be better to count on your presence.'

'I see. Would it be indiscreet to ask what the place is?'

'Just between ourselves, it's the presbytery.'

'The presbytery! That will cause a flutter in the dovecot!'

'Precisely; and that's why I would like you to accompany me.'

'Of course, captain. You can count on me for anything I can do to be of service to law and order.'

'Gracias.'

'De nada.'

After a few more pleasantries, Vargas took his leave, knowing perfectly well that the lawyer would be incapable of keeping his mouth shut; and it was only a short time before Dr. Santillán had the opportunity to share his knowledge with Doña Dagoberta, the wife of Jorge Robles, who came to his office for a certificate and then a bit later with the mayor and the education officer. They too had heard rumours and were keen to talk things over with the temporary judge. And so there was more cud-chewing. There really wasn't much cud, but there was plenty of chewing, completely convincing Juan Ortiz of the priest's involvement with the terrorists. Dr. Santillán inclined to the same opinion, but Don Nicolás Leal was skeptical.

'You mark my words,' said Ortiz pompously, 'in the homily tonight the priest will probably tell us to salute the red flag.'

'Maybe you are right, Ortiz,' murmured Santillán.

'I reckon you are both reading him wrong,' mused the mayor.

And so the eager cud-chewing continued.

As so often happens when rumours circulate, the person most directly concerned remains blissfully unaware of them, and this was the case now. Father Alfonso was ensconced in a stuffy confessional listening to the peccadillos of the more faithful parishioners whilst his name was being taken in vain throughout the town. He had been hearing confessions for well over an hour when Doña Dagoberta and a group of her Ladies of Yanacancha entered the church. The rumours concerning the priest had reached their ears and they were talking animatedly.

'Well, ladies, now what do we do?' asked Doña Dagoberta. 'I was just thinking about preparing myself for the holy sacrament of penance when I visited Dr. Santillán's office and he told me that it is certain that our parish priest is involved with the terrorists. I couldn't possibly go to confession to him now!'

'We've always had our suspicions, haven't we Dagoberta? And sadly it turns out to be true,' twittered her second in command.

'But if Father Alfonso were really a terrorist sympathizer, don't you think that they would have arrested him by now?' intervened one of the more timid members of the group. 'I reckon that what people are saying is probably just another of those rumours that are always floating around in Yanacancha. We all know the popular saying: *Pueblo chico, infierno grande* — A small town is a large hell.'

'Don't be silly, Andrea! I heard it directly from Dr. Santillán when I dropped into his office for a certificate, and you are not going to tell me that such a worthy citizen is going to waste his time spreading malicious rumours.'

'Well, of course not, but....'

'But what?'

'If the rumours are true, why haven't they arrested Father Alfonso?'

'They've probably got a very good reason for not doing so. That Captain Vargas strikes me as being a very sensible young man and the colonel is an excellent person. They both know what they are about.'

Whilst Doña Dagoberta and her ladies were talking they had also been walking slowly towards the chapel now filled with a complicated confection of satins, lace, tulles, flowers and candles that was the Altar of Repose. As the ladies arrived they were met by the architect of all this, Doña Felipa Salaverry.

'What do you think of our humble efforts?' she asked.

'Lovely, my dear!'

'Father Alfonso has said that it's the best Altar of Repose he's ever seen.'

'Did he!' sniffed Doña Dagoberta. 'Well, I can assure you that whatever he says won't count with my approval.'

'Why ever not?'

'Haven't you heard?'

'I haven't heard anything. I've been working here all morning.'

'Well, much as it may shock you, it seems that our parish priest is a supporter of the *terrucos*.'

'Rubbish! He's over there hearing confessions.'

'That may be, but it's all over the town.'

'I don't believe a word of it!' snorted Doña Felipa. 'Stupid rumours are the stock in trade of Yanacancha.'

'That's what I think,' intervened the timid Andrea. 'But nobody takes any notice of what I say.'

'If you don't want to believe me, then nobody is going to oblige you to do so,' sighed Doña Dagoberta with offended dignity.

And so commenced a division of opinion and the bonds in favour of the rumour began to go down in value. Those who believed the rumour to be true pointed out that the red flag had been hoisted on a flagpole in the square just in front of the parish. Those who rejected the rumour insisted that Father Alfonso had not been arrested and was sitting in the confessional hearing confessions like the worthy priest that he was.

WITHIN THE CONFESSIONAL, Father Alfonso found it increasingly difficult to concentrate on the sins being whispered, on suitable words of advice, comfort or admonishment, or on the absolution and the penance to be given. It was always difficult to hear confessions on Holy Thursday because of the crowds of people milling about in the church, the continuous banging that came from the chapel where the Altar of Repose was being built, and other comings and goings in preparation for the ceremonies to be held later on. The priest could also hear one of the men of the Fraternity of the Blessed Sacrament rehearsing with the altar boys. Furthermore, this year a sixth sense told him that something else was happening. From the confessional he could see people walking back and forth, and he realized that a lot of glances were being thrown in his direction. He had no idea what they were talking about or why they should keep looking towards the confessional, but something must have happened.

Another person entered the confessional and the usual opening dialogue followed. Then came a slight variation: 'Father, I don't really know whether this is a proper confession or not, but I need to talk to you.'

'Go right ahead and take your time. I'm listening,' he replied gently and tried to tear his mind from wondering what Doña Dagoberta Castillo and her ladies were talking about.

'I came to Yanacancha a few days ago.'

There followed a pause.

'¿Sî?

'I wanted to see a special friend.'

Another pause.

'Yes?'

Bit by bit the whole story came out about the friend who had joined *Sendero Luminoso*, about her death, and about the involvement with Captain Vargas. 'He's a handsome brute,' she murmured, 'but I can't understand how I've become so caught up in a strong physical attraction to him, and probably all this sounds terrible.'

'Don't worry what it sounds like, good or evil, sensible or stupid. Just let it come out and then we'll try to sort the grain from the chaff.'

She told him how she seemed to have become several different people in one body: 'I'm a close friend, a coquette, a whore even. I'm someone who loves passionately and someone who hates with equal passion, someone who is coldly calculating and someone who has completely lost her head, someone with strong principles, and someone with none. Father, I'm just an incredible mess.' Then she began to cry quietly.

'Just take your time.'

'Other people are waiting, Father, and I find it difficult to go on.'

'Confession is not a mere mechanical routine and one has to take the time necessary. We have the rest of the day if you need it.'

'Gracias.' She went on to explain how she had set out to seduce the captain in order to save her friend. 'But I knew that she was dead by the time he slept with me.'

'How did you know?'

'There are no secrets from the *terrucos*, Father. They have a better intelligence service than either the military or the police.' She stopped abruptly and then whispered: 'You won't tell anyone, will you!'

'Of course not! We're in the confessional and I cannot repeat what you have told me. Whatever you say here will remain an absolute secret between us.'

'Yes, I believe that.'

'You said that you knew that the captain had killed your friend, and yet you still slept with him?'

'Once I knew that I couldn't help my friend Lucha I thought that I might be able to take some kind of revenge. It has been known for a woman to stab the man having sex with her. But it didn't work out like that. Sex with him was marvellous and I actually think I've fallen in love with him. Can you imagine how that feels? If he's a monster, I'm far worse.'

'Do you hate yourself for what you've done?'

'Hate is a very weak word for what I think of myself.'

'Now look, take things gently. I'd be failing you terribly if I just gave you a tongue-lashing and let you leave this confessional hugging your self-hate. I want you to empty yourself of hate.'

'But I'm so awful!'

'No you are not! You are just a very generous human being who suddenly found herself in an extremely complicated situation and got herself into a muddle. Now you can't hate someone who's in a muddle, so you must stop hating yourself.'

'And Captain Vargas?'

'You said that you were falling in love with him. Well, you'll have to choose, either hate him, or love him, but you can't do both at the same time; and I'd recommend the latter, so that you can help him become the person he ought to be.'

'You're asking a lot.'

'Well, that's what Christianity is all about. Try to believe that God has a special mission for you.'

'Is God so hard up that he has to choose me?'

'It would seem so,' said Alfonso with a slight laugh.

There were a few ends to tie up before Father Alfonso gave the girl God's absolution. She left the confessional and another entered. The priest now had to wrench his mind from the complex tale and self-hatred that had just been expressed to the sad tale of Doña

Dagoberta's daughter being made pregnant by the mayor's youngest son who wanted her to have an abortion.

WHILST THE RUMOURS about Father Alfonso spread and multiplied throughout the town, Humfri Becerra occupied himself with formulating a plan to kill Captain Vargas. He was totally unaware that both the military and the police were on the look-out for him, but he had an instinctive dislike of people in uniform and shied at the sight of them. He wanted to get into the Plaza de Armas and discovered to his annoyance that no matter from which angle he approached there were groups of soldiers checking documents, and he saw a couple of *campesinos* dragged off roughly. The square would be the best place to kill Vargas, especially if it could be done during one of the processions, but as things were, he couldn't risk trying to get past a check-point. Then he had an idea. If he could enter the parish house by the back entrance, he'd be able to get into the church and from there walk into the square without the military being any the wiser. So he walked round to the street where the back entrance was and noticed that on the corner there was a policeman. 'Bugger it!' Just at that moment a heavy truck came lumbering down the street, giving Humfri the chance to dash to the door and push it open as he knew that during the day it was kept off the latch. Once inside he saw Pancracio, a youth of about his own age who looked after the small hospice that the parish maintained for the rural catechists when they came into town.

'Hi, Pancracio!' Humfri called brightly.

'Hola, Humfri! Señorita Flor told me you had gone to Llangodén, so what brings you here?'

'Yes I went there, but my granddad sent me down to get something for him so I'll have to stay overnight.'

'No problem.'

'Is Father Alfonso around?'

'He's in the church hearing confessions.'

'It's Holy Week of course, so I expect he's being kept busy.'

'Busy isn't the word for it. I've hardly seen him over the past few days. I'll put your name on the list of those who are staying tonight. Oh, by the way, is there still a policeman at the corner?'

'Yes.'

'He's been snooping around all day. Did he stop you?'

'No.'

'I wonder what he wants.'

'Why don't you go and ask him?' grinned Humfri.

'And have him jab his gun up my backside! No thanks!'

'Well, work hard. I'll see you later,' said Humfri with a cheerful shrug of the shoulders and walked off towards the church.

From the church Humfri was able to stroll calmly into the forecourt and then down the steps into the square. He saw that the check-points were controlling those who entered the square, but once inside people were free to wander about as they liked. He sized up the situation and picked a spot behind one of the hedges that bordered the gardens in the square. Both tonight's and tomorrow's processions would have to pass very close to that spot, which had the added advantage of being higher up than the street. It would be ideal for the public execution of Captain Vargas. After making that decision, Humfri decided to go back to the hospice and keep out of the way. He didn't want to see anyone, especially Father Alfonso. Meanwhile, a light rain began to drift across the town.

'Another bloody tempest,' murmured Humfri morosely to himself.

THE AFTERNOON WORE on and Father Alfonso could hear the rain beating on the church roof. He was kept fully occupied in the confessional and then, as daylight waned, the benches in the church began to fill for the Mass which would start at eight o'clock. It was gone seven before the priest could leave the confessional and he then walked slowly towards the parish house in search of a much needed cup of coffee. He was aware that many of the people waiting for Mass looked at him with a special curiosity, and he wondered why. When he entered the kitchen he found Manuel, half changed into his penitent's clothing and looking decidedly incongruous.

'Hello, Manuel, what brings you here?'

'Mother has sent you some hot food which she reckons you need after hours in the confessional'

'Gracias, Manuel. Your mother is dead right; I feel ready to drop and I wonder how I'm going to get through the next few hours.'

Manuel lowered his gaze and then said: 'We've heard the rumours and we want you to know that we don't believe a word of them.'

'What rumours?'

'That you are linked up with the *terrucos*.'

'Stupid rumours like that have been buzzing around for ages,' rejoined the priest with a shrug.

'It's different this time, Father.'

'What do you mean?'

'The talk is more persistent, as though ...how can I put it?' He hesitated and then went on: 'As though the police or the military really had some evidence. And they are saying that you are responsible for hoisting the red flag last night.'

'That's outrageous!'

'But that's the rumour. Has something else happened?'

'I've no idea. The police seem to think that Humfri Beccrra is involved with the *terrucos*, but apart from that I've been in the confessional all day, so I haven't a clue about anything else.'

'Humfri Becerra; he's Flor Delgado's godson isn't he?

'Sí.'

'So that explains why she's moping in the sacristy.'

'Yes, the poor old thing has been hard hit by that.'

'And Humfri often lodges in the parish hospice?'

'Yes. But fortunately he's not here in Yanacancha at the moment. I don't like the idea of having to turn in anyone to the police.' Then he changed the subject and said: 'Let's see what your mother has sent.'

They enjoyed the hot food and whilst drinking coffee Manuel said: 'I don't understand why people in this town should be gunning for you. What on earth have you done that makes them think you have something to do with the *terrucos*?'

'I seem to have committed the terrible crime of not only speaking out in favour of Human Rights, but actually trying to practice what I preach. I believe in dialogue and tolerance. I try to listen to people and understand what they are saying. I try to practice the equality I believe in, and none of that goes down very well with people who want to hang on to their privileges and power, however insignificant these may be in the world at large, and to their prejudices and sheer bloody blind stupid ignorance.'

'Our local authorities?'

'They, amongst others.'

'Bloody fools!'

'I agree, but how does one make them see it.' Then he added with a smile: 'You know what Einstein is supposed to have said?'

'What?'

'There are two things that are infinite, the universe and human stupidity. With regards to the first he still had doubts, but none with regards to the second. Now if you'll excuse me, I must get a quick shower before Mass.'

'By the way, what do we do if Becerra shows up?'

'I've no idea at the moment. I hope to goodness that he doesn't; but if he does, let me know at once,' answered the priest sadly.

BY THE TIME the Holy Thursday Mass began the church was absolutely packed. It seemed that curiosity had brought out people in even greater numbers than usual. Did they expect to see the priest arrested during the ceremony, or a consuming fire to descend and burn him up? Would he urge loyalty to the red flag? Whatever the motives, the place was crammed, and the civil and military authorities had arrived early enough to ensure they had seats at the front of one side of the church; whilst on the other sat members of the Fraternity of the Blessed Sacrament, plus Doña Dagoberta and *The Ladies of Yanacancha.* Father Alfonso entered with a collection of altar boys.

He was dressed in the prescribed white vestments to express the joy of this Mass, which commemorates in a special way the Last Supper of Christ with his disciples. He tried to look across the heads of those in the front benches to the crowd of people behind. As he moved his eyes from left to right he was aware of soldiers standing along the sides of the church. At one point he thought that he saw Humfri Becerra, but quickly decided that he must be mistaken.

Just before the first reading of Scripture, Father Alfonso asked all those present to listen carefully: 'This reading speaks of the Angel of Death striking the first-born of the Egyptians. There is an angel of death amongst us in this town, and we noted his presence this morning when we saw the red flag waving in the wind from the main flag pole in the square. All of us must reject this flag as being totally alien to us as Peruvians and Christians.' Then he sat down and motioned the reader to continue, whilst the mayor whispered to Juan Ortiz: 'So much for your belief that the priest would tell us to swear allegiance to the *terruco* flag.' Ortiz just managed to restrain himself from expressing the expletive that immediately rose to mind.

The reading about the Angel of Death was followed by a psalm and then a second lesson in which St. Paul speaks of the tradition he had received about the Last Supper. There followed the joyful singing of the Alleluia, and, in a cloud of incense smoke, Father Alfonso proclaimed the Gospel with its description of Christ washing the feet of his disciples during the supper. The Gospel over, Alfonso bent and kissed the book, and then invited everyone to sit down.

He spoke of Christ's washing feet as a symbol of service. He too would shortly wash the feet of 12 altar boys as a symbol of his own service to the community of Yanacancha, and he invited the town's authorities to join him in this. The priest let his gaze run along the benches where the civil and military authorities were sitting. Most of them shuffled uncomfortably and lowered their eyes, finding something on the floor of extreme interest. That was all. No resounding denunciations, no dramatic appeals, just a gentle invitation to the powers that be to demonstrate their willingness to serve their fellow citizens.

Father Alfonso then prepared to begin the ceremony of washing the feet of the altar boys, and as he did so, Don Nicolás rose stiffly to his feet and walked over to where the priest was standing. There was a tense silence in the church as the two men greeted each other with an embrace, and suddenly there was a burst of applause which shook the building, drowning in the efforts of the choir to sing: 'Where there is love and the service of loving kindness, there God is to be found.'

The colonel turned to Captain Vargas and muttered: 'What the bloody hell has got into the mayor?'

'I reckon that it's just an empty gesture. He's got nothing to lose by what he's doing.'

'Bloody politician! He'd probably sell his mother if he thought that he'd win a few votes by doing so.'

'She's dead.'

'You know what I mean.'

After washing the altar boys' feet, Father Alfonso went to the altar to continue the Mass whilst Don Nicolás walked over to one side and stood apart from the other authorities. The rest of the ceremony continued as in any other year; so when the Mass itself concluded there followed the solemn procession to the Altar of Repose. As in other years, Father Alfonso invited the faithful to accompany Christ and his apostles in their walk from the Upper Room to the Garden of Gethsemane, and spend a while in silent prayer.

At the back of the church Humfri Becerra waited in the crowd. Then he went with the surge of people out into the forecourt. He had seen Captain Vargas enter the church and he hoped to have a clear view of him when he left the building. Just at that moment one of the soldiers came and stood beside him.

'Are you from here?' he asked.

'Sí,' muttered Humfri morosely, wishing that the soldier would move away.

'I'm from Piura where it's hot. This place is fucking freezing.'

'So you don't like the sierra?'

'Right arsehole if you ask me. I wish the *terrucos* would just bugger off and let us get back to the coast.'

'Shot any *terruco* yet?'

'No, not a sign of the bastards.'

Humfri tried to see whether Captain Vargas was amongst the people still pouring out of the church.

'Looking for someone?' asked the soldier.

'Sí, un amigo.'

The crowd began to thin and there was no sign of the captain. 'Where the bloody hell is he?' Becerra asked himself morosely.

EMOTIONALLY FATHER ALFONSO felt drained by the time he arrived at the sacristy and handed his vestments to Señorita Flor.

'Very nicely done, Father, if I may say so,' commented the old lady.

'Gracias, señorita.'

'You look tired.'

'I feel it.'

There was a moment's silence; then she plucked up courage and asked: 'There's been nothing more about Humfri has there, Father?'

'Not as far as I know.'

'I do hope that the police don't get hold of him,' she said fervently.

'Let's hope that he doesn't commit any crime.'

'And now there are all these nasty rumours against your reverence. Who's started them?'

'I've no idea, señorita.'

'Can't you silence them?'

'I reckon that it would be easier to stop the rain falling over Yanacancha than to silence rumours,' he replied with a tired smile.

She cocked her head on one side and listened. After a few seconds she said: 'It sounds as though it's raining again. It's strange how it always rains during Holy Week, but never during the processions.'

'Thank goodness, otherwise we'd all go down with 'flu or pneumonia. El viejo Catequil, the storm god of our ancestors, also knew how to arrange things. Though with the damage that has been caused by the tempests during this Holy Week make me wonder whether he isn't in league with the Devil.'

Just then, Pancracio put his head round the door and said: 'Father, there are eight in the hospice tonight. Here's the list.'

'I'm too tired to bother about that now. Leave it on my desk will you.'

'Okay.'

'Everything alright in the hospice?'

'Yes, fine.'

With that the youth left them and Señorita Flor said: 'Father, are you going to spend some time before the Altar of Repose?'

'An hour or two, yes. What I need at the moment is prayer rather than sleep.'

'I'll be along myself when I've tidied up here.' She paused for a moment and then added: 'Just listen to the rain, it's really beating down like some kind of dirge!'

LUCIO BENITES HAD passed the whole day mooching about in Yanacancha. His breakfast with Humfri Becerra had filled his stomach for the time being and then he thought of going home, but he knew that he'd be met with weeping and wailing on the part of his mother, looks of reproach from his brothers and sisters, with a general clamour for him to provide money to buy food. He couldn't face it and drifted round the streets. In the evening he went into the church because it was something to do and was free. Towards the end of the ceremony Lucio caught sight of Humfri on the other side of the building, largely hidden by a pillar, but when everyone flocked outside he lost sight of him. 'Bugger!' muttered Lucio as he went out himself. His documents were vetted at one of the check points and as he wandered along a side-street he regretted Humfri's disappearance. 'The lucky bastard's got cash and we could enjoy a piss-up together,' he thought morosely. With that, he found himself outside old Squint-Eye's cantina; which was just the opposite of Ma Vasquéz' place. Whereas Ma served oceans of *chicha* every day to a cantina full of clients, old Squint-Eye never seemed to have anyone in his place; so it was a mystery how he made a living out of it. Since Lucio had just enough money to buy a measure of *cañazo*, he entered and went over to a small table where he could sit and savour the liquor, hoping that it would assuage his loneliness and bitterness.

Another person who went in search of liquor as a panacea for his own problems was Major Telmo Cantuarias. He was convinced that the colonel was totally mistaken in linking Alfonso to the terrorists, and at the same reckoned that Captain Vargas' hatred for the priest bordered on paranoia. But worse than that, he had allowed himself to be drawn into the whole murky mess. Once again his life had become inextricably complicated. He left the barracks in jeans and an anorak, and although he was unaccustomed to drinking in cantinas, somehow he found himself in Squint-Eye's. When he entered he saw that the only other client was a scruffy-looking young man with long hair and dirty jeans, whilst Squint-Eye himself seemed to be a combination of the Sphinx and the three monkeys who neither see, nor hear, nor speak. This phenomenon was leaning at the bar with a cigarette dangling from his mouth and reading a last week's newspaper.

Cantuarias walked up to the bar and ordered a beer. The Squint-Eyed-Sphinx-cum-triple-monkey served him without saying a word and without taking the cigarette out of his mouth. The major tried to make conversation with him, but since this would require a minimum of two people he soon gave up the attempt —the Sphinx, etc. remaining mute. The only other possibility was to join Lucio. Again his initial attempt at conversation only elicited monosyllabic grunts, but after Cantuarias had plied Lucio with several beers the conversation began to flow, and it came to light that Lucio knew Humfri Becerra.

'I think I met him once in a house in San Roque,' lied Cantuarias. 'An interesting guy and I'd like to have the chance to meet him again. I know that he's from somewhere around here.'

'Yeah, he's in town right now,' offered Lucio.

'Is that so? Where can I find him?'

Before replying, Lucio realized that old Squint-Eye was giving him a hard look and shaking his head as if to say 'no.' Lucio stammered: 'Well I don't exactly know where he stays.'

'At the parish house perhaps?'

'I…er….I couldn't really say.' By now his brain was going round in circles and he asked himself: 'What the bloody hell does this guy want with Humfri?'

'Young man, you're coming with me,' said Cantuarias harshly.

'Where to?'

'To the barracks.'

'Why? I haven't done anything. I haven't said anything.' And he looked appealingly towards old Squint-Eye, who remained totally absorbed in what he was reading.

Cantuarias dragged the protesting Lucio to the door and thrust him outside into the rain which was now bucketing down again. As he did so he turned over in his mind whether he could use the young man for his own advantage in his bargaining with Captain Vargas and the problem he had with Miranda. But his thoughts were cut short almost at once when Lucio shouted for help just as a military patrol came down the street.

'Corporal, take this fellow to the barracks at once. He's to be held for questioning.'

'Yessir!' came the smart reply.

'What the hell!' shouted Lucio.

'Shut your bleeding mouth, or I'll shut it for you,' snapped the corporal, hauling Lucio away like a rat in the mouth of a cat. He gave him a kick: 'Get a bloody move on or we'll all be soaked to the skin!'

THE COLONEL AND Captain Vargas were sharing a bottle of pisco and reviewing the situation: 'I've got to give it to you, Vargas, the town is buzzing with rumours against the priest. The only thing that has slightly buggered up the general feeling of hostility was what that stupid bastard of a mayor did in the church, going up to help the priest wash the feet of a group of snotty-nosed kids. What the bloody hell did he do that for? Is he on the side of the priest and against us? I just don't understand, for Christ's sake!'

'Don Nicolás is a sentimental fool, colonel,' answered Vargas. 'With that note he received this morning he's shit scared and knows he's going to have to resign as mayor. I reckon that he wanted to make a gesture; it was a purely political move.'

'Bloody politicians! They're the bane of this country, damn it!'

They carried on drinking and then Vargas said: 'You know, colonel, I'm enjoying this little duel with the priest. When I was a kid I remember seeing a bull-fight, and for months I dreamed of being a picador. The matador didn't interest me, I don't know why, perhaps he wasn't very good because it was a pretty crappy sort of fight, but there was this picador who danced round the bull like a bleeding ballerina, and he had me hooked. I remember that he broke the banderillas in half, and then in quarters so that he had to get really close to the bull in order to stick them into him. Today I've enjoyed being a picador, sticking the banderillas of rumour into the priest and getting him mad.'

'He didn't seem mad to me in the church.'

'Underneath his flowing robes I'll bet he's anxious and angry. Tomorrow I'll enjoy sticking the sword into him.'

'Better I hope than the matador that you've just mentioned. For God's sake man, don't make a botch of it and turn the priest into a martyr, or a hero. I don't want to have clean up any more of your shit.'

'I won't, don't worry, colonel.' Vargas laughed and took another swig of pisco and said: 'Strangely enough I feel a certain admiration for the priest. He's alone and he's got guts. As I've said before, I like an enemy who's well hung. It gives spice to the fight and makes winning more satisfying.'

The door of the room opened and Cantuarias entered.

'Where have you been major?' asked the colonel.

'Out in the town and I've got news for you.'

'Well, spit it out, man!'

'I've detained a young guy who can probably lead us to Becerra.'

'That's great! Who is he?'

'His name is Benites and I reckon that he's a *terruco* sympathizer. I got him a bit pissed and he told how he'd like to screw all the authorities in this town; 'string 'em up,' he said time and again.

'Where is he now?'

'In the interrogation room.'

'Good. Let's hope we can get some information out of him.'

'He's already told me that Becerra is here in Yanacancha. They had breakfast together this morning and Benites saw him in the church this evening.'

'So Becerra must be lodging at the parish,' observed Vargas. 'That's where he usually hangs out according to his godmother whom I interviewed yesterday. In that case we're close to the final thrust in the fight against the priest,' he added, rubbing his hands.

Cantuarias turned away. He felt sick at heart and just repeated sadly to himself: 'Judas, Judas, bloody Judas; that's what I am!'

A MONOTONOUS RAIN continued to fall over the town; not all that heavy for the Andes, but it managed to create a sad atmosphere. Within the church some thirty people were still praying silently before the Altar of Repose. Here one didn't feel the cold damp atmosphere of the town's streets because hundreds of candles were burning. Several members of the *Fraternity of the Blessed Sacrament* took it in turns to watch and make sure that none of the drapes caught fire. All 16 *penitentes* were present, standing stiffly along the sides of the chapel.

Looking through the two slits for his eyes in the white hood he was wearing, Manuel observed Father Alfonso. He was kneeling slightly apart, his head buried in his hands. He seemed to be a man close to God.

Where Alfonso himself was concerned, he couldn't feel further from God. Rather, he felt himself to be in the midst of the dark night of the soul. Everything was black and empty. He wanted to cry out. He felt dry. He looked up at the silver tabernacle surrounded by the silken drapes that had been so lovingly arranged. In the tabernacle was the Host, the Reserved Sacrament, the presence of Christ.

Alfonso's thoughts went to that first Holy Thursday, when Christ was in the Garden of Gethsemane, perspiring blood and offering himself totally to the will of his Father. And then, hardly an hour later, the Temple guards arrived to arrest him as Judas proffered his kiss.

Outside, the rain intensified and Yanacancha became swathed in the black clouds that bore down from Condorrumi and the other mountains.

Seven

AT ABOUT TWO o'clock in the morning Lucio Benites finally slumped to the floor of the interrogation room. He had told everything that he knew about Humfri Becerra, but it hadn't saved him from being humiliated and beaten up. As far as Captain Vargas was concerned, it seemed perfectly clear that if Becerra were still in Yanacancha he'd be lodging at the parish hospice: 'So we must mount an operation at once and grab the bastard whilst he's snoring in bed,' he said to the colonel.

'Fine, Vargas, and make sure there are no cock-ups. Even though the search of the parish will be in the hands of your lot in the police, just remember I'm the supreme authority here; so don't go barging into the place, breaking down doors and smashing furniture. Do everything efficiently and politely.'

'Don't worry, sir,' replied Vargas, thinking 'Bugger you!'

'I've ordered Major Cantuarias to make sure the house is surrounded by my soldiers so no-one can either enter or leave during your search.'

'Very good, sir.'

Rain was still pelting down as the troops set off to surround the parish house, and they were cold and bad tempered.

'Sodding rain never stops!'

'What wouldn't I give to back in good old Piura where it never bloody well rains!'

'Quiet you men!' ordered Sub-lieutenant Álvarez who was in command. Then he turned to the sergeant who accompanied him and said: 'I hope we find this bloody *terruco*. It'll be the first time I've seen one in the flesh,' he added with his boy scout grin.

'Don't worry, sir. If the bastard is in there we'll smoke him out like the rat he is.'

Whilst the troops were occupied surrounding the parish house, Captain Vargas went to Dr. Santillán's house to have him witness the search.

'What do you mean he's not here?' Vargas threw at the seedy woman who stood peering out cautiously from behind the barely opened door of the lawyer's house.

'Emilio sometimes goes drinking with his friends,' she replied, and then added bitterly: 'He also has his lady friends.'

From the little he could see of her, Vargas could understand the lawyer wanting better female company, but at the same time he found it difficult to comprehend what woman would want to share her favours with Santillán.

'Haven't you got any idea where he's gone?'

'He didn't say anything to me, he just went out.'

'Can you give me some addresses?'

Vargas fumed impatiently as the woman spoke in driblets:

'Sometimes he goes drinking with Señor Ortiz ... not the Ortiz down the road here ... he's just a mechanic ... not our class of person at all ... well, not that Ortiz, but the one who works in the Education Office, or whatever it's called now ... you know they're always changing the names of these places and I can never remember them.'

'Yes, yes, I know who you mean, Juan Ortiz,' spat Vargas impatiently.

'That's the one.'

'Where does he live?'

She knew the name of the street, but had no idea of the number. 'You go past the bread and pastry shop at the corner between Ugarte and Bolognesi streets ... you know the one I mean, don't you? Now a few doors further along ... on the right that is, because the shop I mentioned is on the left ... there's a large house ... I can't remember what colour it is ... green? ...No, I think it's pale blue ...'

'Yes, I know it!' Vargas almost shouted, fuming with impatience.

'That's not it, but ...'

'For Christ's sake, woman, get a bloody move on!' he hurled at her, driving her into such a flurry so she had to begin all over again.

And so it went on until he had several addresses.

An hour later there was still no sign of Dr. Santillán.

'Where the bloody hell has he got to?' yelled Vargas at the corporal.

'Can't we just raid the parish house, sir?'

'No we bloody well can't!'

'But if we know that the *terruco* is there …'

'That's just the problem, we aren't a hundred percent certain.'

'But we've also got the evidence to plant in order to arrest the priest.'

'And the military want Santillán to be there so that we have a legal witness giving us a foolproof case. If he's not there, a good lawyer will be able to convince a court that we planted the evidence. I know what I'm talking about because that's what happened to me in Ayacucho and I was nearly booted out of the police. We can't afford to balls things up this time.'

Eventually they found Santillán, dead to the world with drink. They woke him, but he was incapable of standing. They plunged his head into a bucket of cold water and pumped hot coffee into him. It was only then that Vargas was able to get the wretched little man to accompany them.

'It isn't really necessary,' the lawyer pleaded. 'We're under a state of emergency, so you can enter any premises without a judicial order.'

'I told you yesterday that I need you, so you're bloody well coming!'

And with that the sad mess of a lawyer allowed himself to be dragged off.

WHILST CAPTAIN VARGAS was searching for Dr. Santillán and the troops had been distributed so as to surround the parish, inside the church a small group, including Father Alfonso, continued to pray quietly in the chapel of the Altar of Repose. They were totally unaware of the military and police operation until Captain Vargas arrived with the lawyer. On hearing them approach, Father Alfonso stood up and turned towards them: 'Captain, has something happened?' he asked.

'We have orders to search the parish house, Father,' replied Vargas abruptly.

For a moment the priest didn't reply. Then he said: 'Well, there's nothing I can do to stop you, so you'd better come along with me.'

He led the captain into the house, followed by several policemen. The miserable Dr. Santillán was also dragged in and he slumped on a bench in the patio whilst the searchers sorted themselves out. They went into every nook and cranny, opened cupboards and chests, crawled through the attics, and left no corner of the rabbit-warren of a house unsearched. In the church they looked into the confessionals and behind the altars, but there was no sign of Humfri Becerra. The few catechists who were in the hospice and Pancracio, the Jack of all trades, were lined up in the patio. Meanwhile Captain Vargas accompanied Father Alfonso into the latter's study. There he saw on the desk the list of those lodging in the hospice that Pancracio had made. He grabbed it and when he saw Becerra's name he rounded on the priest: 'I told you yesterday that if Becerra showed up you were to inform me at once.'

The priest paled. He realized that he hadn't looked at the list since Pancracio left it in his study. 'Well, he hasn't.'

'Not bloody likely he hasn't! Then what the hell's his name doing on this list!'

It dawned on him that he hadn't said anything to the hospice keeper about Becerra. He tried to keep calm and said quietly: 'Captain, the young man who looks after the hospice put the list here and to be perfectly honest I never even looked at it.'

'Why not? snapped Vargas.

'I was too tired and thinking about other things.'

A noise outside attracted their attention and the police corporal put his head round the door: 'Captain, we've got eight people here in the patio, there are seven *campesinos* and the guy who looks after the place.'

'Becerra?' shouted Vargas.

'No sign of him, sir!'

'You stupid jerk, you've let him escape!'

'All these men were sleeping. No-one has had a chance to escape, sir.'

'Well tear the bloody place apart and find him!'

'Just a moment, captain,' intervened Father Alfonso. 'Before you do that, why don't you ask Pancracio what he knows about Humfri Becerra's whereabouts?' Then he turned to the frightened young man and said: 'Just tell the captain what you know. No harm will come to you because the responsibility for what happens in this house is mine.'

Pancracio hesitated and then explained that Becerra had been in the house and said he would stay the night: 'That's why I put his name on the list. After that he went out and I haven't seen him since. He never came back.'

'Sod it!' snarled Vargas.

'We've still got the *evidence* to plant,' whispered the police corporal to Vargas.

Suddenly, like some phantom, the mayor appeared. He had obviously dressed in a hurry and looked disheveled. He was accompanied by the left wing member of the Town Council, Lenin Izquierdo.

'Don Nicolás, what on earth are you doing here at this hour?' Vargas demanded in surprise.

'I was told that you were here searching the parish house and I was anxious to let you know at once what Izquierdo here told me just an hour ago.'

The captain looked even more surprised. What could have made two respectable citizens of the town run around during the night? 'Well?' he said. 'what is it?'

'I've discovered that my brat of a son wrote a note and pushed it under Don Nicolás' front door.'

'What did the note say?'

'It said that Don Nicolás must resign as mayor and hand over money.'

'Yes, I've seen it.'

'You mustn't believe a word of it. The stupid boy thought it a great joke. I've thrashed him of course, the silly little bugger!'

'Well, thank you for letting us know, Señor Izquierdo. Kids get some mighty odd ideas into their heads.'

As he bade the two men goodbye Vargas thought to himself: 'Blast it! Now we can't use the evidence that we've fabricated.' He turned to the corporal who was still standing close by and said: 'We'll take statements from the *campesinos* and this guy Pancracio and leave it at that for the time being. But I'm going to keep the priest under surveillance.'

The police had now concluded searching the parish house and Captain Vargas said to Father Alfonso: 'Well, that's all for the time being. However, you must understand that the fact that Becerra's name is on your guest list means that I will have to accompany you during your procession and whatever else you do today.'

'As you wish, captain.'

Father Alfonso went back into the church and one of the members of the Fraternity of the Blessed Sacrament approached him: 'Everything all right, Father?'

'I think so. The police got into their heads someone they are looking for was here in the parish house but they were mistaken.'

'As usual, Father.'

Alfonso smiled wryly and said: 'It's nearly dawn, so I must take the Blessed Sacrament away to the chapel in the house, and I'd be grateful if you could put out the remaining candles and clear the flowers away. As you know, The Way of the Cross will start at nine.'

'Okay, Father.'

'In the meantime I'm going to have a shower and drink some much needed coffee.'

AFTER HIS SHOWER and coffee, Father Alfonso rested for a couple of hours. Then he left the presbytery and went to where a group of people were arranging the First Station of The Way of the Cross. In Yanacancha, as in so many towns, the custom was to imitate Christ's journey from the time he was condemned by Pontius Pilate to his death on the cross and burial. There were 14 stations en route and each would have a picture with flowers and candles; a meditation by a member of the parish would take place and prayers would be said.

The First Station was the Condemnation of Christ by Pilate. For some reason, this was in front of a house next door to the cinema. The owner of the cinema had replaced the usual diet of Kung-Fu and pornography with one of the more sentimental Hollywood films about Christ. A large black drape had been suspended from the balcony of the house and pinned to it was the number 1. Below was a table covered with a fine lace cloth, on which had been placed the picture of Christ standing before Pilate. This was surrounded by flowers and candles. There weren't many people other than the group arranging the station —most of them were older women dressed in solemn black. It was always this way and Alfonso knew that as the procession proceed slowly from station to station more and more people would join in, and it would become as varied as the Palm Sunday one.

The man designated to offer the meditation was the town's principal shoe-maker, Don Remigio Fernández who was chatting with Manuel's mother, Doña Leonor. 'Doña Leonor, do you have a copy of the meditations we used to use before Father Alfonso came to the parish?'

'No. What do you want that for?'

'They don't have anything in them that could upset people.'

'What do you mean?

'Now that we've got *terrucos* here, and the military and the police are all over the place, I don't think it's very advisable to talk about corruption in the judiciary, the savagery of the military and things like that. In fact, I know that one could be arrested for saying what the *terrucos* are saying. It would be different if everything were peaceful, but it isn't and I'm not going to stick my neck out and say things that the military and the police wouldn't like: modern Pilates who are unjust and wash their hands, or,' he added, lowering his voice, 'police brutes like young Vargas.'

'I understand how you feel, Don Remigio, but I would have thought this is just the moment when we should talk about these things.'

'I don't want to stir up any more trouble.'

'That's precisely what we Christians ought to do.'

'Well, I did prepare something along those lines, but I'm afraid.'

'Why don't you show me what you've written. I'll give the meditation.'

'Muchas gracias, that's very kind of you.'

'Not at all, Don Remigio.'

Just as Father Alfonso arrived, also dressed in black, out of respect for the town's customs, Captain Vargas approached from the police barracks. He too had taken a shower, shaved, and drunk coffee, so that he now looked the model of clean youthful energy and authority in his *sinchi* uniform. The group of parishioners looked at him with surprise.

'The captain will be accompanying us,' said Father Alfonso, as though this were the most normal thing in the world; and he added no further explanation.

Since the people in the group were aware that something had happened in the parish during the night they began to ply the priest with questions, but Father Alfonso waved these aside and said: 'This isn't the time for gossip, so I'll just say what one says to journalists who pester folk with questions: "No comment." Now, let's start our Way of the Cross. Who's going to give the first meditation?'

'I am, Father,' replied Doña Leonor firmly.

'Fine, so let's get going.'

A hymn was sung and the opening prayers were said. When it came to the moment for the meditation, Doña Leonor began by reading what the shoe-maker had written. Then, suddenly she laid aside the manuscript and throwing all caution to the winds announced: 'I'm one more mother, one more wife, one more working woman, who is fed up with the generations of Pontius Pilates that have run this country for their own benefit and who have condemned Christ wherever he is to be found amongst the poor and the ignored. And no matter how hard these people work, it is virtually impossible for them to escape the slavery of poverty which lies like a heavy cross on their shoulders. We've reached a state of affairs where thousands of mothers cannot put bread on the table for their children, and they are condemned to starvation. Yes, daily Christ is sentenced to death in our midst amongst those who suffer hunger, disease and desperation.'

Whilst Doña Leonor spoke there was total silence amongst the people who had gathered at this first station; but the moment she paused another voice broke in harshly. It was that of Doña Dagoberta Castillo de Robles: 'Father! We have come here out of devotion to Our Lord Jesus Christ to pray, not to listen to political harangues!'

'What I have said is the truth,' countered Doña Leonor, 'and it won't do us any harm to meditate on the truth whilst honouring him who said: "I am the way, the truth and the life".'

'I've come here to find peace of soul and be uplifted, replied Doña Dagoberta. 'This day, above all days, Good Friday, should be respected and venerated. It's my opinion, a very humble one no doubt, but shared by other people in this town, that we should treat this Friday with exceptional reverence, and it is totally out of place to speak of hunger and misery when we should be thinking about the precious wounds of Our Lord.'

'Hunger and misery are two of those wounds!' flashed back Doña Leonor.

'Nonsense!' protested Doña Dagoberta, angry now at what she saw as a travesty of Christian devotion. 'Hunger and misery are repulsive, but the wounds of Christ are pure and sanctifying. We should be asking him to forgive us our sins instead of waffling on about the ills of our society. Yes, I know there are poor people in this town, but they could well ask themselves why they are poor. Drink and laziness are to blame. They are sinful, that's why they are poor!'

'Rubbish!' called back Doña Leonor.

At this point Father Alfonso intervened. He thanked Doña Leonor for her contribution and said to Doña Dagoberta: 'I believe that you will be conducting one of the meditations later on, and there you will be able to do it in the way you think fit. We may not all agree with the style of each meditation, but we should be able to listen to one another.'

More people were arriving and a group of youths passed by on their way to play football. For a moment they paused and wondered what the discussion was about, whilst Father Alfonso decided that the best way to silence it would be to sing another hymn. It was one of the well-known hymns on the passion of Christ, sentimental in style, and the group sang lustily, with the exception of the youths who quickly went on their way and Captain Vargas, who had assumed an impassible expression as soon as Doña Leonor had started to speak. Whilst they sang, Father Alfonso looked across at Doña Leonor and gave a wink of approbation.

Slowly they all moved off in procession to the second station: Christ receives his cross.

SINCE HIS INTERROGATORS had departed Lucio Benites had been left alone. His body ached from the blows he had received, and his mind was dulled by the battering of questions and insults. He had been unable to sleep and could do nothing more than go over what he had said about Humfri Becerra, and ask himself: 'Why was I so bloody stupid to mention him in the first place?' As dawn came up a few rays of light penetrated the store-room of the school into which the soldiers threw him. The hours continued to tick by, but no-one came to see him. From what he could hear he calculated the room backed onto a street. Apart from the sound of passing footsteps and the occasional vehicle, Lucio could hear a couple of soldiers chatting just outside the door, so he knew he was well guarded. Their exchanges about their amorous adventures with a prostitute a couple of nights back irritated him since he had visited the girl himself on a number of occasions. Then he heard a hymn being sung by the people participating in the Way of the Cross as they advanced along the street. The hymn stopped and there were some wheezes as a loudspeaker was turned on, after that came Manuel's voice: 'Jesus falls for the first time.'

There followed the ritual prayers and responses, and then Lucio heard Manuel say: 'Jesus is prostrate. He has fallen under the weight of his cross and is lying face down in the muck of a Jerusalem street.

All around him people push and jostle. Perhaps a few jeer, and the Roman soldiers pull him roughly to his feet. They abuse him verbally and one of them gives a couple of blows with his lash.' Manuel paused and Lucio found himself listening intently, if only because this was a voice that he recognized and he felt some comfort in the proximity of so many people. Manuel continued: 'We can ask ourselves whether we treat people much the same as that crowd in Jerusalem or the Roman soldiers. How many people in this town are down on their knees, or even flat on their faces, in the dirt of the road of life because the cross they are bearing is proving too heavy? We have already heard today of the crosses of poverty and disease, but there are plenty more: the cross of loneliness, that of being unwanted, the cross of ignorance and of vice. Drugs are pushed here in Yanacancha by some of our most respectable citizens, and the victims are people like myself, the youth of this town!'

'Bloody hell!' thought Lucio. 'I never imagined that Manuel Verástegui had taken a trip.'

'My friends, if any of our fellow citizens are crushed by such crosses it's up to us to help them to get up...'

'Get on your sodding feet!' shouted a sergeant who entered the store-room. 'You look a right bloody mess, so we'll have to clean you up a bit; come on!'

With that, Lucio was dragged outside into the bright morning light which at first hurt his eyes. As soon as he could see clearly he noticed that the sergeant was dressed in civilian clothes. He was ordered to strip and wash. Then he was given a clean shirt and an effort was made to brush the dirt from his jeans. After that he was taken to the canteen and given something to eat and drink. As he munched hungrily on a hunk of bread the sergeant said to him: 'Now listen to me, Benites; that's what you're called isn't?'

'Sí'

'I'm a sergeant and you're under my orders. You're coming outside with me and we're going to walk about in this town and try to locate your friend Becerra. If you see him, you let me know at once; but don't try any tricks or to get away, because if you do I'll put a bullet up your arse. Got it?'

'Yes, you want me to spot Humfri Becerra for you.'

'Very good!' Jeered the sergeant. 'For a teacher you're a bloody genius!'

'And what if I don't see him?'

'You'd better, for your own good.'

'He might have left the town by now.'

'We reckon he's here to commit a crime.'

'What crime?'

'Just shut your mouth and don't ask questions. Okay?'

'Sí,' replied Lucio morosely, indicating that everything was anything but okay.

They left the school where the military camp was and walked briskly towards the centre of the town. Within a few minutes they caught up with the procession of The Way of the Cross and Lucio muttered: 'I wonder if Humfri is there.'

'What, saying his bleeding prayers?' mocked the sergeant.

'If he's going to commit a crime, as you say, there's nothing like hiding in a crowd.'

'Bloody hell! I've got sodding 007 with me!'

They tailed along with the procession, now making its way towards the fourth station, but there was no sign of Humfri Becerra, so they turned away and decided to scour the town from one end to the other. Meanwhile, their quarry was sitting in the Plaza de Armas. He had spent the night in a disused shack on the edge of town and breakfasted again in the market. Now he was planning how he'd shoot Vargas. After an hour or so he decided to leave the square, and as he stood up he caught sight of Lucio Benites who was walking beside a close-cropped guy with a hard look about him. He didn't call out because he felt that he could do without the bloody silly questions that a creep like Lucio would be bound to ask. However, just at that moment Lucio saw him.

'There he is!' he said urgently in a low voice.

'Where?'

'He's slipped behind a tree.'

'Let's get after the bastard then!'

As they started to run, Humfri realized they were coming for him and he ran full tilt into a small shop that sold cakes and soft drinks. He leapt over the counter, scattering plates and glasses, whilst the girl in charge of the shop screamed. The sergeant burst into the shop just as Humfri slipped through a door at the back.

'Where did he go?' he yelled at the girl. All she was capable of doing was to continue screaming.

The sergeant saw the door and rushed at it, giving it a hearty kick. As the door splintered, the sergeant dashed into the small patio behind. It was full of washing hanging on several lines that completely blocked his view. Screaming obscenities, the sergeant lashed at the towels and sheets, but it was no use. By the time he could see clearly there was no sign of Humfri Becerra.

'The bastard escaped, carajo!'

He went back into the shop, treading on the cakes that were scattered all over the floor. Lucio followed him and helped himself to a large cake that hadn't fallen off the counter. The girl was still screaming, and by this time several other people had crowded in. One of them asked the sergeant: 'What the hell's going on?'

'Nothing that concerns you.'

'But look at all the damage you've done'

'Now just shut your fucking mouth and piss off!'

Since the sergeant had a revolver in his hand the man obeyed, muttering something about the bloody *terrucos* and the bloody forces of repression.

Meanwhile, Humfri had jumped from a balcony into a side street and ran as fast as he could. Suddenly he found himself blocked by the procession which had now reached the fifth station and the meditation was all about Simon of Cyrene being obliged to help Jesus carry his cross and how today we ought to help others carry their crosses. For a moment Humfri thought that instead of meekly obeying the Roman soldiers, Simon of Cyrene should have turned on them and how he himself would like to harangue this crowd of praying idiots so that they turn against the capitalists and the government that were oppressing them. No, he couldn't allow himself that luxury. His job was to kill Vargas, not raise the flag of rebellion in Yanacancha, so, reluctantly, he decided to melt into the crowd and keep quiet.

As the procession moved along the street it enjoyed the morning air of the Andean wet season. The sky was a cobalt blue, and the peak of Condorrumi glistened in the distance. Later on this would change and the black rain clouds behind the mountain would burst their contents once more over the unhappy town.

At around mid-morning the girl staying at the Hotel Velezmoro in the Plaza de Armas decided to go for a walk. She felt shut in, claustrophobic and confused. It was bad enough having to accept the news of Lucha's death; then had come her entanglement with Captain Vargas, and after that, her confession yesterday. To some extent she felt cleansed but she had missed the captain last night and now she just didn't know what to make of herself.

She wandered slowly up the street from her hotel, submitting meekly to the identity card check, although she knew that the soldier to whom she handed the card had mentally undressed her. She felt a moment of resentment and then, when he handed back the card and said: 'Alright, señorita,' she managed to give him a smile. She passed by the church and went on climbing. There weren't many people about, just a few children playing in the street and a couple of youths sharing a cigarette and a bottle of beer. The occasional owner sat in the doorway of his shop, minding the few goods on sale since there was no-one around to buy them. She turned a corner and found herself a few metres away from the now quite large crowd making the Way of the Cross.

This was the sixth station and the theme was the incident of Veronica wiping the face of Jesus as he passed along the street. The person leading the meditation indicated that this incident is not recorded in the Bible, but comes from a pious tradition and has inspired many of the acts of the corporal works of mercy, or charity. As she listened to the meditation her mind drifted away and she became oblivious to the people around her, remembering the discussions she used to have with Lucha. How often Lucha had flung at her: 'You

Christians are ready enough to give alms to the odd beggar, but you won't face the fact that we live in a society that produces beggars and which gives you enough money to throw them a few coins. And if that's all you can do to solve the problems of our society I find it disgusting! We need a radical change so that there won't be people with too much and there won't be beggars. That's the kind of society that I want to fight for.'

These discussions had left the girl feeling like some kind of useless egoist, and it was after the last one that they had together that Lucha disappeared. She joined the guerrilla forces of the *Shining Path* and had paid dearly for her convictions. The girl now found herself crying quietly and just as she was turning away from the crowd her eyes met those of the captain who was standing beside the priest. She froze, and then, went along a street that led out of the town.

The town of her childhood hadn't changed much over the years. There were the same cobbled streets, the same crazy leaning houses with their crooked roofs, which always seemed to be on the point of caving in, but somehow never did. There was a delightfully simple air about Yanacancha, and at the same time a closed provincialism that grated and irritated her.

She heard footsteps behind her and turned to see a tallish youth dressed in splotch-bleached jeans and jacket, which gave him an air of freedom and presented a marked contrast to herself, elegant yes, but tense and nervous. He walked rapidly with a springy step. As she looked behind her the youth smiled and said: 'Buenos días, señorita.' She replied and then he asked: 'Going anywhere in particular?'

'No, just taking a breath of fresh air.'

'May I join you?'

'Delighted.'

She was struck by his friendliness and calm air of authority, as though he didn't have to prove anything or impose himself on anyone. He seemed to be about the same age as herself and involuntarily she compared him with Hudson Vargas. They linked hands and walked slowly upwards, side by side over the cobblestones and between the rickety houses. After a short time they reached the top end of the town, showed their identity cards at the check-point, and continued walking. The straight street became a twisting path, weaving its way between dry-stone walls bordering the maize fields, and then between the cactus-like *penkas* and wild blackberry bushes. The day had not yet begun to cloud over as a prelude to the inevitable afternoon's rain, so it was warm and the air smelled sweet. The two walked in silence until they emerged on a small knoll overlooking the town, and they sat down on some boulders. This was where the cross had stood before being thrown down by the storm the week before.

'Poor old cross!' exclaimed the girl.

'The lightning felled it last Friday, but there are plenty of people in the town who believe that the *terrucos* did it,' observed the youth.

'It's a lovely spot,' said the girl. 'I used to come here when I was a child and enjoy spotting everything: the church, the Plaza de Armas with its palm trees, the market, the bull-ring, and the schools. It's a little world of its own that both attracts and repels me.'

'You used to live here?'

'I was born here, but my family moved away a good many years ago.'

'I've done exactly the opposite. I was born down on the coast, but my family moved up here when my father became the bank manager.'

'So you must be Manuel Verástegui.'

'That's right' he replied, plucking a stem of grass and sucking it between his teeth.'

'I've heard about you.'

'That sounds pretty alarming,' he said with mock seriousness, and then his face crinkled into a broad grin.

'Someone told me that you were to take part in the Way of the Cross, so what are you doing up here?'

'I've done my bit, and then I just felt that I had to get away. So here I am.'

She found something very clean and refreshing about this young man who offered such a contrast to the captain with whom she had become entangled here in Yanacancha, and they soon found themselves conversing as though they had known each other for ages. He told her of his ambition to be a first class doctor and she found herself talking about her relationship with Vargas: 'A man whom I both hate and begin to love at the same time.'

'That does sound rather a mess.'

'Yes, that's what life is for me at the moment, a mess.'

'That makes two of us on the same shit-heap; oh, sorry, I didn't mean to swear in your presence.'

'That's alright, Manuel. I think you're right. Life can be a shit-heap.'

He drew closer to her and watched how the breeze ruffled her hair, and how the concentration in her face was all the more desirable. They talked about their ambitions and their frustrations. They smoked together in silence, feeling fragmented internally and at the same time united to each other.

Then slowly the deep blue sky above them began to turn a blotchy grey, and the glistening peak of Condorrumi in the distance disappeared as clouds surrounded it. Half an hour later the first light fusillades of rain came across the countryside and the girl jumped to her feet saying: 'We'd better get moving or we'll be soaked.'

Manuel stood up more slowly and then suddenly took her in his arms and embraced her passionately for a fleeting moment of love. A sharp gust of wind whipped her long hair onto his neck as he kissed her, and it was followed by another stinging burst of rain.

'Come on!' He took her hand and reluctantly led her swiftly down from the knoll into the town.

FATHER ALFONSO FOUND it almost impossible to concentrate on the meditations at each station on the Way of the Cross, and he was only too thankful that the tradition had grown up whereby he was not expected to lead them. However, he still had the main ceremonies to face and the procession tonight. His thoughts floated distractedly from last week's scenes in Chugurmayo, to Lucio Benites, to Humfri Becerra, to Doña Leonor and Doña Dagoberta, then to the sufferings of the province, to the constant petty abuses, to Captain Vargas, to Telmo Cantuarias and the colonel. All this was muddled up with the meditations being offered at each station.

They had passed Christ's second fall and now Flor Delgado was speaking of the comfort that he gave to the women of Jerusalem as he passed on his way to Calvary: 'We are often called the weaker sex. Yet in the Gospel narratives of Christ's passion we read that it was a group of women who stuck closest to him until the end; yes, women, plus the youngest of the apostles, John! In this station when a group of women showed him compassion we see that they were not like the men. Peter had bragged that he would never abandon his Master, and then denied him at the first opportunity. Most of the other apostles just ran away. Nicodemus and Joseph of Arimathea kept quiet. But the women no! These women of Jerusalem were not intimidated by the presence of Roman soldiers, just as today many women turn out on the streets to protest against government policies guaranteed to cause hunger. We women are often the first to protest against the abuses committed by the armed forces, and it is we who do not hesitate to speak up on behalf of the unfortunates who find themselves arraigned before the kangaroo courts of the guerrillas, as happened last week in the cooperative of Santa María del Valle.'

'Politics again!' hissed Doña Dagoberta. 'How can we possibly pray if politics are dragged in every time we stop at one of the stations to meditate?'

Father Alfonso was irritated by Doña Dagoberta's whisperings, but Flor Delgado was not one to be put off by the criticism and continued to speak passionately about women's contribution to a more just and humane society. Captain Vargas was still at Alfonso's side and maintained a stony expression as though he were from another planet and didn't understand anything.

The meditation and the prayers came to an end and everyone took up a hymn as they walked slowly towards the next station, the ninth, which commemorated Christ's third fall. Alfonso looked anxiously at the sky which was now clouding over and already the peak of Condorrumi was no longer visible. Rain would start to fall shortly and they still had a number of stations to visit.

The third fall was precisely the station outside the Robles' house and it was now Doña Dagoberta's turn to lead the proceedings. She stepped forward to take the megaphone and at the same time pulled several closely typed sheets of paper from her handbag. Any hopes the priest had that the proceedings could be speeded up to avoid being drenched by rain were dashed. However much Doña Dagoberta could irritate him, he had to admit that whatever she set about doing, she did with thoroughness. Here, the station of Christ's fall was elaborately decorated, whilst the typed sheets indicated that she had carefully prepared what she was going to say. He was right.

Doña Dagoberta took her listeners to the Via Dolorosa in Jerusalem with a graphic description of the narrow cobbled street, the overhanging oriental balconies, the crowd, the curious, our Blessed Lady, the soldiers, the heavy wooden cross, the sweat, the filth —'much of which would not be a bad description of some of the streets of this town,' thought Father Alfonso.

'Then he fell! His sacred body embraced the mud and dirt of the narrow street! The cruel thorns pressed even harder into his divine brow! Oh, the agony!' The emotion which Dagoberta put into her description might have struck an outsider as exaggerated, or even rather ridiculous, but this certainly wasn't the reaction of the Yanacanchinos who were listening to her with deep and respectful attention. Doña Dagoberta's baroque phraseology was as much part of the local culture as ponchos, *chicha*, and the crazy pantile roofs of the houses. So she continued to wax eloquently on the Divine being besmirched by human sin

Strangely enough, Doña Dagoberta's discourse had the effect of making Father Alfonso feel mentally closer to Captain Vargas. This flowery flight of speech was all very beautiful, but in practical terms it had little or nothing to do with solving the problems that present day sin created. The humiliation, the pain, the suffering, the dirt, all remained as though in a classical painting, staying remote from the reality of Yanacancha; and all this was probably what the captain thought about all religious and political discourse —mere bla, bla, bla which changed nothing. The priest smiled and turned to look at the captain, and, for once, the captain smiled back. 'Well,' thought the priest, 'if dear old Dagoberta hasn't done anything else, she's managed to draw the two of us closer together.'

When at last Doña Dagoberta finished, Father Alfonso thanked her for her meditation, bowing graciously. She, for her part, assured him that it was her duty to make unsparing efforts on behalf of their holy faith.

The crowd moved on to the tenth station, commemorating the stripping of Christ of his garments. The speaker, a man this time, did not try to emulate the elegant flights of Doña Dagoberta's meditation, but spoke simply of the poor of Peru who were unable to clothe themselves decently, because clothing had now passed into the realm of luxury goods. 'We could never buy wine or choice cuts of meat, even though both are produced by our country. Many of us could never afford to travel by bus and have always walked or gone by truck. Now we can't even afford to clothe ourselves. Just as Christ was stripped of his garments, so we are stripped of our dignity as human beings. Under the circumstances, it's no wonder that the *terrucos* go from strength to strength.'

A frisson ran through the crowd and suddenly the rain struck, dispersing them and making them run for cover.

THE OFFICIAL GOOD Friday ceremonies as prescribed for the Latin Church are thought to contain some of the oldest formulations of Christian prayer, and they are expressed very well in the dry formality of the Roman Rite. However, they are far from suitable as a mode of expression for the emotive people of the Andes. The Andean Indian is not conceptual in his thought patterns, but, like the ancient Semites, he moves within a concrete world. So, although Father Alfonso was faithful to the ritual norms of the Church, he also included local customs and traditions. One of these was a lengthy homily on the Seven Words from the Cross, and another was the solemn lowering of the figure of Christ from a cross and placing it in a coffin, as a prelude to the Procession of the Holy Sepulchre which would take place in the evening and well into the night.

Billowing clouds of cold grey rain were sweeping across the town by the time the ceremonies were due to start, but they didn't prevent people from crowding into the church, and even all the local authorities had turned up in accordance with the tradition dating from colonial times. There were six policemen lined up by the still empty coffin, an elaborate piece of gilded wood-carving and glass, enabling the faithful to see the prostrate figure once it was laid inside. The entire scene was dominated by a large cross on which the figure of Christ hung, but for the moment covered with a purple velvet cloth. Everything was now ready for the priest and the *penitentes* to make their solemn entry. However, there was a slight delay because Captain Vargas presented himself in the sacristy and insisted that the identity of each of the *penitentes* be made known to him and that they be searched.

'It's against all tradition that anyone other than the parish priest knows who the *penitentes* are,' protested Alfonso to the captain who had managed to find time to change into his formal uniform.

'I don't want to offend your tradition, Father,' replied Vargas coldly, 'but a dangerous man is loose in this town and it's my obligation to take every precaution to prevent a killing. We'll both look bloody silly if one of the *penitentes* were to shoot the mayor.'

'That's preposterous!'

'So are a lot of other things that have happened this week.'

There was nothing for it but let the captain make his inspection. When he had finished he thanked them formally and said: 'I'm sorry to have to interfere with your traditions, but I cannot afford to take any risks.'

None of the 16 men replied, but Manuel grinned at Alfonso just as he slipped his hood back over his head. The priest gave him a weary smile in return, and then the *penitentes* clanked and swished their way into the church and took up their positions in a semi-circle, forming a dramatic back-cloth to the great crucifix under its purple drapes.

Father Alfonso entered the church and, to a total hush on the part of the packed congregation, prostrated himself before the crucifix. After a few minutes he got to his feet and led the ceremonies with their readings which climaxed with the Passion according to St. John. His mind was in a daze most of the time and at one point he thought that he had caught a glimpse of Humfri Becerra. When it came to the moment to preach on the Seven Words he climbed up to the old baroque pulpit, hardly ever used now. The first three Words slipped by conventionally; Alfonso spoke well and his people listened attentively. But when he came to the fourth, 'My God, my God, why have you forsaken me?' His tone changed completely. He sensed as though his own faith had suddenly exploded into fragments. There surged up in him a tremendous urge to tear off the vestments and to blaspheme against the Master of the Universe. Or was there a Master? If there was, what the bloody hell was he doing? Violence swelled up in him on a scale that Alfonso had never experienced before. Blackness engulfed him and outside the tempest raged furiously. The rain clattered deafeningly on the roof and Alfonso sensed that the old pagan god Catequil had really got into form and would strike him with one of the shafts of lightning that were always depicted in his hands. Alfonso was shouting now because of the deafening roar of the storm, but he had little idea as to what he was actually saying, and the faces of the people in the church were just a blur. He poured himself out in a sweat of images that identified suffering humanity with the crucified Christ.

The tempest slackened slightly to a steady drumming of the rain and Alfonso passed to the Fifth Word, 'I thirst'. He spoke in a parched voice of half the world clamouring for a decent life. He reached a new crescendo as he pronounced the triumphant Sixth Word, 'Everything has been accomplished', his ideas weaving a tapestry of hope, whereas before he had pictured chaos, destruction, and desperation. Finally came the epilogue with the Seventh Word, 'Father into your hands I commend my spirit', and Alfonso felt the calm that had enveloped Job when God spoke to him out of the whirlwind. No rational explanation was given to him, just the intuitive knowledge of the Majesty of God before whom he could only bow his head and adore.

By the time Father Alfonso had finished, the tempest had abated and several people came forward to lead the intercessions. One of the altar boys handed him a glass of water which he gulped down gratefully. Following the intercessions there came the veneration of the Christ figure after the crucifix had been unveiled, and the ancient texts were solemnly proclaimed. Finally there was the communion, and when the official ceremonies had concluded there came the solemn lowering of Christ from the cross, with each nail being taken out and passed from hand to hand of the members of the special fraternity of The Holy Apostles — not that they stood out as being very holy; quite the contrary. Then came the laying of the Christ figure in the gilded and glass coffin.

When Father Alfonso finally made it the sacristy and laid aside the heavy ornamental vestments, Flor Delgado came up to him and said: 'Father, what a great sermon!'

'Was it?'

'I think that you moved everyone as never before.'

A look of blank surprise crossed the priest's face.

'You took us down into the depths of suffering, into the deepest anguish, and showed us that it is the cauldron of love in which our Father draws us closer to him. You spoke of the purifying of gold, the beating of silver, the polishing of diamonds and the creation of the chalice which each one of us is called to be and to be filled with the wine of Christ.'

'I said that, did I?'

'Of course you did, Father.' She looked at him, puzzled. Then she said: 'I think I'll be able to bear now whatever suffering Humfri's actions may bring upon me.' She watched the priest who had slumped into a chair. 'I'm sorry to chatter on so, you must be very tired.'

In fact, Flor Delgado's words had restored Father Alfonso to a calm frame of mind by the time he re-entered the church to watch queues of people still coming forward to pray before the figure of Christ in the coffin. There were old ladies who found it painful to walk, mothers giving suck to babes in arms, the ladies of the town, the none too frequent attenders at Mass, the gum-chewing youths and girls, and the solid ranks of the faithful who could always be relied upon. His heart warmed towards all of them. There were no obvious saints, but nor were there any desperate sinners either, just a great variety of infuriating and strangely loveable human beings. So, in the midst of what is the saddest day in the Church's calendar, Father Alfonso felt a peculiar happiness.

Now that the rain had stopped, Humfri Becerra sat on a bench in the small square where there was a statue of the Yanacanchino poet Juan Carlos Losada Aguilar. He was nervous and kept looking about him anxiously, afraid that he might be spotted again by someone who knew him, just as Lucio Benites had; though fortunately darkness was already descending. He had a clearly formulated plan. He would shoot Vargas when the procession of the Holy Sepulchre moved up one side of the Plaza de Armas. He had picked his vantage point and reckoned that he'd be able to escape easily in the confusion that would ensue.

It began to rain again and Humfri had to seek shelter under the broad eaves of a house in one of the darker streets. There were great flashes of lightning. Then suddenly it stopped and Humfri could hear the band which meant that the procession would soon be on its way.

The procession left the church at exactly eight o'clock, a long black serpent of people with almost everyone holding a candle. At the head came a cross, escorted by two tapers held high. Behind that came a special black banner, only paraded on Good Friday. It was made of fine velvet, into which the face of Christ was stitched in gold thread. From the banner trailed lengthy black ribbons, each held by one of the notable ladies of the town — principally Doña Dagoberta and *The Ladies of Yanacancha.* The faithful came in a dense column, their candles flickering in the night wind. The crowning point of the procession was the gilded coffin of Christ held high by the *penitentes,* and escorted by police with their guns turned to the ground. The *penitentes* were playing their last official role this Holy Week and they walked even more solemnly and slowly with their majestic claank, claank, swiissh!

Hours ticked by as the procession made its lengthy way through the town's half-lit streets. The night was cold and the stars were bright, bright as only an Andean sky can show them. The procession was an impressive sight: the black centipede-like mass of people, the hundreds of flickering candles, and, high above everyone's heads, the glass and gilded coffin on its own ornate platform. The pointed white hoods of the *penitentes* created a special atmosphere and contrasted sharply with the smart green capes of the police escort. Immediately behind the coffin came Father Alfonso, wearing a heavy black embroidered cope, with Captain Vargas in his smart uniform at his side.

When they reached the Plaza de Armas the procession turned up towards the church at the head of the square. Humfri was standing behind a bush and a whole crowd of kids swarmed into the gardens that filled the square. Humfri watched carefully. Yes, the heads of everyone in the procession stood out clearly. It was going to be easy. The coffin drew level, with Captain Vargas and the priest behind. Becerra waited for them to pass so that he could fire at an angle. Just as he was about to do so he was spotted by Lucio Benites who was still patrolling the town with the military sergeant. 'There he is!' shouted Lucio. Both he and the sergeant ran forward and Humfri turned his head as he fired. Precisely at that moment Vargas lent forward and the coffin shuddered. Then bedlam broke out.

Father Alfonso heard the shot above the music of the band and at the same time saw one of the *penitentes* at the back right hand corner of the coffin collapse onto the ground, causing the coffin itself to lurch violently. He rushed forward, but Captain Vargas was there before him, stripping off the hood. Blood was streaming down the side of the penitent's face.

Alfonso turned ashen and gasped in horror, 'Manuel!'

Eight

$\mathcal{M}$ANUEL WAS DEAD by the time they got him into the patio of the Velezmoro Hotel. Outside, in the Plaza de Armas, everything was confusion, with both the police and military firing, whilst the panic-stricken crowd that had formed the procession ran in all directions. Many ran up the steps into the church, others threw themselves onto the ground amongst the bushes and flowers of the square's gardens, whilst the majority fled down the side streets. The *penitentes* managed to lower the coffin to the ground without breaking the glass and then scattered.

'He must have died instantly,' commented Captain Vargas to Father Alfonso as they stood helplessly beside the corpse lying on a bench in the patio. The priest was completely numbed. He couldn't pray; he couldn't even cry until Doña Leonor, her husband and their other children, came running into the hotel. Then the tears flooded down his face as he embraced each one in turn. It seemed ages whilst they just stood there crying, and it took the arrival of Dr. Santillán and the hospital doctor to stir them.

'Father, I think my heart is broken,' whispered Doña Leonor between tears.

'Mine too.'

'Why did they kill my son?'

Father Alfonso just shook his head and then looking at Captain Vargas, asked: 'Did Humfri Becerra do this?'

'Probably.'

'I just can't believe it!'

'Now do you realize what we're up against?' asked the captain bitterly.

'This time it has hit me personally, but I still can't accept that the only response is more violence.'

They were interrupted by Dr. Santillán who seemed to have shriveled inside his worn-out suit: 'You can take him away now. The doctor has certified instant death from a bullet wound; assailant unknown.'

'Gracias,' replied the priest. He looked across to where the Verástegui family stood in a sorrowing huddle and said to Vargas: 'We must ask them what they want done.'

The captain walked over to them.

'I'd like my boy to be carried home for the last time,' wept his mother.

With that, Father Alfonso came more to himself and said: 'If the *penitentes* are still around, it would be fitting that they carry him.'

It took a short time to find the *penitentes* since they had scattered in the panic, but eventually they were brought over to the hotel. There the priest told them to unscrew the coffin from its platform. 'Four of you can easily carry the coffin to the church and the rest will carry Manuel on the platform to his parents' house.

The coffin was duly unscrewed and the platform was brought over to the hotel. They laid Manuel's corpse on it gently and covered this with a drape. Then they lifted it, and to the accompaniment of the mourning family, the priest, Captain Vargas, a crowd of the curious who had overcome their fear, the procession set off and once more could be heard the mournful claank, claank, swiissh, of the *penitentes*.

By now the night sky had clouded over and the rain began to fall in a steady curtain as the cortege walked slowly through the streets.

No SOONER HAD he fired than Humfri Becerra started to run. He was certain that he had seen Captain Vargas keel over, and he felt satisfaction that he had completed his mission. He fled towards the upper part of the town, hoping to gain the woods where it would be easy to evade his pursuers who had broken away from the procession as soon as they saw him run.

'That's the bastard!' called the sergeant who was with Lucio Benites, and immediately several soldiers and police set off in pursuit. They fired at the fleeing figure, but they couldn't see clearly in the badly lit streets, and the bullets merely ricocheted off the walls of the houses, or shattered an occasional window. Behind the police and soldiers several civilians also took part in the chase, one of them being Lucio Benites. Suddenly a bullet got Becerra in the leg and he fell sprawling, his revolver flying from his hand.

'Got the bastard!'

They came up to him, gave him a number of kicks and dragged him to his feet. Amongst the small crowd that assembled quickly were Corporal Sánchez and Martha León who had come down from Llangodén. Sánchez pushed his way through the people surrounding Becerra and ordered: 'Hands up, *terruco de mierda!*' Slowly Becerra raised them.

'So we've got you, you bastard!'

Humfri summoned up enough courage to spit, provoking the corporal to give him a kick in the groin which sent him sprawling again.

'Get up on your bloody feet!'

Humfri struggled up and recognised Lucio Benites in the small crowd. Lucio had seen Humfri's revolver and picked it up. Humfri laughed: 'Bloody Benites!'

'Shut up!' ordered Sánchez. Then, before he knew it, Martha León hurled herself at Humfri, throwing him to the ground again and screaming: 'Kill him!'

The corporal dragged her off the prostrate Humfri and snarled: 'Woman, keep quiet! Becerra is under police arrest!'

'The *terrucos* had no mercy with my husband, and shot him like a dog. I want to see this *terruco* die. Then, before anyone could stop her, she leapt at Lucio Benites, grabbed the revolver and shot Humfri who was still prostrate. Martha León let out a peal of hysterical laughed and shouted: 'My Gilby's got his revenge!' She threw the revolver onto the ground and let herself be seized.

Corporal Sánchez and the military sergeant who had accompanied Lucio Benites had to struggle to disperse the crowd and get some of them to carry Humfri's corpse to the police barracks. The rain helped, scattering the last of the curious and washing Humfi's blood from the cobblestones. Lucio Benites shivered. No-one seemed to be interested in him now and he turned towards Ma Vasquéz' cantina. He had no money, but perhaps he'd find someone there to stand him a drink, or perhaps even Ma herself would take pity on him. He turned and ran down the street as the rain intensified. 'Sod this bloody tempest!'

THE TRADITION IN Yanacancha on the morning of Holy Saturday was for people to go early to the church in order to offer their condolences to *La Dolorosa*, but this time they made their way to the Verástegui house where the *capilla ardiente* had been installed in the main room. All the furniture, except the chairs, had been taken out. A large black drape had been extended across the end of the room, in front of which hung a majestic crucifix. In accordance with Doña Leonor's instructions, Manuel had been laid out in his penitent's clothes, except for the hood, and placed in an open coffin that rested on a catafalque in front of the crucifix. Round the coffin burned candles, and many of the mourners arrived with bunches of flowers or wreaths, so that before long the room was heavy with their scent.

As each group arrived they lingered before the coffin to say a few prayers, and then they dispersed, the ladies to sit in chairs in the room or to go to the kitchen to help prepare food, and the men to take their places in the wide corridors round the ample patio of house. There they could smoke and drink small glasses of *cañazo*.

The rain had backed off well before dawn and as the first light began to flood into the house there was the special luminosity of an Andean dawn. The buzz of a low hum of conversation amongst the mourners filled the air, and the sweet scent of the smoke from the wood fires in the kitchen, laced lightly with that of roasting goat drifted across the scene.

Everything was in accordance with the funeral customs of Yanacancha, except for one distinctive feature, which was the honour-guard that the *penitentes* had arranged amongst themselves. Their hooded white presence gave an eerie touch to the proceedings, standing out against the prevailing black of the rest of the mourners.

Father Alfonso was present and prayed the first mystery of the Rosary, then Manuel's father came up to him and said: 'My wife and I would like a word with you. Perhaps you could come to my study; Leonor is there.'

'Of course!' Even though he was extremely tired he followed the bank manager across the patio to his study.

Doña Leonor was sitting in an armchair and although she had obviously been crying, she was composed and said: 'Father, thank you for coming over. Felix and I want to talk to you about Manuel's funeral.'

'I'm at your service,' replied Father Alfonso taking a seat.

The bank manager said: 'We feel that to bury our boy this afternoon would be very hasty...'

'Yes,' intervened his wife. 'It would be less than twenty four hours since he was killed and it wouldn't be right. You know how we feel about these things here.'

'I quite understand.'

'But we can also see that there is a problem, because tonight and tomorrow the Church celebrates the resurrection of Christ.'

'Sí,' said the priest tiredly. Since the moment of Manuel's death he had not wanted even to think about the Easter Vigil this evening. Normally he looked forward intensely to the blessing of the Easter

Fire and the lighting of the Paschal Candle. He enjoyed the incense and the masses of flowers and candles, the bells and the joyful singing, all signifying that 'Christ has risen!' How was he going to be able to go through all this knowing that Manuel was lying in his coffin waiting to be buried?

'We've had an idea, Father,' said Doña Leonor hesitantly.

'What is it?' he asked gently, noting her hesitation.

'We'd like to go down to the church with Manuel's body so as to participate in the Easter Vigil together and then go on to bury him. Would that be allowed?'

'Frankly I haven't a clue whether it would be allowed; but I can't see anything wrong with it. In fact it strikes me as being a beautiful idea.'

'Gracias, padre!' murmured Manuel's father.

'You see, Padre Alfonso,' continued Doña Leonor, 'we feel that if the Resurrection Mass could be our boy's funeral Mass perhaps some good could come out of the terrible tragedy that has hit us. When I saw Manuel's body stretched out on that bench in the patio of the Velezmoro Hotel, my first reaction was to curse God, because I'm sure that I've never done anything so bad to merit such a punishment. I wanted to curse you; I wanted to curse the Church, to curse everyone. Then came to my mind everything that you had said during the homily and suddenly a kind of sound barrier broke and I was in the presence of God. The world is his; we are his, as St. Paul says, in life and in death, so it's up to him to make sense of it. Manuel's 22 years with us have been pure joy, so blessed be the name of the Lord!'

'You know, Doña Leonor, you make me feel very small and ashamed of myself,' replied Alfonso quietly. 'In circumstances like these I am supposed to be the one who helps the anguished come to terms with their grief and their sorrow. However, so far all I seem to have been able to do is to feel sorry for myself and sorry for the uselessness of my own faith. I've never been so close to total unbelief and I had begun to see tonight's resurrection ceremony as a charade through which I would have to drag myself unwillingly, and then perhaps throw off my priesthood. I saw myself as a peddler of empty dreams.' He paused and then laughed gently before going on. 'Only a few days ago Manuel asked me to help him with his own crisis of belief and I told him that God was asking him to plunge into a deeper faith. I suppose that I ought to have listened to my own words; and now you have helped me see that we can celebrate the Liturgy tonight as it has never been celebrated before in Yanacancha. I have been so busy following the fashion of cursing the darkness that I have forgotten that the resurrection of Christ is all about lighting a fire and a light, no matter how small, that will conquer the cold and the dark.'

A communion of silence then fell between the three of them and the sun's rays filled the patio of the house with their warmth. After a while, Father Alfonso said: 'I must go and see Flor Delgado, she must be distraught.'

HE FOUND THE door of Flor Delgado's house open so he walked in called out: 'Señorita Flor, it's me, Father Alfonso!'

She emerged from the kitchen at the end of the corridor, wiping her hands on an apron. Her furrowed cheeks were glistening with tears and her voice cracked as she said: 'Buenos días, padre.'

'I'm sorry that I didn't come down earlier, but I've been with the Verásteguis at the wake for Manuel.'

'I quite understand, Father. Now perhaps you'd like a cup of coffee, or something to eat.'

'If the coffee's ready, that would do fine.'

'I've just made some.'

'Then I accept with pleasure.'

Señorita Flor returned to the kitchen and Father Alfonso observed that there were none of the quick hoppity movements that had always been so characteristic of her; just a slow shuffle of her shapeless little body. Whilst he waited for her to return he watched several birds flitting between the branches of the two orange trees in the patio, and a humming-bird darting at the honeysuckle.

The old lady returned with a tray in her hands and served the coffee with her customary precision and neatness. There was the delicate porcelain cup and saucer, and also a tray full of a variety of sweetbreads. The hot liquid was aromatic and the priest drank it gratefully. Then he said very gently: 'Doña Flor, what can I do to help you? Do you want to talk? Do you want to keep silent? Do you want to be alone?'

'Father, I honestly don't know. Ever since Captain Vargas came here and gave me the awful news of Humfri's probably being linked to the terrorists and planning to commit some crime, I have been steeling myself to face the worst. I imagined him shooting Don Nicolás, or the colonel, or the captain himself. I even imagined him shooting you. And in each case I tried to imagine how I would cope with the bad news. But I never imagined that he would do what he has done. It has been so awful that I can't really take it in. I keep hoping that it is all a terrible nightmare from which I am going to wake; and then I know that it isn't. It's an appalling reality!'

'I hope you aren't going to blame yourself in any way for what has happened.'

'Of course I am. I've asked myself a hundred times why I didn't let Humfri grow up like any other boy in the country, to work the fields and tend his animals. If he had stayed in Llangodén doing that he'd never have done what he has. I now see that it was my pride that pushed him through school and on to the university. If he had never gone to San Roque he wouldn't have learned all about the *Shining Path*. He wouldn't have had his mind warped by terrorist propaganda.'

The priest tried to make her see things differently, but to no effect. Then he raised the question of Humfri's burial.

'Perhaps it was better that he was shot dead and not captured,' said Father Alfonso.

'I agree with you. They say that terrible things are done to any terrorist that is captured, and I pleaded with Captain Vargas that he wouldn't torture poor Humfri.'

'Fortunately that hasn't been put to the test. Do you know where Humfi's body is? Is it in the military camp or in the police barracks?'

'Nobody will give me any information in either place. I've been told that only next of kin have a right to it.'

'And in my experience they too are kept in the dark, just as happened in the cases of Pablo Huamán and Eriberto Huaripata. Anyway, I'll see what I can do.'

'Gracias, padre. In the meantime, I think I'll go to Chuncazón.'

'What on earth do you want to go there for.'

'It's the only place I know where *claveles moros* grow. You know, they are tiny red flowers and very beautiful when they are massed together. I want to make a wreath out of them for Manuel; something different and something special from me.'

'A beautiful idea if I may say so.'

Now it was her turn to smile, and she almost hopped along to the door to see him out.

THE GIRL WAS sitting in the patio of the Velezmoro Hotel, still numbed by the death of the young man she had chatted with so easily yesterday. He had been full of life and light-heartedness, and now he lay dead. What surprised her most of all was the depth of her feeling: 'We just met once and chatted for a while, and now I feel as though I've lost someone whom I've known all my life.'

After a while, she decided that she would go up to the Verástegui house and participate in the wake being held there. As she walked slowly through the streets she was struck by how few people she saw and how little activity there was. Yanacancha lay silent, almost dead. She had no difficulty in spotting the house because it had the traditional light burning over the door to indicate that a wake was being held. In the doorway itself there was a small group of men and youths, mostly dressed in mourning, smoking and chatting. There was a sudden burst of laughter, and the girl recalled the strange custom of telling jokes during a wake. She went in and was greeted by the low murmur of all those sitting in the patio and in the room where Manuel's body lay. On entering, she made the sign of the cross and then knelt at the prie-dieu at the foot of the coffin. After that she stood up and lent over the open coffin, letting out an almost audible sigh of relief on seeing that the face didn't seem to belong to the Manuel whom she had met yesterday. Similar, yes, but not the same.

The girl turned and left the hot sickly scented room, and when she emerged in the wide corridor of the patio was surprised to see Captain Vargas stand and offer her a seat: 'Señorita, please!' It was almost a command.

'Thank you, captain.'

She sat and murmured a few pleasantries to the people on either side of her, whilst the captain remained standing. He leaned over and said: 'So you knew Manuel?'

'Only very slightly. We just met once.' She looked at him. Still the same clean-cut *sinchi*, but something was missing, the aggressiveness perhaps, or some of his previous overbearing self-confidence. There were also shadows of tiredness etched round his eyes.

Plates of food were brought to them and they ate, continuing to converse in a desultory manner. After a couple of hours, the girl decided to leave and stood up.

'Are you leaving?' asked Vargas.

'Yes, captain.'

'May I accompany you?'

She hesitated for a moment and then said: 'That's most attentive of you; yes.'

And so they left together. The mourners in the patio murmured amongst themselves and shook their heads.

THE INEVITABLE AFTERNOON rain fell heavily over Yanacancha, and then, around six o'clock, it backed off. As soon as the clouds began to disperse and the rays of the setting sun made the cobbled streets shine like silver, Manuel's body was brought down to the church and placed on a catafalque in the nave. Señorita Flor Delgado arrived with her own special wreath. For a few moments she stood before the coffin which was surrounded by elaborate flower arrangements and wreaths, wondering where to place her own, very small in comparison with the majority. Doña Leonor saw the old lady standing uncertainly and came up to her. Seeing the wreath she embraced her and said: 'It's lovely. You must have gone especially to Chuncazón to pick those flowers because that's the only place where they grow.'

'Sí,' murmured Flor Delgado.

'And you went in the pouring rain?'

'Sí,' said again. 'It was the very least I could do for Manuel.'

'Because your godson killed my boy?'

'Sí.'

'I hope that what has happened will not separate us but unite us more.'

'Please God!'

AFTER MAKING SURE that everything was ready for the Easter Vigil Mass, Father Alfonso went to his study to rest and prepare himself. He turned on the radio to listen to the news and learned that 'in the province of San Agustín de Yanacancha, in the Department of San Roque, there has been a terrorist attack causing the death of one civilian. A terrorist known as Comrade Pedro, was also killed in a brilliant counter-attack organized by Captain Hudson Vargas. We are confident that the captain will shortly be rewarded by promotion to major. Meanwhile, the military commander of the province has expressed his satisfaction and wishes to commend especially Major Telmo Cantuarias for his excellent detective work which enabled the counter-attack to take place.'

'My oh my!' sighed the priest.

IT WAS A CLEAR star studded night when Father Alfonso commenced the Easter Liturgy in the forecourt of the church. The fire was lit and blessed, as was the Paschal Candle representing the Risen Christ. As he lifted the candle high and sang: 'The light of Christ!' Everyone responded loudly: 'Thanks be to God!' Then they crowded round to light their own candles.

The Easter Vigil ceremony is a lengthy one, with the chanting of the *Exultet,* a hymn of praise sung beside the Paschal Candle lauding God's saving acts and ending with an invocation that the candle be a symbol of Christ's unending light. There are many readings from Scripture and the singing of the Gloria whilst the church bells are rung, joyfully announcing that Christ has risen. There is the Litany of the Saints and the blessing of water for baptisms, plus the baptisms themselves and the renewal of the baptismal vows by all those present; and, of course, the Eucharist with the consecration of the bread and the wine.

In his homily Father Alfonso said: 'I am convinced that the force behind the bullet which killed young Manuel was not simply that of another young man of this province pulling the trigger, but was the accumulated sin of all the ill that has been committed here over the centuries. Evil has been present, and now it is up to us to make the Risen Christ present in its stead. That depends on all of us, and we make our promise to that effect as we renew our baptismal vows this night. I will conclude with words from the Prophet Micah: "He has shown you, O man, what is good; and what does the Lord require of you, but to do justice, and to love kindness, and to walk humbly with your God".'

When the ceremony concluded prayers were said over Manuel's body lying in its coffin. After that there came the last procession of this Holy Week. The *penitentes* stepped forward and hoisted the coffin onto their shoulders, and then began the slow walk to the cemetery.

This time the procession wasn't one of human joy and exultation, nor was it like the Good Friday one; rather it was an expression of determined faith and hope.

The night remained cloudless and star-studded. Father Alfonso sucked in the sharp Andean air and felt that old Catequil, the pagan god of the storm and lightning had been replaced in the hearts of many by the Risen Christ.